THE WITCH'S CURSE

TJ Lee

Thank you for going on this journey with me.

Prologue

Captain Andrew Hill

“You all good, Alpha?”

My wolf turned our head and looked at the vampire standing on our side. I may be nothing more than a child to him, seeing as he was over a thousand and I was only 29, but he had become a close friend these last few weeks.

I never thought I would ever call a vampire my friend.

Maybe it was the end of the world.

While my pack never had too much to do with vampires in general, I had heard many horror stories from other packs. Shifters, like me, were often seen as Speed for vampires. Or maybe more like catnip. Even the oldest among them struggled with control around us. Well, the Nightwalkers anyway. None of the Vampire Borns seemed to have that difficulty.

I just had to hope that once the fighting started, they didn’t sink into their baser instincts. The coming battle was important. Not just in the sense that we were saving human lives and holding back the spread of the Nightwalkers. More in the sense that it would also prove to the human government that we could all work together. And the other Alphas.

I'd spoken to the other Alphas many times after Curtis started his revolution. The debate to get involved had been heated, to say the least. No decision could be made.

Then, Prince Deacon of the Vampire Borns resurfaced.

With a pregnant mate, a *fated* one at that. Neither of those things had been seen in centuries.

His father, King Dominic, asked if we wanted to team up. So, the Alphas met again.

Then came the assassination of King Dominic.

The Alphas who thought Curtis would leave the other magical races alone, realized just how wrong they were. They completely ignored the fact that Curtis had been holding many wolves hostage at that moment. Something we didn't have concrete proof of, which was the point they kept arguing.

The decision quickly became unanimous after Dominic's death though. If Curtis was going to be killing members of his own species, what would keep him from killing ours? The time had finally come for the shifters to step into the open once again.

Even still, the fear and doubt that the vampires would be honorable was there. This wasn't the first time I went on a mission with the Vampires Borns. But it was the first time we would actually be fighting. Blowing up the Mojave wall and rescuing the human teenagers had been surprisingly easy. Of course, the Nightwalkers had been trapped by the sun at the time. It was like shooting fish in a barrel.

Well, that was what my human soldiers told me when we got back. Gleefully, I might add. My soldiers had enjoyed themselves immensely.

While the Vampire Borns helped me search the neighborhoods, and collected the kids playing at being spies, my men threw grenades into the makeshift tents and makeshift wall. My men had more than a little bit of fun shooting grenades launchers and rifles at them. Some even went up close to the tents, taunting the Nightwalkers. They had already used all the ammo they had when my soldiers were further away. All the Nightwalkers could do was stand there until they got blown up and pray they didn't blow right out into the sun.

They were soulless creatures. Their prayers went unanswered.

This mission was different though. A storm was rolling in. My little spy on the inside tipped us off to Curtis' plans. To back it up, she sent back my men. My pack. The ones Curtis had been holding hostage for months. He planned to ship them up here, to Seattle, as a gift to his fighters. They had a lot of ground to cover, they would need extra energy. My little spy diverted that shipment, at great risk to herself.

I hadn't heard from her since.

I wanted to message her. I wanted to ask what she meant when she told my Sergeant that it was too late for her. I wanted to know if she was okay.

I wanted to hear her voice. Something I had never heard before, not while awake anyway. I'd never seen her while awake either. But that didn't stop her from haunting my dreams.

It was from the guilt. I knew it was. I felt guilty for allowing her to do this.

I passed the message onto the General.

I told them about the teenagers who were placing themselves close to Curtis in order to spy.

I passed the phone to the boy.

Why did I ever call it in? I could have pretended that the government said no. That they refused to back up a bunch of kids. Teenagers.

"Alpha? You still there?" Colton, my new friend, asked me again.

I tried to clear my throat, which probably sounded more like an odd growl to those around us. My wolf shook our head, trying to clear it.

Yes. Sorry. Just a lot on my mind.

Colton nodded his head while he rubbed the spot right over his heart and turned back to look toward the port we were guarding.

We had no idea how many Nightwalkers were coming, or how Curtis had planned to hit the ports. We only knew the where (sort of) and when (vaguely). That being said, we had to do some major splitting up.

The human General and American President sent us two squads of Marines. They spent the last two months training with pure silver swords and daggers.

Colton, the Vampire Born General to the Royal Born Army - and mate to their King and Queen - was able to bring in nearly thirty Vampire Borns.

I brought all twenty of the shifters my little spy released to me. They had a hunger for vengeance.

We split into groups of five to ten and spread up and down the coast. From the Northern tip of Washington, down to the most Southern tip in Oregon. Each group had a little of each species. We told the humans it was so we could prove that we could work together. In reality, it was so we could protect them.

Humans were not fast enough to kill a Nightwalker on their own. No matter their skill level with a sword.

I watched Colton rub his chest again, a small grimace on his face. I couldn't help the envy I felt toward him. Yes, he was separated from his mates, but at least he had mates.

For most packs, tradition stated that the Alpha be mated *before* taking his position. It wasn't the same for the Army pack. Once the eldest son reached a certain rank in the Army, they were given the honor of taking over for their father. Unless he died before that.

We mated when we mated. There was no time crunch for us.

I wanted my mate though. My wolf wanted his mate.

I could have settled for anyone by now. There had been more than a few offers from other packs. But my wolf said no. While a fated mate had become rare, he insisted ours was out there. For the last few months, he had been swearing that she was close.

Which was also making him pretty irritable. The only times he was calm lately were the times we could exchange messages with my little spy. But after… well, let's just say no one wanted to train with me anymore after those messages. He was also known to outline the wall keeping us away from our spy. The wall that kept everyone out of California. My wolf was protective of her. He saw her as an equal because of the sacrifice she was making. She was the bravest person he had ever heard of. Of any species.

Even just thinking about her was making him antsy. He was bothered by Sergeant Morris' report more than I was.

You are rubbing pretty hard there. Everything all right back home? I needed to redirect my mind onto other things before we both lost it.

Colton huffed. "I believe so. It's harder to tell who is feeling what from this distance. It's fuzzy, something that will grow stronger with time, or so we have been told. But knowing my mates as I do, I'd say Carrie is worried but calm. Deacon, however, is anxious and frustrated. They both have fear in them."

My wolf and I both laughed.

He is still not happy you made him stay behind?

Colton chuckled. "No. He is not. He only agreed to stay so that we did not leave Carrie alone. She would have worried more, and we need her safe. But he knows that was not the main reason. Deacon is strong. Even stronger now that he feeds from his fated mate every day. But he is not a fighter. Never has been. And, for now, he is the only King we have. Our sons will not be ready to wear the crown for many years."

I mentally tskd. *It is not in a King's nature to let his men go into battle without him.*

"No. It is not. But there are times when they must. Deacon never liked hiding. He won't say it, but that is what he is feeling right now. That I am forcing him to hide." Colton sighed sadly. "Ever since Dominic died, Deacon has blamed himself."

My wolf tilted his head. Both of us confused by this. *Deacon had nothing to do with that.*

"No, but it was his choice to not see or speak to his father for the last century. He feels guilty and ashamed. He feels like he was a bad son. A bad heir. He feels unworthy. He wants to prove himself to our people."

We nodded our head. That was something shifters understood well. A leader had to be worthy to lead. Strong.

Alpha, we can smell the Nightwalkers. A truck just pulled in. A human dockworker is driving. The Nightwalkers are probably in the back.

I let out a low growl before passing the message on to Colton and the others. We took our positions inside various shipping containers that lined the main pathway from the entrance and waited. With my fur being so dark, I was able to keep my door open. I wanted to be able to see which way they went.

The Corten steel walls hid our scents perfectly, I just had to stay far enough inside. The winds from the approaching storm were strong enough that the scent trail we left behind would be gone before they arrived.

Early this morning, we cleaned the ports out as good as we could, getting all the civilians to safety. The Marines changed out of their uniforms, and into clothes more fitting for the humans that worked on the ports.

From where I was located, I could see a large U-Haul driving closer. I purposely had one of my men stationed at the gate. I was glad I did too. We weren't completely sure whether they were already here, and hiding in containers like us, or if they were arriving another way. They came later than I expected them too. The sun had risen hours ago, and the storm had already begun.

The truck drove deeper in, coming closer to us. At some unseen signal, or possibly rearranged drop off, the human driver jumped out of the cab and ran to the back. He flipped the metal anchor that kept the rolling door from opening and stepped back. The occupants inside pushed it open roughly and jumped out of the truck.

I watched as the human held his hand up, most likely asking for his fee. The wind carried the dark chuckle from the vamp over to me. By the time I heard it, his teeth were in the human's neck.

Now. I growled out, grateful that I could speak to more than just my own pack. It was fun freaking the human soldiers out the first few times. The Vampire Borns especially loved when they would shiver. I did it enough on the way there, that the humans should be used to *hearing* my commands by now.

As one, seven container doors swung open, and our own small, but powerful army stalked forward. The Nightwalkers were surrounded. This couldn't have worked out better. It was almost too easy.

The dozen Nightwalkers spun in circles, growling at us. They only stopped when their glowing eyes rested on Colton, who was taking his sweet time joining us.

He walked like a King.

Like a man who knew he was in charge.

Like a lion stalking his prey.

As he stepped to my side, the sides of his lips curled up into what could only be described as an evil grin. Followed by a deep chuckle.

"You screwed up." He told them his smirk fading fast. "Who's in charge?"

"I am." The vamp who killed their driver stepped closer, trying to impersonate Colton's confidence. It was more of a parody than an imitation. "Who are you?"

"My name is General Colton, of the Royal Born Army."

The Nightwalkers all looked at each other, some shrugging. The head vamp turned back to Colton.

"Never heard of you."

Colton chuckled darkly. "No, you haven't. Because your creators failed to teach you properly. My men and I are born vampires. Nightwalkers, that's you," he pointed to them, in case they doubted, "were first created to serve us. *We* are your masters. We are stronger. We are faster. And we are not limited by the sun."

"We serve no master. We are free now. Or have you not been watching the news?" A female vampire snarked with attitude. The

Nightwalkers all laughed, some more out of fear and duty than others.

"You will serve as you are told, or you will die. Take your pick."

"We don't know you. We've never heard of you. And we have no reason to believe you. Curtis has been good to us. We feed when we want. We screw when we want. We do what we want, whenever we want."

Without another word, the Nightwalker supposedly in charge, stupidly raced toward Colton. He really should have listened. Colton, who's hands had been empty seconds before, met the vamp with a silver dagger. The vamp ran right into it.

The rest of them hissed and screeched in anger before running at us.

My wolf lowered his front down and prepared to jump, there he paused for the count of two, waiting for the stupid Nightwalker to get closer. Then he pounced, ripping the snarky female's head off with our teeth as he went over her.

Right as my feet landed on the ground, I felt a sharp pain rip through my chest. I froze, mentally taking inventory of my body.

Where is that coming from? I asked my wolf.

He didn't respond, he only tipped his head back and howled into the dark sky. His howl sounded painful, as though he had just lost someone dear to him. The pain in our chest deepened, a crack splitting down the middle.

"Andrew! Andrew!"

I could hear Colton calling to me, but my pain was so intense that I could not think straight long enough to respond.

"Alpha?" Morris called to me next, no longer in wolf form.

I was vaguely aware of him putting a hand on my shoulders, and of the other wolves howling in response to my pain. The Vampire Borns rushed to protect them in their weakness, as well as the humans who were getting a wakeup call. They ended the fight quickly. The humans surprisingly got a couple of their own, their speed and agility better than I gave them credit for.

"What's wrong with him?" Colton asked, his worry for me evident. "I see no wounds, but he sounds like he is in pain. Was one of your men hurt?"

"No." Morris sighed deeply. "This is not a physical wound. I experienced it myself once upon a time. It is the howl of mourning. The sound of someone who felt the loss of their mate."

"I thought he didn't have a mate yet."

"He does, he just hasn't met her. When I met the little spy, she said she kept seeing visions of the Alpha. She described him perfectly. I wondered, but I wasn't sure."

"You think the little witch is your Alpha's mate?"

Is she our mate? Did something happen to her? I pleaded with my wolf.

I don't know. But something is wrong with our mate. I can feel it. Something is pulling her away from us. I had never heard my wolf speak so morosely, painfully, emotionally.

How would we be able to feel that if we've never met her? A bond has not started yet.

If the little spy is our mate, then a bond has *already started. We communicate with her. We are protective of her. We care for her.*

But not in the mate sense.

It would not matter to fate. A bond has begun. If she is our mate, then something is wrong. With that last thought, his howl turned into a whimper as he dropped us to our stomach in defeat. He no longer had the ambition to keep us up.

He didn't care who was around.

He didn't care if he looked weak.

He no longer cared about being the most dominant in the room.

Morris dropped to his knees, softly pushing a hand through the fur on my head. "Alpha, I know you are in pain. I know this is confusing. We will figure it out, I promise. But we need to move. If the little spy is your mate, then don't let her sacrifice be in vain. She sent us here to save these people, to stop Curtis. We need to help her finish this, so we can save her next. We need you, Alpha. Your mate needs you."

Get up. We can't let her down. There will be plenty of time later to wallow in our sorrows. Morris is right. She needs us now more than ever.

My wolf wordlessly followed my command, pushing us to stand on all four paws. It took a great deal of effort to accomplish such a small task.

"There we go, Andrew. Come on. This isn't over yet. We need to call the other teams, see what's going on at the other ports. Then we can get home. I doubt that Nightwalker was in charge of the whole mission. Probably just this group of misfits." Colton spoke with the voice of one trying to instill courage in his men.

My wolf let them lead us back toward the vehicles we brought. I wasn't up for shifting, but there was no way we would have fit if I stayed as a wolf. Colton steadied me, while Morris helped put my pants on. It was pathetic, and not the actions of an Alpha. But the pain in my chest, in my heart, made it so I didn't care.

I sat quietly in the middle seat, while Colton contacted the other teams. I vaguely heard him gathering reports. The Nightwalkers had split into three groups in Seattle. We were the only ones who lucked out from the beginning like we did. Our group showed up late. The others had attacked earlier or been hiding before they arrived. In comparison, our total losses were minimal. Two of the human soldiers were lost and one of the Nightwalkers managed to bite one of my packmates. He didn't die, but the Nightwalker got a boost and sped out of there.

The teams at the other ports were instructed to stay until the storm was over, just to be safe. We were hoping that the Nightwalkers that had already hit would have moved onto them later, but no one wanted to risk it.

I waited until Colton hung up with the last one before I spoke. "I don't even know what she looks like. I dream of a woman all the time, but by the time I wake up, I can't remember her face."

"The first time I saw your wolf, I had to laugh."

I turned and looked at him in confusion.

He chuckled and rubbed a hand over his short hair. "Grace has black hair, about to her shoulders, with the tips dyed purple. Your fur reminded me of her."

I huffed a small laugh, which quickly turned into silent sobs. "Something isn't right."

"Nothing is right. But we will get her back. We have to, or my mate will go on a rampage. Carrie won't settle for anything less than getting her sister witch back."

I sniffled and wiped my eyes.

"She isn't the only one."

I lifted my head and met the eyes of my Sergeant, looking back at me.

“I made a promise and I mean to keep it. If that little spy is our future Luna, then I have even more reason to get in there and pull her back out. You have my word, Alpha. We will bring her home.”

I swallowed and gave him a short nod in thanks. I knew if I even opened my mouth right then, I would lose all the control I had over my emotions.

PART I

1000 years ago, give or take a century,
(People weren't great at tracking time back then)

Chapter One

Conrad

"Conrad!"

I laughed as I stepped through the front entrance to my parents' home. Then braced myself for what I knew was coming. Sure enough, a few seconds later I was knocked breathless from a four and half foot firecracker. Also known as my younger brother.

"Hey, squirt." I ruffled his brown hair, the exact same shade of brown as mine.

He tipped his head back far enough to look up at me but did not release his grip on my waist.

"How long are you staying? Wanna go for a run with me?"

I chuckled at his youthful exuberance. We had a fairly large gap in our ages, but that was common among our people. I hit 100 last week, whereas my younger brother will turn 12 next month.

When you lived as long as we did, the centuries-long age gap was to be expected.

"Not today, Dom." He pouted and let go of me. I squatted down to be on his level. "Hey, I will be back in a few days, and then what do you say, you and I, go camping?"

His frown quickly flipped back to a smile, not much was able to keep this runt down. "Can we go hunting and swim in the river?"

I laughed and stood back up. "Sure, bud. Whatever you want."

"Hope you aren't making too many plans for the near future." A firm but loving voice said from the entrance to the kitchen.

"Good morning, mother." I stepped toward her and kissed her cheek.

My mother was pushing her first millennium, and still didn't look a day over 25. That was another thing about our people, once we hit our mid-20s, we stopped aging. At least for a thousand years or so. After that it began again, only very slowly. I'd met a few men who were already gray by then, but most held it together well.

"Good morning, son. Have you had anything to eat recently?"

I smirked. I hadn't lived at home for over a decade, and she still babied me. "I ate some bread this morning, mother."

She clicked her tongue and turned to the kitchen. "Sasha?"

A young human girl with curly red hair came into the room. "Yes, my lady?"

"Conrad needs to eat before he sets out."

Sasha walked over to me, a blush on her cheeks. "Yes, my lady."

Being as my parents were actually the King and Queen, our human servants weren't just for cleaning. We cycled through them on a regular basis. Mainly, it was the unmarried humans who worked for us, up until they were ready to move on.

Sasha was about average height. Her hips were the perfect size to carry a human child. She could have been every other human female, except for the red hair. It wasn't seen as often in this area of our kingdom. She was pretty, I'd give her that. I took her by the hand and began to lead her to another room.

"Thank you, mother." There were some things I just wasn't comfortable doing in front of my mother. The others? Sure. My mother? Not even close.

I led Sasha to a room we often used for this purpose. In case we desired privacy. After I closed the door, she turned around to face me.

"Does his lordship have a preference?"

"Yes. Come." I had a bit of a sweet tooth this morning.

I led Sasha over to a small table in the room, then lifted her up and set her on the table. I could smell a small hint of fear wafting off her and I stopped.

"I won't hurt you, little one. You have no need to fear me."

"I know, my Lord. I'm just still new to this."

"Ah. Well, I am going to feed from you, right here." I kissed her neck softly, causing shivers to run through her. These ones weren't from fear. "While I feed, I am going to be doing something else, something you will enjoy very much." I lowered a hand to her thigh, and she shivered again.

I laughed softly at the little gasp she made when my hand slid up her skirt. It didn't take long for the sweet scent of dopamine to permeate the air in the room. As soon as it hit the right strength for me, I sank my fangs into her neck.

The initial spike of fear blended well. It soon disappeared altogether as she gave into the feeling. I was sure she would be staying with my parents for a long time. I couldn't help but wonder if Dom had learned how to sweeten the blood yet. Was he even old enough for that? Hmm, something I would have to discuss with him when we went camping after my return.

I licked her neck softly when I finished, sealing the holes. I laughed as we had to wait for her to finish shaking.

"Have you not fed anyone before?"

"No, my Lord. I've only been here a few days."

"And?"

She laughed. "And I may stay for a while. I did not know how good that could feel."

I laughed with her and kissed her neck again. "It can get so much better. Maybe another time I will show you. But I need to leave soon."

"Whatever you wish, my Lord." She blushed again and I helped her down.

By the time I rejoined my mother, my brother was long gone, but my father was there.

"Good morning, father. I wanted to let you know that I am headed out to check on the Southern Territories. I should be gone for less than a week."

My father had one hand running through my mother's dark brown hair, the hair we took after. He smiled at me.

"That's fine. Just remember to be home before the new moon. Yolanda and her parents will be coming to stay for a time."

Dang, I forgot about them. Seeing as I had made it this long without a mate, my father had taken it upon himself to arrange one for me. I would prefer to wait until I found my fated one, the other half of my soul, but that could be anytime between now and a thousand years. She may not even be born yet.

"Yes, father. I will do my best."

"I know you aren't fond of this plan, son. But you are nearly old enough to take over the throne. You need a mate. You need to settle down." He gave my mother a soft smile. "Besides, your mother and I would like to travel for a time. Maybe hide in the woods for a few months."

I chuckled. "Are you trying to give me a sister next?"

My mother's eyes glazed over. "A daughter would be lovely. I've had enough of being the only woman in the house."

"What about Sasha and the other servants?" I of course was only being dramatic about it. I loved it when my mother laughed.

Which she did. "You know what I mean. A vampire woman would be nice. And since I won't be having a daughter anytime soon, how about you just give me a daughter-in-law?"

I snorted and shook my head. "Ganging up on me now, are we?"

She shrugged, then leaned over to kiss my father's cheek. "I've got some gardening to do."

She bade me farewell and walked out the door I came through not too long ago.

The amusement slid from my father's face. "There have been rumors of unrest in the Southern territories. The witch city is not far from there. I heard they just lost their King and Queen. A daughter is set to take over, but she has yet to find a mate. This could cause problems for us. We need to make sure we are stabilized, ourselves. Humans are fickle creatures. We are all counting on you, Conrad."

I nodded solemnly. "I know, father."

He sighed and stood up, leading me outside and toward the barn. "It's all this mess with mixed mating. I blame it on that. Bloodlines are getting tainted. If fate destined for you to be together, then fine, but not chosen. I fear a war between the kingdoms will soon be on us if it keeps happening. Not everyone agrees that fate would give someone a different breed for a mate. With how often you are checking on the Southern Territories, some are speculating that you are seeing a witch."

I stopped and gave my father a confused look.

He laughed. "I guess there's my answer to that. As the next heir to the throne, it will be your job to keep the lines pure, to set a good example. I trust you will do that with Yolanda."

Our stable hand met me at the door, a horse saddled and ready for me. The bags I dropped off before I went inside my parent's house were strapped onto the back.

"Yolanda is a beautiful woman, father. I'm sure we'll work it out somehow." I climbed on the horse and leaned down to shake my father's hand.

"Good. I'm proud of you son. You will make a fine King one day."

I chuckled. "Thank you, father. I will see you in a few days." I clicked my tongue, and my horse took off in a decent trot.

We barely made it to the end of the path before a small brown head popped up next to me.

"Bet I can beat your horse!"

I laughed as Dom took off running. I kicked the mare with my heel, and she took off after him. By the time I reached the bottom of the hill, he was sitting back chewing on a piece of grass. Little skunk.

"Bye, Conrad!"

"Bye, squirt." I leaned down and ruffled his hair as I passed.

It took me over a day to make it to the village closest to our border with the witches. I set my things up in a cabin kept empty for my use, then headed out. Over the next few days, I spoke to the human leaders in the village. I spoke to the local vampires. And I hung out with some friends and played games with some of the local children. All in all, it was a nice visit.

The day before I left, I decided to go for a walk further into the woods. There was a waterfall with a small lake nearby. It would be a good place to just relax and reset myself before returning home to my parents.

I made my way through the thick trees and leaves, passing through the natural territory line between us and the witches. It was usually pretty easy to tell where our land ended and theirs started. Nature. They were really big on nature.

Not that I could blame them. I always felt like I could breathe better there.

Technically speaking, I was trespassing. But I had done this a few times now and not once had I seen another person, of any species. I wouldn't dare do this if it were the shifters. With their noses, they wouldn't have to see me, they would smell me.

Last thing we needed right now was a war with the shifters. Or the witches. They may not be able to hold their own in a physical fight, but they played dirty with their magic.

Their blood had a way of healing us as well, so we were keen on keeping the treaty with them.

Fifteen minutes after passing the border, I could hear and smell the water. I stopped and took a deep breath. Fresh water always smelled the best to me.

There was something different about it today though. Another layer I never noticed before. I sniffed deeper as I followed the trail closer to the waterfall. The closer I got, the stronger the scent became. I was practically drooling by the time I reached the small shore.

My ears pricked up when I heard soft singing. It was too low for me to understand the words, but the voice was soothing. I felt my limbs begin to relax little by little. All the tension I had been feeling just melted away.

I watched carefully as a head of black hair appeared under the waterfall. There must have been a rock under it, as she slowly stood up, her head tilted back so the water was brushing her hair down her back. The sweetest smile crossed over her face.

I watched the water trail from her hair, down her bare sides, and over those perfectly proportioned curves. Every inch of me screamed to join her.

As though she heard my thoughts, she turned to face me. Instead of panic and anger over being spied on in a private moment, her smile grew wider. Slowly, as though she were afraid of startling me, she raised her right hand. Inviting me to join her.

I knew at that very moment that I would never be able to deny this woman. Nothing else mattered. No one else mattered. She was fated to be my everything. And I would move mountains to make sure she always knew that.

Chapter Two

Angela

I needed an escape.

A fortnight ago, we sent my parents back to Mother Nature. One minute, I was a spoiled princess, free to roam the countryside, free to be who I wanted. And in the next, I was the Queen.

I was responsible for the safety and protection of my people.

It was my duty to continue on the bloodline of my people.

It was my duty to hear them out when they had disputes.

It was my duty to comfort them when they needed it, to give them advice on things I knew nothing about.

It was Queen Angela this, and Queen Angela that. And "Oh no, your majesty you mustn't do that! That is not befitting your station!"

Well, you know what else was not befitting my station? Running away when no one was looking. Bathing in the middle of the forest.

But I needed this. I needed time to myself to rejuvenate. To mourn the passing of my parents.

Like all magical creatures, we were given the gift of a true mate. That one person who held a power that matched our own. The person who was created to balance us out.

Yes, well. I'd been all over our kingdom. I met every man living within it. They all sucked.

The downside to a true mate, and binding yourself to them, your souls were literally bound together. When one went, so did the other one. Hence losing both my parents at once.

We may not live as long as the vampires did, but our life spans were still longer than the humans. Easily double their average life span. So, when my mother decided to try for another child, her fifth, at the age of forty-five, no one batted an eye. It happened all the time.

My father was the born prince. He met my mother at the market when she was seventeen. I was born a year later. My two sisters and one brother came every few years after. Randall, the youngest, was now ten. Thankfully, my grandparents were still alive. They were helping raise the rugrats.

Unlike my parents, I passed into my twenties without a mate. According to my council, the kingdom was in an uproar. The heir was not supposed to ascend without a mate. They were now trying to push me toward a chosen mate. Something that strictly went against tradition.

And against my heart.

I wanted my mate. I wanted what my parents had. I wanted the companion to my soul.

I sighed with relief as my dress and undergarments fell to the forest floor. There was nothing like the cool clean air against your naked body to rejuvenate you. Okay, well, there was one thing better.

I giggled for joy as I walked into the cool water. As soon as I was deep enough, I slowly made my way toward the water falling from a rock overhang. This beat a bath in the large pot we called a bathtub.

I sang softly to myself, a lullaby my mother used to sing while putting us to sleep at night, soothing our sorrows, or just because she felt like it. I kept it low, not wanting to draw attention to myself. Last thing I needed was for the others to find me out there, naked. No doubt, I would get a lecture about that.

I thought I was supposed to be the one in charge. You know since I was the Queen now.

I found a large stone on the lake bottom and stood up. There was a time when my chest barely came out of the water when I stood there. Now, half my body came out. With no one around, I didn't care.

I had been under the waterfall for nearly a minute when I felt a shift in the air. Something, or someone, was nearby. I pretended not to notice, while I pushed out my senses.

I couldn't see the person just yet, but I could feel their eyes on me. I could feel their heartbeat as though it were right next to me. Goosebumps traveled up and down my skin, and it had nothing to do with the cool air.

Slowly, I turned, wanting to see who was spying on me.

Half hidden by a tree near the water's edge, stood a man. A very well put together man. His hair was dark brown, reminding me of the tree stump he stood next to. Or chocolate. When our eyes met, his began to glow.

Vampire then. I had met a few over the years. Not too many, as I hadn't traveled outside of my kingdom since I was a little girl.

My brain told me I should be afraid. I was alone in the woods, with a vampire. One who did not belong on this side of the border. But my heart, my soul, was telling me otherwise. They were telling me that this man, this vampire, was my protector.

When he didn't come to me, I raised a hand. I was on the verge of begging him to come. He seemed almost shy about it. Or he did. Until I raised my invitation for him to join me.

A giant grin appeared on his face, making those strong features soften. He had to be the most handsome man I had ever met. More so then any of the unmated men in my kingdom, that was for sure.

I kept my hand up as he quickly stripped out of his clothes. The speed he used made me giggle. Then he waded into the water and swam to me, painfully slow after his previous speed. I was beginning to think he was trying to torture me.

When the man got close enough, he slid his palm into mine and up over my arm. I stepped back as he joined me on the rock. He stepped forward again, until we were both under the overhang, the waterfall blocking us from outside view.

His hand slid up to my shoulder and then down my back, until it gripped my bare butt. With one swift move, he lifted me and pressed me against the wall. A little afraid of falling, I wrapped my legs around his waist. The smallest of whimpers passed through my lips when his manhood brushed against me.

His grin grew. He was a cocky vampire. And I did mean that in every sense of the word.

Again, he moved slowly, as he lowered his head to mine. His nose bumped mine and I moved it back just a touch. Very lightly, he pressed his lips to mine, like he was unsure of whether I wanted him to kiss me. I was a little nervous up until then. That soft kiss was my undoing. I wrapped my arms around his neck and pulled him closer to me, our lips moving in perfect synchronization.

I only ever kissed a few boys growing up, we liked to experiment. They called it practicing for their mates. I called it fun. Tradition called it forbidden. Which made it even more fun.

We had never gotten to the tongue part though. My, as of yet, unnamed mate obviously had no problems with it. He was a master at it.

We broke apart minutes later, smiling, and breathing heavily.

"I have searched high and low for you, my dear." His voice was soft and deep.

"I have been right here, waiting for you, my love."

He threw his head back and laughed before kissing me again. He balanced me with one hand, while his other explored my body.

We stayed under that rock, just as we were, for hours. We talked about anything and everything. He told me about his brother and his kingdom. I told him about the sorrow I had been feeling since my parents died. I told him about my concerns and my fears. Things I had not told anybody.

"If you do not want to be Queen, then why do it? Surely your sister is of age?"

It wasn't the first time I had thought about it, to be honest. "She has always been the more diplomatic one. She would make a good leader, much better than I would. I am far too rash, as I am told on a nearly daily basis. Unfortunately, Carolyn does not turn 21 for another season."

We were silent for a time, both lost to our thoughts. Not that that stopped his lips from moving along my neck and shoulders. I could die of happiness right there.

"What are we to do? We just met, and I already don't want to part from you. Yet, you have your kingdom and I have mine." Just the thought of it hurt my heart.

"Bond with me, we will never have to be apart."

I gasped. "And where would we live?"

He thought about this for a minute and then grinned. "I have a cabin, not far from my parent's castle. Come with me, run away from here. Your sister will soon be old enough. Your grandparents can guide her, as will the council."

It was a very tempting offer. I shook my head. "I cannot leave them like that, not without saying goodbye at least. Our parents just died."

He sighed and laid his head against mine. "I cannot come back with you. I am due home tomorrow. But I can come back in a few days, a week at the most. Would you be able to leave with me then?"

I bit the corner of my lip and thought about this. Carolyn really would be a better Queen than me. She would also tell me to follow my heart.

I grabbed both sides of my mate's face and kissed him hard. "I'll do it. I will talk to my sister and get everything set. One week."

Conrad growled deeply, sending shivers through my body. "I don't know if I can wait one week to bond with you."

I grinned at him cheekily. "Who said anything about waiting to bond?"

I barely spit out the last word before his mouth was on mine again. I snapped my head to the rock wall behind me as his body entered my own.

Now that was what I was talking about!

I whimpered when his hand left my body and he chuckled. I watched as he placed his wrist inside his mouth and sliced it with his fangs.

"You are going to need to drink my blood, love. This is how vampires bond."

I nodded, really not caring about anything but our intimacy at that point. I attacked his wrist, ready to tie this man to me for eternity. I hadn't thought much over how it might taste. Surprisingly, it was like melted chocolate pouring down my throat.

Conrad tipped his head back and groaned, before lowering his fangs to my neck. I never would have thought that having my neck sliced open would feel so good.

It could have been minutes or hours before he moved his wrist from my lips, replacing it with his own lips. I felt his heat enter me numerous times, my body shaking uncontrollably against that wall.

At one point, he even stopped moving, and yet our bodies continued reacting. It felt like ocean waves were rolling throughout the inside of my body.

"That was… holy crap that was hot." I leaned my head against the rocks, trying to catch my breath. "How are you able to keep holding us up like this? My legs are practically numb."

He laughed breathlessly. "It is not without great effort. But I would suffer the torments of hell if it kept you from getting harmed."

I grinned and looked at him. "I love you."

He grinned back and moved in to kiss me softly. "And I love you. Come, let's go back to the lake edge."

I nodded and let him lower me down. Together, we swam back to the shore. I dropped to the dirt and laid down. He laid next to me, propping his head up with his arm, looking down on me.

His eyes roamed my body, up and down. His left hand grazed me from my head to thighs.

"You are perfect. Better than I ever dreamed."

I blushed and laid my arm over my eyes. My body was something I had always been self-conscious of. I was not as skinny as Carolyn, nor as fair. My skin was a tone darker, and my waist a few inches wider.

He tried to pull my arm down, but I refused to let it budge. He chuckled.

"Angela, my love, why are you hiding from me?"

"Because I'm embarrassed."

His chuckle deepened. "Of what? Of me complimenting you?"

"Yes. It doesn't happen very often."

He leaned down and kissed my arm, since he couldn't access much else. "That is the worst travesty in the world. Witch males must be blind to not see your beauty."

I snorted and moved my arm down.

"There they are. Those warm brown eyes that suck me in."

I blushed again, groaned, and covered my face with both hands this time. Conrad laughed harder than ever now. It was a joyous laugh, one that I could feel in my heart. Actually, I think I was feeling it in my heart.

I rubbed my chest and looked at him. “Is this normal?”

“Yes. As fated mates, we can feel each other. The longer we are together, the further away it will work.” His eyebrow creased into a slight frown. “I don’t think we will be able to feel each other once we separate today.”

I lifted my hand to his cheek, wanting that uncomfortable sadness to go away. “Just a week. You will be back in a week and then we will never part again.”

His smile was still sad, but he leaned down and kissed me again. I pulled away laughing when I felt his body ready for another round.

“Already?”

“Yes,” oh, boy, was that voice deep. His eyes sparked up again. “I don’t think I will ever be able to be near you and not be ready to claim you.” His lips hit my neck again and soon other places.

I wasn’t exactly planning to say no. So, I didn’t.

A little later, he held me in his arms. My head on his forearm.

“The sun is beginning to set. I have been gone longer than I should have. Carolyn will be looking for me here soon.”

“I should hit the road. The sooner I get home, the sooner I can come back.”

“Before you leave, we need to do the witch’s bonding. It will double our bond to each other.”

Conrad smirked in that adorably sexy way he had. “I don’t think anything could bind me more to you then I already am.”

I laughed and pushed to sit up. I crawled over to my clothes, laughing at the growling animal behind me. I yelped when his hand swung and hit me hard.

"Watch it, mister. You are going to have to wait just a few more minutes before we do that again." I searched through my dress and found my hair ribbons. Then I crawled back to him. His growl got louder and deeper.

I folded my legs in front of me and waved for him to sit up. "Sit like this, right in front of me. Good. Now, we are going to tie these ribbons around our wrists and then you will repeat after me."

"That's it?"

I winked at him. "The fun part comes after." My smile shrank as I looked down at the ribbons in my hands. "Tradition dictates that parents bless the ribbons used in a mating ceremony. My parents blessed these two months ago. A psychic in our coven saw that they wouldn't be here for most of our matings. To be safe, they blessed ribbons for each of us. They didn't know when or how they would go, the psychic refused to tell them that."

Conrad reached over and held my hands in his. "At least they wanted to honor you with this."

I sniffed and nodded. I tied our hands together, with a mix of my hand and my teeth. His eyes were glowing again by the time I was done.

"What?"

"I'll show you when we are done."

I grinned and then worked to school my face.

"Alright, so. I am going to say this line, then you will repeat after me. Then we will say it together. Got it?"

"Yep, fairly simple."

I grinned again, then closed my eyes and focused my breathing. When I opened them again, I saw nothing but love shining back at me from his eyes.

"What's mine is yours, what's yours is mine, together we make our souls combine." I gasped for air as I felt a pull, like someone was trying to rip my soul right out of my chest.

"What's mine is yours, what's yours is mine, together we make our souls combine." I looked up when Conrad gasped in surprise as well.

It took a whole minute before we were able to repeat the line together. We held tight to each other's hands as the pulling suddenly stopped and then something else pushed against us like it was trying to shove the soul back in. If it hadn't been for his grip on me, I would have fallen backward.

We sat there, huffing and puffing. Then, slowly, with his eyes not leaving mine, he used his teeth and untied our ribbons. Then he pounced on me with the speed of his ancestral heritage.

The sun was completely set before either of us put our clothes back on. We stood near the tree he had been hiding behind earlier, just wrapped in each other's arms. My tears silently ran down my face.

"Angie??"

I sighed. "Carolyn has come to collect me."

Conrad gently kissed the tears on both my cheeks. "One week from today. I will meet you right here, high noon."

I nodded and sniffed.

"Angie?" Carolyn was close enough now that she could see us and was most likely confused.

"One week. Now go, before I change my mind and don't let you leave."

"That is not a threat I would mind succumbing to." He kissed me again quickly. "I love you, don't forget that."

"I love you, too." And then he was gone. One second he was standing in my grasp, the next there was no sign of him.

I fell to the ground and sobbed. I didn't know how Carolyn managed it, but she got me up and walked me back to the castle. She even managed to sneak me in a side door and to my room. I sobbed out the story to her as we walked.

Chapter Three

Conrad

The hardest thing I ever had to do was pull away from my mate while she was crying. If I hadn't gone at my top speed, I never would have been able to do it.

I didn't even give myself time to think. I packed my bag, loaded up my horse, and took off. As Dom proved when I was leaving home, we run faster than the horses. But we tried not to scare the humans if we could help it.

Sometimes, I was honestly surprised that they lived so close to us. We needed them though, so we did our best to keep them somewhat comfortable. We did get the occasional vampire succumbing to bloodlust. And all the Nightwalkers had to be watched of course.

A Nightwalker was a human that we turned into a vampire. We did it for a variety of reasons. The biggest was for warriors. They weren't as strong or as fast as us, but their strength rivaled that of the shifters. The one downfall for them, they could not walk in the sun.

Well, maybe two downfalls. They needed the blood more than we did. And they succumbed to bloodlust faster. Hence, the need to monitor them.

Humans were also changed if they asked, paid, or whatever reason we could think of. Oftentimes, it was to prolong the life of a dear friend. Or as a reward for a servant who did well.

I rode my horse faster than normal, something I had never done. Therefore, I was slightly surprised when she began to wear out. Begrudgingly, I pulled her toward a stream of water I could smell nearby and let her rest. I was too restless to sleep, not that we needed much. Instead, I sat on the edge of the water and stared into it, letting my mind wander back to just a few hours before.

I had never imagined my mate would be a witch. And what a beautiful one at that. She was perfect in every way. I loved the softness of her body, and the way it molded itself to my own. Her taste was incredible. Both blood and otherwise.

I chuckled to myself when I remembered her reactions to how else we could pleasure each other.

I once thought witches were stuck up, a bit prudish and thought highly of themselves. I was so wrong. At least, I was with my girl. She loved to laugh. She wanted to have adventures. We would not be bored spending a millennium or two together. We would need at least that much since I may not let her leave the bedroom for a century.

And with her being closer to a human than me, I wouldn't need to use servants anymore. I could go to my mate. I could feed the best way there was, with our bodies entwined.

I let my horse have until the sun rose, and then I reclaimed my position on her back. I allowed her to control the pace this time. I was happily lost in thoughts of my mate.

I couldn't wait to tell my father that I finally found her. My mother would be so excited to have another woman in the house. And Dom, well, I didn't know if it would even phase him much. He was still too young to care much about mates. I would have to make sure to still spend time with him though. That he would care about.

It was mid-morning by the time I arrived back home. My parents must have heard me coming, as they both came out to greet me. I dropped the horse off near the barn and flung my saddle bags over my shoulder.

This time I caught Dom before he tackled me. I swung him up into my arms and tickled him.

"Put me down! I am too big for you to carry."

I threw my head back and laughed as I set him back down.

"You smell different."

I grimaced. I forgot about that. Looked like I would be telling them all straight away then.

We approached my parents together, both of them looked very happy. I wondered if they had been paying attention and heard Dom's comment. If they did, they may have already figured it out. That would sure make my life simpler.

"Mother, father." I greeted them.

Before my mother could get a word out, a squeal came from the house. Followed by a stick figure with blonde hair rushing at me.

"Conrad! You're home! I can't tell you how sad I was to find that you weren't here when I arrived!"

Yolanda.

I mentally cursed at myself for forgetting that she was coming. Our fathers had made a deal for this arrangement. I hadn't cared much either way. She and I typically had a tryst when we were around each other. It wasn't uncommon for vampires to do that. We celebrated nature in our own ways.

Not for the first time, I recognized the severe differences between the witch culture and ours.

I turned my face in time and made her kiss land on my cheek.

"Yolanda. It's good to see you."

She gave me a frown and then an odd look. She sniffed quietly, then snarled. My eyes glanced at my parents, who were standing near the front door, still a good bit behind her.

"I think you and I need to have a talk." She hissed through her teeth low enough for only me to hear.

I sighed. Maybe we should discuss it before I tell my parents. I did owe it to her in a way. Our mating had been coming for nearly a year now. Mostly because I kept dragging my feet.

I gave her a tight smile, waved at my parents, and then led her to my cabin. She kept a tight grip on my arm the entire way. Thankfully we didn't pass anyone else along the way. No worries on the word of my change in scent reaching my parents before I did.

My door was barely shut before she started snarling at me again.

"How the hell could you mate someone else? And when? I have been with your parents all morning and they haven't said a word! In fact, your mother and I have been talking about ways to fix up this place. What the hell, Conrad?"

I lifted my hands in a placating way, trying to calm her down. "I can explain, but I need you to calm down first and listen."

I waited while she tried to steady her breaths, and then collapsed onto a chair in my sitting room. I pulled a chair in front of her and sat down, bracing myself with my arms on my knees, I leaned forward.

"I never meant to hurt you. This wasn't planned, Yolanda. It just happened. I went for a walk in the forest near the Southern Territories, and there she was. I came home to prepare my parents for her arrival. She needed to prepare her sister to take her place in the family. I am going back next week to get her. Look, you know the call of a fated mate is the strongest thing in the world. Nothing can break that. Nothing can compare to that."

I couldn't resist the grin pushing to come out.

"There is nothing like it, Yolanda. I hope you can experience it one day. It's the best feeling in the world!"

I laughed, feeling light and free, being able to share this news with her. She had always been a good friend to me. Despite her own disappointment, she couldn't fight the smile at my obvious happiness.

"I can't say I'm not disappointed." She took a big breath, letting it out slowly. Her eyes creased. "Wait, that smell. There is something different about it. Something sweeter."

She tilted her head and I waited with a slight grimace for her to place it. Yolanda had never been quiet on her opinions on mixed matings. Fated or not.

"Did you say you were in the forest?"

I gulped. Here it comes. "Yes."

She was silent for a split second then dramatically gasped. She jumped out of her seat and took a couple steps back, putting more distance between us.

"You mated a witch." She spit out with venom. "How could you? You are a traitor to your crown!"

I jumped up and blocked her as she headed for the door.

"Woah! Wait a minute. I haven't betrayed anybody. And I would never betray the crown. You should know that better than anyone."

She huffed and folded her arms. "You want to prove you aren't a traitor, then reject your mate."

It took me a moment to comprehend what she was saying. I kept trying to make sense of it, but it didn't.

"You want me to *reject* my fated mate, the one I have already sealed myself to, in order to prove my loyalty to my own crown?"

"Yes, Conrad. Of course."

"That is the most ridiculous thing I have ever heard. That makes no sense at all."

Yolanda sauntered toward me, like she held all the power, and placed her hand on my chest, picking at my shirt.

"Sure, it does. You know how your father feels about pure bloods only on the throne."

I closed my eyes and cursed silently to myself. He did have strong feelings regarding that. Just before I left he kept going on and on about it. He didn't care what the lower ranks did in their matings, but when it came to the royal line, we needed to stay pure.

"He will understand, she is my fated mate." I was grasping at straws, and my voice showed it.

"Will he though? I don't. I don't see that it matters."

I scoffed and pushed her away. “Cut the crap, Yolanda. You just want to be Queen. That is all you care about.”

She grinned, like I was finally understanding. “Of course. What girl wouldn’t?” She then looked me up and down. “My King isn’t exactly a second-place prize either.”

I rolled my eyes and stepped away from her, rubbing both hands over my face.

“It doesn’t matter. I have bonded with my mate. The moment I am near my father, he will smell it. I will make him understand. And I’m sure, once he meets her, he will realize she is perfect for our family. That she is perfect for me. Fate selected her for a reason.”

Yolanda took quick steps to me, a snarl on her beautiful face once again, and slapped me hard.

“If you won’t reject her for the crown, then do it for her safety!”

Say what now? I guess she could read that on my face as she huffed haughtily and shook her head.

“It’s simple. Either you reject your mate and bond with me, or I go on a hunt and kill your mate.” She shrugged, like this was no big deal.

“And then you would die for murdering the crown prince.” Duh.

Her grin was so evil. “No one would know what happened to you. You would just suddenly fall dead. Splat!” She gave a mocking pout. “Everyone will be so sad and confused. What would they do?” Her pout morphed slowly into a grin again, as she closed in on me. “You want your mate to be safe. Then you will bond with me.”

My voice barely made it out of my throat. “I cannot. I told you, I already bonded with her. We cannot bond with more than one mate.”

Yolanda waved a hand, pushing the thought away like it didn't matter. "We aren't fated. We just need to trade blood regularly. It will weaken your bond with her. Her scent will eventually fade from yours. The more we trade, the sooner it goes away. We just hang out right here in your cabin for a few days. When we emerge, everyone will have assumed that we bonded." She tapped my chest with her last few words, emphasizing her point. "No… one… will… be… the… wiser."

She giggled and wrapped her arms around my neck.

"What do you say…mate?" She cackled again. "Me or the death of your fated mate?"

I scowled. I couldn't believe I was going to do this. My only saving grace was that Angela had performed the witch's bond. One way or another, we would always be tied together. I just wished I knew what all came with that. I just needed time to work this through and find a way. I had a week until I left to meet with Angela. One week. I could fix this before then. And pray she didn't kill us both when she found out what I had to do in order to save us.

"Fine. You win, Yolanda."

She jumped off me and clapped with glee. What had I ever seen in her before?

Chapter Four

Angela

I paced back and forth at the edge of the small lake. My sister Carolyn stood not far off watching me warily.

"I'm sure Conrad will be here any time now, Angie."

I rubbed my upper arms and looked up at the sky for the millionth time.

"The sun is setting, Cary. He was supposed to be here at noon. Do you think something happened to him?"

Carolyn walked over to me and grabbed my hands, loosening the grip I had on myself. "What does your heart tell you?"

My voice cracked as I spoke. "That something is wrong. I've been feeling it for days. I don't understand any of this. When he first left, I felt sadness because he did not want to leave me. He said we wouldn't be able to feel anything because it was so far. Not yet anyway. But I still feel this pit in my stomach that breaks my heart."

My younger sister pulled me in and held me against her tight. One hand trapped my face in her neck, the other rubbed my back.

"I say, we give him one more day. If he doesn't come tomorrow, then we go find him. It won't be hard to do. We can place a tracking spell. You two have bonded through your magic, it will be simple enough."

"Do you think Grams will be willing to help like that though? None of them seemed all that thrilled with you taking my place." That was an understatement. There was a good deal of yelling. Especially when they saw the marking he left on my neck.

Carolyn laughed softly. "It was only because they love you and we will all miss you when you are gone. No one would want to keep you from your fated mate. Fire and ice, remember? That's what we decided."

I gave her the best smile I could, which was not more than a grimace. The first night, after I finally stopped sobbing, we talked it all through.

Carolyn theorized that his matching power was his fire. Vampire Borns had fire running through their veins. My power was more like ice. I could freeze time. I could freeze anything. It came in handy a few times when I needed a break from my grandparents nagging this last week.

"Do you think he's discovered that he can freeze things yet?"

I snorted. "I never did get a chance to tell him he would have my power. I only told him what it was since I told him stories of us growing up. He laughed, saying we could freeze our kids when they cried or fought too much." I blushed. "He also said we didn't have to bother with getting a room when he wanted me, I could just freeze the room, and no one would ever know."

Carolyn laughed with me. The laughing helped ease my discomforts. Still, I wasn't sure about leaving our meeting place just yet. The moon was high in the sky when she finally convinced me to leave.

First thing the next morning, I was back at our lake. I waited all day, but Conrad still didn't show.

The next morning, we sat down and cast a tracking spell. My grandmother was a pro at these spells. She used to tell us stories of using this spell to find our dad when he would wander off on his own. She only stopped after he met mom.

Grandma learned her lesson on tracking him down then. That was also how they found out that dad had met his true mate.

"It will take you all day to get there, so you better get started."

My Grams handed me the gemstone that would act like my beacon and kissed both my cheeks. Carolyn insisted on coming with me. We saddled two horses and a change of clothes for each of us. I debated on taking all of my things with me, that way I wouldn't have to make the trip twice, but something was telling me not to. I didn't like feeling pessimistic. But the feeling was strong within me. Like a darkness that refused to budge.

The stars were bright in the sky by the time we entered the last village. We could see the castle, and we both snorted. Vampires had large egos. I didn't mind so much though. It was beautiful.

My gemstone led me to the right of the castle and down further. It was a bit down the road, but at the end was an adorable little cabin.

"Is that it?" Carolyn asked.

I nodded, a smile on my face. "Yes. I can feel him now, too. I think he is sleeping." I gave a peaceful sigh. "It feels good to have him back in there."

"Maybe he just got caught up getting the cabin ready for you?"

"Maybe. Hopefully."

We stopped the horses at the gate to the yard. Carolyn was still sitting on hers after I got down.

"I'm nervous. Will you come with me?"

"Of course. Whatever you need." She giggled as we got closer to the door. "I think you should just sneak inside and climb into bed with him."

I couldn't help the grin that took over. That was the best idea ever. I hugged her quietly, before turning the small knob to open his door.

We were both smiling as we walked through the small home. It was just the right size for us. And it was beautiful. Conrad even had a wooden rocking chair in a corner, something that would be perfect for rocking a baby to sleep at night.

I stopped a few feet from a closed bedroom door, the other two had been empty. At the foot of the door was a woman's brazier. I looked at it cautiously, afraid to touch it. The tears were threatening when I looked back up at Carolyn.

She lifted a hand, silently reminding me to wait and not jump to conclusions.

I closed my eyes and took a minute to steady myself. Surely, I was overreacting.

Carefully, I turned the knob and pushed the door open. Carolyn and I both gasped at the same time.

Conrad was sleeping alright, but he wasn't alone. And neither of them were wearing clothes.

I felt the sharp pain hit my heart at his betrayal. A sob tried to break out, but it kept getting stuck. Conrad jumped out of bed, his hand over his heart. When he looked at me, I saw nothing but panic and regret.

"Angela, baby. I can explain." He tried to step toward me carefully.

The woman woke up and sat on the bed with a haughty look.

"I don't want to hear it. Carolyn, go untie the horses."

I heard her sniff as she turned and ran out of the house.

"I can't believe I trusted you. I can't believe I worried about you when you didn't show. How long did you even wait before jumping into bed with her?"

"The next morning." The vampire whore happily told me.

Conrad winced when he felt my pain. "Baby, please. I can explain."

I threw my hand up. "I don't want to hear it. There is nothing you can say that will fix this."

Unable to control my tears anymore, I spun and ran out of the house. Conrad ran after me, calling my name. I jumped onto my horse with ease and grasped my sister's hand. She knew me well enough to know what was coming.

There was only one way to escape a vampire chasing you. And thankfully, I had been born with that talent.

I lifted my freehand into the air and whimpered out one word. "Freeze." The whole world froze around my sister and me.

I fell apart right then and there. Carolyn grabbed the reins for my horse and clicked her tongue. Without a word, she steered us back toward home while I sobbed. I waited until we crossed our own borders to unfreeze the world.

My Grams was shocked when we opened the door and walked in. She took one look at my face and held me tight. Carolyn filled her in on what happened. By the time she was done, I was angry. Angrier than I had ever been in my entire life.

"I want him to pay. I want them all to pay. I want to rid this world once and for all of the vampire menace. I want them to suffer the same pain that I have felt, what all the mates have felt when they betray us. Call all the women together."

"What about the men?" Carolyn asked carefully.

"I don't want to see another man anytime soon. It's only women who will understand my pain, who will understand the betrayal. Besides, the men will want to kill the lot of them all at once. I only want the women, at least for now. In time, the humans will take care of the rest. I want the males to suffer first."

An hour later, all the women showed up in our meeting house. They sat down and waited. I stood up and addressed them.

"As many of you know, I met my true mate only days ago. He was supposed to meet me the other day, but he did not show. I grew concerned and went to find him. And I found him in bed with another woman." I snarled while they gasped in shock.

I waited out the murmurings, most growing angry with me. A true mate was to be treasured, not tarnished.

"The vampires have infested these lands for long enough. Their immorality and disrespect of nature and other species needs to end. They torment the humans, they betray their mates, they have no hearts. It is time we step up and rid this world of their treachery."

"About time!" An older woman shouted from the back. "My daughter was hoodwinked by one of them once upon a time. He fell into bloodlust while they bonded. All I got was an oops!"

My heart cracked for the woman and her daughter. I had heard rumors from other villages, but nothing so close to home.

“What’s your plan, your majesty? You have our support.”

I nodded. “Thank you. My plan is simple. We rid them of all their vampire women. We also curse them that they can have no more. If they get any other woman pregnant, she will only give them a son. In time, the humans are going to revolt against them. They are already beginning to wake up to the true nature of the vampires. We will just make it nearly impossible for them to continue their lines.”

A younger woman raised her hand nervously.

“Yes, Rachel.”

“For the spell to remain strong and last longer, they have to be given a way to break it. A balance in everything. Do you know how we will balance a spell like that?”

I chuckled. “Yes. I have the perfect counter to it. One that will require them to change who they are and repent.”

We spent the rest of the night planning. Then rested the next day. We gathered together once more as the sun set. This time, we had a large cauldron in the middle of the room. Grams and another of the elders in the village mixed the ingredients we would need.

Right as the sun started its last decline behind the mountains we began to chant.

“As the sun sets on the earth, so does the reign of the vampire. From here until the curse is broken, not one female child shall be born.” I sliced my hand with the blade and let my blood drip into the bubbling water. Then passed it on.

Each woman added her own part of the spell, and their own blood. The gray smoke grew thicker with each drop and each word. When it came back to me again, I sliced my other hand and held them both over the cauldron.

"From now until the curse is broken, not one female child shall be born to a vampire. The curse will be broken when the hidden vampire prince accepts his witch mate and humbles himself to her. Only this can break the curse. Only his humility and willingness to accept what fate has given him will lift this curse from them. With the blood of the witches, we seal this curse."

"With the blood of the witches, we seal this curse." The others repeated in unison. The smoke lifted into the air and drifted out the windows.

We all ran to the wagons, which we had previously loaded with everything we would need. The men argued that they should come with us. It was their job to fight after all. Not one of the women took that well. Instead, the men stood sullenly off to the sides.

"Ladies, the time has come for us to seek our vengeance for the plague that has spread through our lands."

With everyone gathered, we held hands, some held the wagons with the oxen, and I closed my eyes focusing hard. I had never done it this way before, but it was necessary. The vampire lands were so vast, it would take weeks to get all the women. So, we sent a message through a dreamwalker, each village had one. It made it easier to communicate.

In my right hand was our dreamwalker. She linked with me mentally, and then with the others.

"Freeze."

The wind had been blowing lazily, brushing against the leaves in the trees. The water in a small waterfall that provided clean water to the village had been gurgling nearby. All of it froze. The wind mid blow. The water mid gurgle. Even the smoke from the spell froze. I wasn't concerned, once I released the spell it would continue on until it reached every vampire in the world.

I focused on the women in the dreamscape, waiting to hear if it worked.

"Well, done, my lady." They each bowed and then blinked away.

I laughed with triumph and commanded my own team to load up.

We rode in the darkness, everyone taking turns driving. When we reached the Royal village, we pulled over and let everyone rest.

I worried some may not be able to handle it, but their faces were firm and their grips tight on their weapons.

Darkness still reigned over the earth as we approached the castle. We divided up and headed in different directions. I only had one place in mind.

I stalked through the small house that should have been mine. I looked at the rocking chair that I should have been sitting in with my babies. I stared at the fireplace where Conrad and I should have been cuddling every night when it was cold, talking away the hours. Just as we had under that waterfall.

I pushed the tear away, refusing to let my sorrow take me again. It wasn't hard to do. All it took was opening the door to the bedroom, where my mate was frozen in his sleep. The whore still next to him, her hand resting on his back.

It took no effort at all to raise the sword over her frozen, sleeping form and bring it down, severing her head from her body. Who needed a silver dagger when you had the power to freeze?

I pulled the note I'd written for him out of my pocket and laid it on the side table near his bed. The bed where we should have created our many babies.

I stood over him, staring down at the face that I still loved so much. I felt the crack in my heart, the one I had been using to inflame my anger. I felt my body begin to crumble as I fell to the floor.

My sister, though, knew me well. She was right there, ready to catch me. I let her lead me out the door and back to the wagons. We waited as the women came back victorious.

We stopped at every human village we passed and looked for their vampire overlords. Everywhere we found a female, someone went inside and dispatched them.

The older witch who lost her daughter greedily took out the female vampire who had taken her daughter's place. She said she didn't regret not killing the male who killed her daughter. She wanted him to suffer the loss just as she had.

Oncc homc. I waitcd ncxt to my drcamwalkcr, both of us sitting under a tree in the center of our village.

"The job is done. You may release your spell, your highness." She told me tiredly.

I nodded once. "Unfreeze."

Chapter Five

Conrad

I awoke with a start in the middle of the night, my heart aching once again. It hadn't stopped for days. I knew the reason. And it was all my fault.

I should have tried harder to get to her, to protect my mate. I failed. And now I'd broken her heart. Her dear, sweet, heart. I knew she would never forgive me.

I tried to follow her, I planned to chase her all the way home if I had too. But with a blink of an eye, both witches and their horses were gone. I didn't understand at first. Then I remembered something she had told me, about her and Carolyn stealing sweets from the kitchen. She would hold her sister's hand and freeze the room, only, the whole world would freeze.

The only thing that made sense was that she froze me. Who knew how long ago that had been? I wouldn't blame her if she kept us frozen until she was home. I could sniff her out. I could go to the waterfall and then follow her scent from there.

But I wouldn't. I couldn't.

I needed to give her space. Space to calm down so she would listen. In the meantime, I needed to find a way to get rid of Yolanda and to protect us from her.

Right before I fell asleep, I decided to suck it up and speak to my father. I needed his wise guidance on this. I should have sought his help to begin with.

I rolled over in the bed, pushing Yolanda's hand off my back in disgust. I had hardly touched her in days, much to her dismay. She kept trying. But I couldn't do it. I never should have in the first place. I only wanted my mate.

It wasn't easy, but I almost made it back to sleep. Until I heard the first scream.

And then another.

And another.

Soon, the whole village was screaming. Only, they were all men and boys screaming. Not one single female voice was rising into the air. Why?

I jumped out of bed, preparing to go find out what happened. I was confused how Yolanda could sleep through it all.

"Yolanda. Yolanda! Wake up!" I cursed under my breath as I walked over to her side of the bed and nudged her shoulder.

I jumped with a scream of my own as her head rolled off the bed.

"What the hell?"

I pulled the curtain on the window, bringing in the moonlight so I could have perfect eyesight. I could see decently enough in the dark, but some things needed to not have shadows. I walked to my side of the bed and opened the other.

I stood back in shock at the blood all over my bed. I looked down and saw it on my side. I turned, trying to get a look at my back. I couldn't see any signs of a splatter. Only the pooling. And it was still wet. As though it had just happened.

How could that be? There was no scent trail of someone having been there besides us.

How did I sleep through this?

I looked around the room frantically, desperate for some answer. My eyes found nothing as it went over it the first time. The next time, I spotted something small. I picked up the paper off the side table and stared at it, unable to make the words sink into my brain.

No. This didn't make sense. Angela couldn't do this. She wouldn't. She was too pure. Too sweet.

I staggard backward a few steps, a hand over my chest as though a dagger had just been shoved through me. My back hit the wall, and I slid down, tears falling down my face.

What had I done?

This had to be some kind of nightmare.

The sun was breaking through the windows when I heard my front door open from a distance.

"Conrad? My Lord?"

I didn't bother answering him. I just sat there in my frozen silence. Why didn't she just kill me and leave the rest alone?

"My Lord?" Lucas choked on the question as he took in the sight of Yolanda on the bed. He then looked down at me and squatted down.

"I'm so sorry, my Lord. The same thing has happened all over town. All the women are dead. Nobody knows why."

"I do." I croaked. "Because of me. Because I didn't protect her. I betrayed her."

Lucas, my best friend since he came to work in the castle five years ago, sat on the floor next to me. "Who, my Lord? Yolanda?"

I shook my head and handed him the note. "My mate. I met my fated mate and I betrayed her."

Lucas read the note out loud, he never was one to keep his thoughts inside his head. It always made me laugh in the past. Not this time.

"Because of your betrayal, your kingdom will wither and die. Your females are gone, and you will have no more. The curse will be broken when the hidden vampire prince accepts his witch mate and humbles himself to her."

Lucas read it over and over again, mumbling to himself.

"I don't understand, Conrad. Was your mate a witch?"

I nodded. "Yes, and she had the power to freeze time." I gave him a look and he cursed.

"We need to tell your father. Now." He practically pulled me off that floor and threw my pants at me.

Numbly, I slipped them on.

I barely made it through the front door of the castle before Dom ran to me and held on as he sobbed uncontrollably. It wasn't until I saw my father sitting much like I had been on the floor, that it really hit home.

All the women had been killed… including my mother.

“Yolanda?” He croaked from the floor when he saw me.

I shook my head. He sighed and his head sank down.

“I don’t understand. Every woman was beheaded sometime in the night. Not one man woke up. Even the ones that were awake and sitting in the same room as them, have no idea how it happened. One minute, the woman was laughing, and the next… I don’t understand how this is possible. Why?”

“I… I… do.” My voice shook and croaked. I didn’t care if I sounded weak. “It’s because I made a mistake. A very grave mistake. I have been trying to fix it. I swear. Just last night I had finally decided to come to you for help. But it looks like I was too late. If I had known this was even possible, I never would have given Yolanda what she wanted.”

My father slowly pushed himself up and walked over to me. “What happened? What did you do?” There was a low threatening growl in his voice.

“I met my fated mate in the southern territories when I was there last week. I went for a walk in the forest, and there she was, like an angel swimming in the water.”

My father shook his head. “I don’t understand what this has to do with anything.”

“I planned to tell you when I got back. I wanted to bring her home with me, but she had to make sure her people were cared for first. Yolanda smelled my scent change before I could get to you. She threatened to find Angela and kill her if I did not give her what she wanted. I had a few days. I thought I had time to figure it out. But when I didn't show up, Angela came to find me, worried something had happened." I swallowed the lump in my throat.

"She found Yolanda in my bed with me. I tried to chase after her, but she just disappeared. I decided to give her space before I hunted her down, giving her time to cool down. I didn't know this was even possible. I didn't know she would take her pain out on others. I swear father. I thought I was doing the right thing!"

He thought carefully, before shaking his head slowly, dismissing me. "No vampire is fast enough to kill all the women in one night, without alerting anyone. Awake or asleep."

"Angela isn't a vampire, father. She's a witch. And she can freeze time. That's how she disappeared on me. I think the male mates survived because they were frozen. Their mate bond was unable to kill them with their mate. When I woke up from the screaming, I saw this on my side table."

I waved to Lucas, and he handed my father the note.

My father's face paled as he collapsed onto a chair. "What have you done?"

"I'm sorry, father. I truly am."

"Get out." It was barely a whisper, something Lucas probably didn't even hear. But he might as well have yelled it in my face.

"Father, please!" I stepped toward him only to be stopped by his growl.

"Guards!"

I stepped back in shock when the others came in, confused as to what was going on.

"Conrad is banished from the lands. He is no longer my son."

"Father, please! Let me try to fix this."

He laughed darkly. "There is no *fixing* this Conrad. Your mother is dead, all the women are dead. And if I am reading this right, we will never have another female vampire again! Who is going to carry on our bloodlines? Humans? They rarely survive as it is."

"Where am I to go, father?"

"I don't care. Live among the Nightwalkers, live in a cave. I don't care. But if you hang around long enough, the others will kill you for what you have done. Now begone!"

The guards walked toward me, angry because they were already catching on to what happened.

"I'm sorry, father. I will fix this. I promise. If it is the last thing I do, I will lift this curse."

I turned and ran out of the house. I stuck to the forests, and off the main trails. I ran until I reached the border to the witch territory. I kept running, until I hit a wall made of air. I hit it with such force that I flew back six feet and landed on my butt.

"What the hell?"

I stood up and walked slower, my hand out in front of me. Sure enough, my hand hit a wall. I walked to the left, dragging my hand along, trying to find an opening. No matter how far I walked, or which way I turned, the wall would not let me pass.

"She didn't believe me, but I knew you would come."

My head snapped up at the voice. It took a second, but soon I placed the girl with blonde hair.

"Carolyn? Where is Angela? I didn't mean to hurt her."

Carolyn lifted a hand to silence me and shook her head.

"It's a little late for apologies, don't you think?"

"Please, Carolyn. Let me pass. Let me see my mate." My legs started bending, the need to beg her on my knees, if I must, growing stronger.

Carolyn took one step forward and snarled at me. "It is too late for that now! Because of you I lost my sister!"

I stepped back and gasped in shock. "No." I shook my head, that couldn't be true. I rubbed my chest, remembering the sharp pain from earlier. No, that wasn't it. I refused to believe it. "Surely I would have felt it if she died. Surely she would have taken me with her."

"And did all the other males die with their mates?"

I shook my head again, no. No!

"Search your cold heart, Conrad. Do you feel her now? Do you feel any piece of my sister?"

I huffed, the emptiness preparing to overwhelm me. Carolyn nodded like I answered her question.

"Go, enjoy the freedom you wanted. Without your fated mate, Conrad."

She spun, creating a small circle in the dirt. I tried to call her back, but she ignored me. I dropped to my knees and stayed there until the sun and moon both passed through their daily cycles.

A month after my banishment, I set myself up in a small cave that I used to camp in with my father. I was there for a week, before I heard a familiar voice.

"I had a feeling you would find your way here eventually. I've been coming out every few days, just to check."

I smirked and looked at the dirt I was drawing in with a stick.

"It's good to see you, Lucas. How are you?"

He dropped down next to me with a depressed sigh. "I've been better. And you?"

"I've been better."

"I take it you tried to talk to her?"

I nodded.

"And?"

"I'm sitting alone in a cave, depressed. You tell me how it went?"

He gave a sardonic chuckle and turned to lean against the cave wall. "I'm guessing you ran into that invisible wall they have around their lands now." I raised an eyebrow at him. "Did you think the others weren't going to try and retaliate? Every woman is dead. The witches left the human and witch mates alive. There had been hope that the ones who were pregnant when the curse hit would give birth to girls, but alas, none of them did. The human died in the process. The witch not long after."

I groaned and buried my head in my hands. "What do I do now?"

"Well, the way I figure it. You bide your time. You hide out with the Nightwalkers until the heat dies down with the royals. An opportunity will present itself."

"That could be centuries."

"Yep. So, I guess it's a good thing that I will be by your side."

I scoffed. "You never wanted this life, Lucas." I had offered more than once before.

He shook his head. "Nope, but I'll take it. You need someone to help you. Someone who knows the real you."

I licked my lips. "You would do that for me?"

"Psh. Who says it's just for you? Immortal life full of women and money. What's not to love?"

I chuckled. "Do you want to do this now, or wait a few days?"

He shrugged. "I have no reason to wait. Might as well do it now." He scratched his jaw. "How exactly does this work?"

"It's simple. You feed from me, then I feed from you."

He nodded once, then pushed himself to a standing position. "Alright, where?"

I waved for him to follow me deeper into the cave. "I must warn you though. Vampire blood heightens many feelings. You are going to want to do things you may not have wanted before."

"What do you mean?" Lucas asked, somewhat warily now.

I could have told him, possibly even turned him off the idea, but I was being selfish. I was lonely. Lucas was my best friend; even closer than the few vampire ones I had had. He was also the only person who hadn't cut me out of their life.

I winked at him instead. "You'll see. Just act on what you feel at the time. That is one of the joys of being a vampire. No more morals and judgements to worry about. You, my friend, are about to enter a world of self-gratification."

We both laughed. Ironically, I would have given it all up to spend an eternity gratifying my mate. I would have given her everything. I thought I was.

I directed him to sit against one of the cave walls. I kneeled in front of him and punctured my wrist with my teeth. I pushed the memories of doing this with my mate aside and focused on the present.

Lucas apprehensively took my wrist and placed it against his mouth. I could have done it for him, but this was his choice to make. It was his last chance to change his mind.

He didn't.

Within the first few drops, his eyes rolled to the back of his head. I laughed a minute later when he reached down and pulled himself out of his pants. He whimpered, trying to take care of his own issues.

"Would you like some help, my friend?"

His suction on my wrist lessened but did not stop. There was both wariness and desire burning in them.

"As I said, my blood is going to affect you. There is no shame in having a need. As long as it gets taken care of, what does it matter where, or who, did it?"

He was still wary, so I reached my other hand down and grabbed him. His head fell against the wall and his suction sped up again. I began to move my hand back when his problem finished, but he grabbed it and put it back. I laughed and obliged. He always had been a bit of a lady's man in the village. Although I may have just made that worse.

When his eyes had a low glow, and I was feeling weak from the blood loss, I took both my hands back. I didn't even wait to seal my own arm before I leaned in and bit his neck.

I guess I should have warned him about the effect of that too.

Lucas was a quick study though. His hand found me with no issues, pushing my pants down in the process. It had been some time since I had both fed and let someone take care of my needs. It was a good thing he had fed first, I might have accidentally killed him.

I hadn't realized how hungry I was. I hadn't eaten in over a month. Not since I bonded with my mate.

Nobody appealed to me. I held no desire to feed from anyone else.

I drank until his body began to shake uncontrollably beneath me, the sign that he was going through the change. Then I drank a little more, until I could taste my own blood coming back to me.

I sealed his neck and rocked back to my heels. When his eyes met mine, the whites of his eyes were glowing. He gave me a tired smile, and I spotted four teeth that were now slightly pointed and sharp.

"You need to feed from me one more time." I pointed to my neck, and he shook his head. "Lucas, you have to drink a little more of my blood to make the change permanent."

His laugh was darker this time as he put a hand to my chest and pushed me with more strength then he would have been able to do before. I laughed when I landed on my back. I laughed harder when his fangs sank into my thigh.

I didn't have to tell him when to stop this time. His body knew when it was done. He slowly sealed my thigh, and then repaid me in a much better way that time.

When we were both done, he collapsed against the wall again. I stayed where I was, neither of us caring about the state of our undress. When he was still human, he would have cared. He didn't anymore. With such a drastic change, so quickly, I had to wonder if it was always in him somewhere. Maybe the pressures of human society made him ashamed to act on what he wanted. Such a shame. I was glad that he let me free him from those constraints.

"How do you feel, my friend?" I asked after a long moment of silence.

"Hungry." He growled with a laugh. "And very horny still. Is this normal?"

I smirked with a nod. "Pretty much, yes. It's the blood. Come, let's go find you a nice unsuspecting human female to feed from."

Lucas' chuckle sounded more like a growl. For the first time in weeks, I felt my load lighten just a little bit.

Over the next two centuries, we traveled the world, feeding, screwing, and doing anything we wanted. We turned men and women in every country, in every city. They were my army, strategically placed.

We returned home 427 years later, when we heard the humans were revolting. Lucas and I took an army with us, prepared to help, but it was too late. My father was already dead, and our people were hiding in the mountains.

I sniffed around until I found a familiar scent. I smiled as I followed it. I hoped he would see sense. That he would see that I could help.

I found him, sitting on a cliff, throwing rocks down the side.

"Long time no see, Dom."

His head snapped around. He smiled at first and then it shrank.

"You are not allowed to be here, Conrad."

I huffed. "Now that is a name I haven't heard in a while."

Dom pushed himself to a standing position. "So, we've heard."

I lifted an eyebrow and he continued, as he passed me.

"Did you really think that we would not hear of your… adventures?" He stopped and spun around to face me.

It was a little disconcerting to see my baby brother all grown up, and nearly the same height as me. I was still larger than him though. It took a little work, but I had bulked up.

"What the hell happened to you? I remember you being happy and kind to people. You never took more than what was offered. You never hurt the servants. And you always had time for me."

I scoffed and threw my arms out to the side. "I grew up, that's what happened. I tried to protect someone I cared about, and it backfired. The world wants to see me as the bad guy, fine. I'll be the bad guy." I shrugged, dropping my hands back to my waist. "It's more fun anyway."

Dom gave me a look of disgust. "Why are you here? Why did you come back now, of all times?"

"I came back to help you. I tried to get here sooner but traveling with a hundred Nightwalkers isn't so easy."

That seemed to confuse him more. "Why would you bring all of them with you?"

I laughed out loud. "Why do you think? To help you win this war and get our homelands back."

It was his turn to scoff at me as he turned and walked away again. "We don't need you. We are fine how we are."

"Dom! You are hiding in a hole like wild animals! That is not living."

There was venom in his voice, something I had never imagined would come from him, when he spun around this time. “That is King Dominic to you. And I do believe that you were banished from these lands and our people centuries ago. I was there, Conrad. I remember the death, the destruction. All because you betrayed a witch. You and your *army* are not welcome here.”

I snarled. “You will regret that decision one day, *your highness*. I will get my throne back, and I will bring vampires out of hiding. And, for the record, the name is Curtis.”

Chapter Six

Angela

Carolyn kept the wall up for a year after what we did. I knew she led Conrad to believe I was dead. It was my choice. I used the ribbon that had once bound us together to hide myself from him. Carolyn had helped me put a different kind of binding spell on it and tied it to my wrist. Conrad would never feel my presence again. To him, I was dead.

It would also help keep me sane. I would not have to feel him anymore either.

It didn't take long before I regretted my rash decision on cursing the Vampire Borns or killing all their women. Not the vampire whore, of course, just the rest of them. They had been innocent in all of this.

Well, mostly.

I stepped down, as planned, and let my sister have the throne. I wouldn't be able to carry on the line anyway. I would never be able to take on another mate again.

I was already bound to the devil.

I settled for living in my forest, keeping myself away from other people. Every day, I prayed for mother nature to take my soul. Every day, I prayed for death. I did not want to live with the guilt and the blood on my hands. I did not want to live knowing that my mate was still out there somewhere, living it up.

I watched as one by one, my siblings passed on with their mates. I watched as the throne passed from generation to generation.

I watched as the humans revolted against the vampires.

From time to time, they would attack us as well. When that happened, I acted as a third mate to the royal couple. It was not something that was spoken of to everyone else. It was dangerous as it made the mates more powerful. It also protected them if one should die in battle.

I learned many new things during those times.

The male mate, Trent, in the second royal couple I helped had the gift of sight. I saw more than I cared too. I saw the real devastation that my spell was going to cause. I turned Conrad into a monster. The thousands of people he would kill in his journey to take back what should have been his would all be on me.

We kept that mating open for nearly a month. A month of seeing the havoc I had caused. By the end, I was ready to kill myself, hoping I would take him with me. Surely that would save everyone.

Trent came to me, having seen what I had planned. He stood in my doorway and gave me the pitying look I was accustomed to.

“It won’t work.”

“What won’t work?”

"Killing yourself. For one, you are bonded with us."

"We won't be bonded forever. The humans are beginning to back off again."

He sank down to the floor, across from my cauldron, where I was making myself soup for dinner. Mine was a simplified life.

"True. And you probably would take him out. Unfortunately, the flood has already started. He has already created a following. They will pick up where he left off. To truly fix your mistake, you are going to have to find another way. You are going to have to step forward."

I thought about that, then tipped my head to the side, intrigued. "How?"

"Let's see. Hold my hands and close your eyes."

I did as he said, and my soup bubbled higher.

"Spirits of witches past, guide our eyes to the proper path. Mistakes have been made and a devil created. Guide us to how we unmake it."

"That was a horrible rhyme." I teased.

He squeezed my hand. "Shut up. Take a deep breath, clear your mind."

I felt a little foolish but did as he said. It took a few moments but soon, the visions came flooding in.

I saw a young blonde woman, who looked so much like my dear sister, sitting at home with her parents, watching the horrible things going on elsewhere, through some sort of box. Her mother was the witch queen. She tried to rally her covens, but many had already turned to the other side. She would fail in her attempts. Her daughter refused to believe in her heritage for so long that she was unable to help.

I saw an even younger woman, barely into adulthood. She had black hair with what looked like purple on the ends. She had the power to see the future. And she had a stubborn streak a mile wide. She looked a lot like me. Even had a bit of my impetuous spirit.

She and her friends would take on a dangerous task, one that would get more than one of them killed. It was risky, and only showed a slight possibility of them succeeding.

Suddenly the visions spun, and I was there. I met with the witch queen and her mate somewhere. I explained about what they already knew was coming and why. Then I left them there to die. I watched as their daughter mourned her parents. I watched as she finally accepted her powers.

I saw her running down an alley, screaming for help. I saw a vampire with black hair pull her to safety. Mates. I saw another joining them. I saw her guiding the younger girl. I saw her stomach expand. I saw battles upon battles.

I saw myself speaking to each of them. The youngest changed her plans, she stood under the waterfall, she repeated my steps. Conrad melted. Her scent, her looks, her actions, he took her in and made her his. Gave her the life that was meant for me.

I blinked as the sob took over.

Trent broke our contact, taking the visions away. He crawled over and held me as I cried. In time I calmed down. It had been a long time since I last let myself cry.

"Thank you."

"Did you get what you needed?"

I pushed away from him, wiping my tears. "Did you not see?"

"No, they were for you, and you, alone. You know what you need to do now to call the power. While you still have it, use it. Make your plans."

I nodded as he left. A week later, we cut the ribbons that bound us and burned them in the fire. It only worked because we each cut one of them and threw it into the fire. Their original bond remained intact, thankfully. Not that they would have complained redoing that one.

I sighed with relief knowing the visions were gone.

During the witch trials, I bonded with the royal couple as we all helped to relocate many of their coven members. We were able to freeze many fires, hangings, and even drownings. We pulled out our sisters and brothers and helped them flee to safety. Whether they be witch or human, it didn't matter. We adopted them. The humans wanted to convict the innocent, then we would protect them as though they were our own.

Ashley, the queen at the time, was a dreamwalker. She was a near replica of my dear sister Carolyn. It seemed our genes were going to stay strong throughout our family line. She begged me to bond with them, so her husband/mate would not die with her if something happened.

By that time, humans had invented a horrible weapon called a gun.

I froze everyone but the coven nurse, in effort to keep the blood where it belonged. We got the bullet out, we stopped the bleeding, but I could not stop the infection.

"Keep my gift, Angie. Use it on your journey. Use it to save our daughters."

I tried to break the binding with her husband, but he refused to do it. Since I was still somewhat bound to Conrad, I did not die with her mate. He left me with the power to track someone without the use of a spell. I could now call to people in their sleep and find them when they were awake.

I had my weak moments at first, but only once did I cave. Conrad still dreamed of me. Still dreamed of us at the waterfall. I couldn't relive that without going mad, and never returned.

As technology advanced, so did Conrad's tactics. If he was getting stronger, why couldn't I?

I cried as I met with the last royal couple. They had already seen that they needed to die and had already taken the measures they felt necessary to help their daughter. I just gave them the answers they needed to give them peace in their passing.

I watched as both girls struggled to overcome their unique trials. It felt fitting that Grace looked so much like me, and Carrie looked so much like Carolyn. We had come full circle.

Carrie accepted what fate threw at her and ran with it. She grew stronger in her powers. I hadn't seen any queen have double powers before. The only other queen to be fated to a vampire was me. And I had the power to freeze, he had the power to burn. I froze the vampire line, and he burned the world down.

Because Carrie had so much power in her, her body created two babies. Two powers, two mates, two babies.

Gracey, oh Gracey.

She had such a strong spirit. She was stubborn, and she had the desire to be rash. There were times when she would act rashly. But she was better than me in many ways. She thought before she spoke. Before she acted.

Most of the time.

Her future was undecided after the war. I had never been able to see that. Just the possibilities. The fates only let me see the paths to fixing my mistakes.

I gave the girls what they needed, and now I could do nothing but sit back and wait. Wait until my turn came, my turn to right the wrongs of the past.

Our lake was long gone. It dried up and then was turned into a shopping center. But in my mind it still existed. In my mind, my mate and I never left. We never parted ways. Because that was where everything went wrong.

Mates were never supposed to part from one another.

PART II

Present Day

Chapter 7

Grace

I had only been asleep for mere minutes before Lucas came storming back into the room, a slew of curses coming through his mouth. I kept my eyes closed, too tired to bother opening them. He wasn't worth the effort anyway.

"Shut the hell up! What is wrong with you?" Curtis hissed at him as he tried to slowly extricate himself from me.

Just to be a brat, I gave a complaining whimper and held on tighter. Curtis chuckled and kissed my head.

"I won't be gone long. I just didn't want him to wake you up. Go back to sleep, love."

I blinked my eyes open and looked at him pitifully. From the corner of my eye, I saw Lucas roll his eyes, rub a hand over his face, and open his mouth.

Curtis knew his friend well. Even though he couldn't see him, he still held a hand up to silence him.

“Promise you won’t be gone long? It’s cold without you.” I pushed out my bottom lip in a dramatic pout.

He was the one whimpering this time.

I giggled as he leaned down to bite my pouty lip before kissing me one more time. “Promise. I won’t even leave the room. Now, sleep. You need to make sure you are getting plenty of rest.” He pulled the blanket down and kissed my stomach, making me giggle again.

Lucas sniffed the air then smiled. “So, it worked then?” His voice was at least calmer this time.

Curtis grinned at him as he stood up and moved him a little further from the bed.

“Yes. It was one hell of a ride too. Now, what do you want? You know better than to storm into my room like that?” Curtis turned enough to look at the door. “When did my door break?”

Lucas huffed and shook his head. “About three hours ago. You weren’t answering your phone, or the door. I could hear you two in here, and I got worried.”

Curtis frowned. “You knew about the vision. You should have known I was busy.”

Lucas smirked at him. “I have seen you answer your phone mid climax many times. Hell, you prefer to handle all your business that way.” His smirk fell. “It was an emergency. One I knew you would want to know about. But when I came in, you didn’t even notice me. It wasn’t until I saw you both in the middle of the blood trade that I remembered the vision. I also know that those moments can be intense. Or so I’ve heard.”

Curtis grinned, too happy to let his friend’s anxiety get to him. “Very intense. Now what was the emergency?”

Lucas grimaced and looked away for a second. "Ryder called. They were ambushed in Seattle. He barely got away."

Curtis wasn't grinning anymore. "The humans?" He placed his hands on his hips and started pacing back and forth.

Lucas nodded. "And the shifters, and the royals. Best I can figure, Franks said something."

Curtis froze then spun back to look at him. "How did he even know anything?"

"He, uh, helped Kyle transport most of our men there on a ship. He got them through customs. He didn't know much, but they must have put two and two together."

"I can see that, but the timing? How did they know when they would attack? Or where for that matter?"

Lucas just shrugged. I worried they would find a way to put it on me, I had to spin this just right.

"The shifters." I mumbled softly from the bed.

Curtis shook his head, looking at the ground. "No, they wouldn't have known."

I pushed to sit up, slowing when I got hit with a wave of dizziness. "That's not what I meant. The shifters knew they were being sent somewhere. And then the storm hitting Washington, mixed with what that guy Franks would have told them." I shrugged. "It all adds up. They probably figured it was better to play it safe. I mean, what better time for you to attack than during the day? The humans wouldn't expect it."

I nibbled on my lip as I held the blanket over my chest. They both kept staring at me. I shrank back to the headboard when Curtis started walking around the bed to my side.

"I'm sorry. Should I not have said anything? It just made sense to me. I was just trying to help." I pled with him, on the verge of a complete panic attack.

Curtis frowned as he lowered himself to my level. "When are you going to stop fearing me all the time?"

A freaking tear slipped out. "I don't mean to be. It's just… that's the story of my life. And I don't know what my role is. I don't want to disrespect you by accident again."

His eyes sparked and I shrank further back. Maybe I went too far that time.

"Lucas? Meet me in my office. I need to speak to Grace alone for a minute." His eyes never wavered from mine.

I felt stupid when I waited for the sound of the door to close. I could have smacked myself for that one.

Curtis sighed and pushed my messy hair behind my ear.

"I told you I was sorry for that. You don't need to be afraid of me, Gracey. I won't ever hurt you. Nor will I let anyone else ever hurt you. Especially now." He flattened his palm over my stomach, and I put a hand on top of his, holding him tight.

"Baby, I love you. You are my Queen. I will even let the others know. My time hiding who I am is over. You are carrying my son. I can't hide anymore. The three of us are a family now. Before, I was doing all this for power, for revenge. Now I am doing it for us. I will make sure that you are the one stepping on others. They should fear you, not you them. We will make this world pay for the way they have treated you. And we will make sure that our son has a better life than what we ever had. Understand?"

My heart pounded, and not from fear this time.

Curtis leaned over and pulled the blanket down enough so he could kiss my heart. Subtly, letting me know that he could hear it. I didn't know what to say to that. But I did know what to do.

I slowly slid down to lay on my back, and he followed, still leaving kisses around my heart. Once we were flat, he looked down into my eyes.

"Can you trust me with your heart, love? Trust me with your life? Trust me not to hurt you, to protect you and love you?"

It was hard to deny the sincerity in his eyes. The pleading for me to trust him.

I nodded mutely. He smiled softly and started kissing a path up my neck. Slowly, he pulled the last of the blanket from between us. My legs moved of their own accord, welcoming him home.

"Say it, Gracey. I want to hear you say it." He was to my ear now and beginning on my jaw.

"I trust you, Curtis. I trust you."

"And?" He hovered over my face, his eyes pleading with mine again.

"And I love you."

And neither of us spoke again for the next fifteen minutes. Pretty sure I was going to sleep for a week after that.

"I need to go clean up this mess that Deacon created. I swear, I have been cleaning up his messes for 400 years now." Curtis moved to sit on the edge of the bed, but he still had one hand on my stomach, and his eyes were on me.

I laughed. "Just how old are you?"

He gave a mock grimace, pretending he didn't want to answer. Maybe part of him didn't. "Let's just say I am older than everyone else."

I giggled. "I never thought I would be one of those girls who slept with the creepy old rich guy."

He laughed. "At least I am in better shape than the rest of them."

I made a show of looking him up and down, licking my lips. He laughed, kissed me, and then stood up with a groaned whine.

Seconds later, he was leaning over me again, fully dressed.

"Sleep. I'll be back to check on you soon. I don't want you to leave this room, or be around anyone else, until I tell them who I am. Are you okay with staying in here?"

I nodded and wrapped my arms around his neck. "If that is what you think is best, then I will trust your judgment." I kissed his lips softly, causing him to whimper again. "I am sorry if I upset you earlier, by interrupting your discussion with Lucas. I will try to do better."

I was surprised when he dropped down to his heels again.

"No. Do not apologize. Do I want you interrupting? No. It is my job to run our kingdom. It is how I will protect you. But you thought of something we hadn't. We needed to hear it. And you didn't do it in a way that disrespected me. On the contrary, you were trying to help. Just like a good Queen does."

I sighed with a relief I felt deep into my bones and melted into my pillow. He kissed my forehead one more time.

"I love you, sleep well."

Before I could even open my mouth, he was gone. Somehow he even managed to at least get the door to stand up in its frame. If anyone touched it, I was sure it would fall, but he was trying to give me a semblance of privacy. It was the thought that counted.

I rolled to my back and placed both hands over my stomach. And that's when it hit me.

I was pregnant.

I had a baby growing inside of me.

My heart warmed at the thought of my own child, my own baby to love and to raise. I felt like my heart doubled in size.

Feeling peaceful and beyond exhausted, I passed out.

Chapter 8

Andrew

"Alpha?"

I looked up from behind my desk to see Morris standing in my doorway. He had picked up a lot of slack for me the last few days, trying to give me time to pull myself together. Which was proving difficult to do. I'd spent most of that time sitting at my desk, staring at my phone. Willing Grace to message me.

"Yes, Sergeant?"

"The General and President are here. They are ready to talk terms, I believe. They are more subdued and respectful this time."

"Good. And the Royals?"

"I sent someone to grab them." He chuckled softly. "The three have not come out of their room since we returned. Clint confirmed that his people have sent food over to the Queen, but other than that…"

I surprised us both when I barked out a laugh. It felt good to laugh. Morris grinned, his eyes losing some of the tension they'd held since Seattle, at the sound of it.

Whatever caused my pain had decreased, which meant Grace was still alive. But we still didn't know what happened to cause it.

"The witch healer believes Colton and Deacon are experiencing some of Carrie's pregnancy hormones through their bonded link."

I laughed harder, that would explain a lot. Vampires, of both races, liked to live in the moment, they did not push off gratification for any reason. If they felt it, they did it. Carrie's rise in hormones would only multiply that.

The moment our plane landed upon our return, and we stepped off, Carrie was running and jumping on Colton. Deacon wasn't far behind her. It made for one interesting scene. It was sweet in the beginning…until it wasn't. I, for one, was glad when they moved it to their room. At Carrie's insistence of course.

I pushed back from my desk, putting the phone in my back pocket. Where it had been for almost four months now, with only a two-day interruption. Carrie had taken possession of it while we were in Seattle. I trusted her more than anyone else when it came to Grace.

Carrie was as worried as I was.

Morris blocked my path out the door, his eyes looking deeper into mine, studying me. The Sergeant was a career man like me. He loved the Army life. Before Curtis' little tantrum, I thought about making him my Beta. While it was common in other packs to have a Beta and Gamma, we didn't always have one of either.

"How are you, really?"

I sighed. "I'm better. My wolf is taking on more of the pain than I am, he is trying to protect me so we can do what we need to."

He lifted a disbelieving eyebrow at me. I huffed.

"I've showered. I've eaten. And I am not hiding under my covers in the dark. I'm functioning." I took a breath and let the sudden irritation drain out of me. "I'm dealing. Which I wouldn't have been able to do without your help these last few days."

He bowed slightly at what he knew was a compliment and my gratitude. "You are my Alpha, and my friend."

I needed a change of subject. "Speaking of which. There is something I wanted to discuss with you before we go in. I was going to speak to you about this when you came home for leave in September."

He tilted his head, probably smelling the slight nervousness I felt.

"How would you feel about being my Beta?"

His eyes widened and he took a step back.

"You have been my right hand for years. I would like to make it official."

"I… I would be honored, Alpha. Are you sure? The Army pack hasn't needed one before."

"Not recently, no. My grandfather had a Beta during World War II. I can't help but wonder if my wolf felt the wind changing when he suggested it. The world is changing, and I am going to need some help. I would greatly appreciate your input and having you on my side. Now more than ever."

Morris dropped to a knee in front of me, bowing his head. "We are more than willing to serve an Alpha such as you. It has always been our honor to serve in your pack. We will do our best to serve as your Beta." His voice carried the double layer, his wolf speaking with him. They were united in this decision.

My wolf surged forth, causing my eyes to darken and my fingers lengthen. "Sergeant Roger Morris. We accept your fealty and your service. From this time forth, you will be the Beta to the Grand Lupine Army Pack. Second only to us, the Alpha. Now, raise your right hand, so we can mark you as such."

Morris lifted his right arm, his head staying bowed toward his knees. My wolf and I smelled two vampires and a witch walking toward us, but we held no fear of them. My partially transformed fingers wrapped around his wrist and pulled it to my partially transformed canines. Morris barely flinched as they sunk into the underside of his wrist. It was quick, just an in and out, twice. This marking officially took him out of his home pack and moved him to mine. Morris now belonged to my pack, permanently.

Once I released him, I gave him a moment, as he worked to control the shift that wanted to take over. He snarled, his fingers lengthened, and small bits of brown fur started shooting from his pores. When the shaking subsided, he raised his head from the floor. His eyes were black as night, and his canines were hanging over his bottom lip.

I lowered my right arm, his fingers wrapped around my wrist. I didn't flinch when his canines sank into me, only once. My wolf hummed, feeling the presence of his brother wolf.

"You are now tied to me, as I am to you. If one of us should fall, the other will know. Together we will lead this pack, and our people into freedom. We will protect them. Rise Beta Roger. My friend. My brother."

We both blinked a few times, our wolves retreating, as he slowly pushed to stand up. We grinned and I pulled him in for a hug.

"Thank you for your trust, Alpha. I won't let you down."

I shook my head and patted the side of his head as he stepped away from me. Obnoxious clapping and cheers came from next to us. I rolled my eyes.

“You are all lucky my wolf trusted you. If anyone else had walked up during a shifter ceremony, they would have been killed.” I gave them half a smirk.

“So, the only people not to drink blood around here are the witches then?” Carrie asked, a grimace playing on her lips. She was leaning against Deacon, his left hand around her waist, and resting protectively on her stomach. Which had nearly doubled in size since I last saw her.

“No, we didn’t drink the blood. We just marked each other. Kind of. It’s hard to explain. And don’t forget, witches use blood in their spells all the time.”

She scrunched her nose, knowing I was right, and she couldn’t argue. Deacon and Colton laughed. We all knew that was one of the reasons why her ancestors had always been hunted by vampires. Their blood was used in the curse that kept them from having more female children. The scent of it drove the vampires mad with need, more so than the testosterone in our shifter blood.

The curse had backfired a bit, and hit a few of our packs, the ones closest to the border with the vampire kingdom. Over the centuries, packs relocated, blended into other packs, or pulled away to create their own. The curse passed onto nearly everyone. We still had female pups, but very few had the ability to shift. They were simply not born with a wolf spirit inside them. In time, we discovered that the only other species, besides our own, capable of producing shifters was witches. Humans gave birth to only humans.

Strong witches, and females that could shift were often mated to two or three males. They had better odds of producing more female shifters, and stronger males. The extra mates provided extra protection - as desperate shifters would try to take them for their own use - and higher chances of reproduction. My mother could shift. And as she was fated to be mated to my father, the Army pack Alpha, she only had the one mate.

My sister could shift as well. She was mated to two males in the Rockies pack in Colorado. So, seeing Carrie with her two mates did not make shifters blink an eye.

Seeing her two mates together… did. While it was not unheard of for the males in the mating to be involved as well, it was rare, and hardly spoken about.

As long as all parties involved were happy, I didn't care.

"That was it? You aren't going to kiss him or anything?" Deacon's voice said he was shocked and a little disappointed. His eyes on the other hand, were clearly amused.

Colton elbowed him. "They are not as greedy as you." Now that man sounded and looked serious.

Until Deacon slapped him on the butt and gripped him. Colton's body rocked forward, and the fire in him sparked to life behind his eyes, making them glow. His head snapped to Deacon, whose eyes sparked right back at him. Carrie just giggled and sighed.

"Darn right I am."

Morris and I both choked on the laughter, more to his word choice than his actions. I coughed and worked to clear my throat.

"Darn?" I kept my eyes on Carrie, who started blushing.

"Ye…" She cleared her own throat, then tried again. "Yeah. We aren't sure where the babies are, in regard to their senses developing. They decided to start watching the words they use now." She shrugged. "I told them they had to curb their tongues once they were born. They started early."

Both of them looked down at her, their eyes somehow darker and yet brighter at the same time. Pretty sure it was due to the tongue comment.

Morris shifted uncomfortably when Deacon's hand began to slide south, off her stomach.

"Deacon…" She half warned, half whined, when he began dipping his fingers under the waistband of her leggings. He ignored her.

A throat cleared from down the hall. Carrie squeaked and jumped away from her mate, slapping his hand.

"The humans are waiting, your majesties." Clint, one of the head Vampire Born guards informed us, an amused smile on his face. He didn't bother trying to hide it.

"Yes, thank you, Clint. We are on our way." Colton responded, blinking his eyes a few times. "Did you place what I asked for inside?"

Clint bowed slightly. "Yes, my Lord."

"Good. Thank you."

"What did you ask for?" Carrie questioned him, trying her hardest to lift one eyebrow.

"You'll see." He leaned down and kissed her head. "Shall we?"

"Wait." I raised a hand to stop them, they had already turned to follow Clint back to the conference room. "We need to talk first."

I stepped back into my office. Deacon and Carrie followed, while Colton said something to Clint. Morris waited until he joined us before closing the door.

"Clint will tell the others that we got held up and will be there shortly. The humans can deal with it. Is everything alright?" Colton studied me carefully, not much different than the way Morris had. They both had to help me when I was at my lowest in Seattle. He even protected my back when I could not.

"Yes. I just wanted to make sure we were all on the same page when we go in there. We should have spoken sooner, before they came. But I think we all were a bit preoccupied."

Carrie blushed and looked at a spot on the wall. Her mates on the other hand looked proud.

"What are we asking for?" I asked them. "What do the witches and vampires want?"

"I spoke with Kristine and the coven leaders before they left. They wanted to get back to their covens, spread the word of me and the babies, and seek out who is willing to help. They are going to speak to their covens about what they want to do. Even the coven leaders are not all on the same page. A few wanted to relocate their covens behind the wall. They do not believe the humans will be very accepting of us. While others believe they will be able to continue their lives as they are, only not hiding what they are."

"Which is why we are thinking of asking for California." Deacon added solemnly. His mates did not react in any way.

I was sure they had downtimes to talk the last few days. They did stop for her to eat after all.

"What do you mean?" Morris asked, stepping forward as my Beta.

Deacon looked at him. Since they saw me elevate him to Beta firsthand, they would not question his involvement.

"Shifters and Witches will not see the backlash the way vampires will. Whether we help or not. We cannot hide, we do not blend in as well as you all do. Nor do we want to. Our way of life is too different. *We* are too different. The wall can keep us safe. We can also use the wall to keep the Nightwalkers in."

"The humans will not want to relinquish an entire state." I reminded him.

"No, and that is where negotiations will have to come in."

"If you are all in one place, how do you know the humans won't drop a bomb or two on you?" Morris asked, leaning against my desk.

"That shouldn't be a problem. In my mother's books, I found a spell that creates a magical wall. It would take many of us, but we could layer it on top of us, protecting us from anything unnatural getting in. If it is not nature made, it will be stopped by the wall." Carrie answered.

"What are the shifters going to want?" Colton asked, his hand rubbing absentmindedly down Carrie's back. Was she nervous?

I took a deep breath and released it. "We are like the witches. Many packs want to stay where they are, where they have been for generations. Their Alphas believe we *will* be seen as the heroes in all this. Then there are those who are not as naive."

"And what do you want?"

I looked at Deacon, thinking about that for a minute. "I am not as naive. But I love being in the Army. This is how I was raised. This is how I planned on raising my pups, with my…" My breath caught and I had to work to steady it again.

Carrie silently stepped forward and wrapped her arms around my chest. She hugged me tight without saying a word. I gently patted her shoulder, not sure how much of a hug I could return before my arms got ripped off. When I looked up, Colton was smirking, Deacon was frowning. Neither seemed defensive. So, I hugged her in return. Only after that did she step back.

"Don't worry. They have my powers now too, remember? They can feel only friendly intentions coming from you."

"Ya huh." I felt awkward but smiled my thanks to her anyway. "We should get in there."

"Joy." Colton sighed. "Let's just hope they are more inclined to side with us now."

I chuckled. We both had been stuck in a room with the General for three very long days, less than a month ago. Some of the players were different now though. King Dominic, Deacon's father, was gone. As well as the elected President.

The General, the most stubborn out of all of them, had had a few eye openers since. We could only hope they would be more willing and accepting.

Hours later, it was obvious that they still weren't. They did not like Deacon's demands. Not in the least bit.

"You're talking about handing over the third largest state! Over 30 million people!" The General just couldn't get over that part.

The President sighed and leaned back in his chair. He was a lot quieter than the General, who we all recognized as the most dominant male between the two.

"Would you rather the vampires live amongst all 300 billion people? Hunting in the night? The lid has come off the can, beans have been spilled. Everyone knows we exist now. They know what the Nightwalkers are capable of. Either we lock them behind that wall, and monitor them, or you deal with a country full of people always in fear for their lives. You do remember how long it took to recover from the COVID outbreak don't you? People will stop going out at night. Possibly even during the day once they learn that some of them are not restricted by the sun. Then of course, you will have the hunting parties. Remember the witch trials? More innocents than witches were killed in those. How many lives can be saved by letting us keep them locked behind that wall?" Carrie passionately told him, her hands pressed into the table, holding herself up.

Deacon had said many of the same things. But hearing it from her, a pregnant woman (who had gone through a crate of strawberries and half a dozen bowls full of French Fries, not to mention all the Teriyaki chicken, Beef and Broccoli, and Fried Rice she ate during our dinner break) who looked and sounded like any other pregnant human, carried a different weight.

COVID was a good point too. The economy was still recovering from that.

The General deflated as he fell into his chair again.

"What are we to get out of this deal? One way or another, the vampires will have California. What does the rest of the U.S. get?" The Acting President asked, sounding defeated.

If his General was losing, how was he to win?

"Allies. As long as you are not the tyrants, then you will have us to help you. Imagine how quickly you could have eradicated Bin Laden after 9/11, with our help. We will come to your aid, but we are independent of your control. Many of your unsolved murders will also decrease."

"But they will continue and probably increase behind those walls." The General interrupted with a bite.

"No, they won't. Vampires only hunt when they have no other choice. When Nightwalkers hunt, they relinquish control to their animalistic instincts. More often than not, their victim does not survive. Believe it or not, fear tastes awful. It might help spike the taste, but blood filled with fear is like drinking straight Vinegar. Most clubs and bars have been supplying vampires with willing donors for decades. Before that, most whore houses and brothels did the job."

The President grimaced at the picture Deacon was painting. The General didn't seem phased.

"The donors are well paid. Depending on who they work for, they are given a choice of how that blood is taken. We will ensure that they always have that choice. If a Nightwalker hunts and kills, they will be taken out immediately. The humans left in California will not see much difference in their daily lives."

The two human representatives looked at one another for a few long moments. When done, the President leaned forward, his hands folded on the table. It looked like he was taking charge, and the guard dog was taking a step back now.

"We know what the vampires want. What about the other two? The witches and the shifters."

"We are a divided people. The packs have been in their homes for many generations. They have lives. Many do not want to leave them. At the same time, we know the history with humans. At first, the humans may accept us, because they will not see us as the bad guys. But how long will that last?" I answered him solemnly.

"The witches are the same. They want to live their lives, free to be who they are, just like everyone else. But we still have scars from the past. Some may choose to move behind the wall, while others will not." Carrie's voice came out stronger than mine.

"If, and that's a big *if*, we sign over California, what rights would the humans inside have. Would they be allowed to leave?"

"Some. You do not have room for 30 million people to migrate into the United States, especially if we are taking so much land. They would need to apply for relocation, just the same as with any other country. You will be surprised how many will choose to stay. Curtis' tyranny hardly touched the smaller towns and cities. The hunting stopped after three days, for each of the three main regions, as he called them. San Francisco, San Diego, and Los Angeles have probably been cleaned out of all humans but donors, by now."

The humans' expressions darkened. Deacon quickly raised a hand to calm them before continuing.

"They were not killed. Only a few hundred were killed during the hunting raids. And that is statewide. Those that survived were to be moved. You knew this already, as he saw fit to have a drone deliver the message to your men outside his wall. People are working and living like normal over there, just in new homes. He will try to determine their jobs for them, I will not. I will allow them to move home if they so desire. Which they probably won't considering how the Nightwalkers will also be there. There will be places that are reserved only for the vampires and those who are willing to donate." He smirked. "Or just want to play."

The room was silent for a time, we wanted them to think everything over. By this point, they knew our hearing was better than theirs. Even Carrie's was better. The only person in the room that never heard their whisperings was Clarise, and she was reading a book on her phone, in the corner of the room. Only half listening. Her only concern was Carrie and the babies. So, the humans tended to write notes to each other.

The President stood up, soon followed by the General, and put the suit coat he abandoned hours ago back on.

"I will report back to the Senate. I do not feel comfortable making an executive decision on something like this. I need the backing of my people behind me."

We stood with them. "Understandable. We all have to make sure our decisions are based on what is good for those who put their trust in us, not based on what we want." Deacon nodded his acceptance to him.

"We will be in touch when we have a decision." The General half growled out.

We all waited, while Clint escorted them out. Carrie reached over and picked up a half empty box of Sweet and Sour chicken. We chuckled as she picked up a piece with her bare fingers. The men all laughed harder when she spit it out into a napkin with a disgusted look on her face, shaking her head.

"Alright, time for the Queen to rest." Clarise stepped around us all and lifted Carrie's shirt and started feeling around her stomach.

Morris' eyes grew, his eyebrows hiding in his hair. "Did her stomach get bigger in the last few hours?"

"Yep." Clarise answered, not sparing him a glance. "These boys are sure in a hurry to grow." Her eyes traveled up to Carrie's. "You need to rest tonight. Like, really rest."

Carrie groaned and sagged into Colton, who was behind her. Deacon grinned ear to ear.

"Does that mean I have permission to knock her out?"

Clarise laughed quietly. Colton's wasn't as quiet during her response. "Yes. Her body needs real rest. It has been through a lot today."

Carrie was still frowning when she relented. "We will discuss all this tomorrow, then."

We separated at the front door to the pack house, the others all going to their cabins. I went for a run. I missed being in Mojave. The wall was closer.

Grace was closer.

Over the next three days, we waited and waited. But no word came from the humans, or Grace. Eventually, the vampires returned to their home in the Rockies.

Chapter 9

Grace

When I woke in the evening, Curtis was already gone. I spent the last two weeks hidden inside our room. I was tired of it. I needed out.

His council was here, doing their monthly check in. That meant that anyone who did not live here was kicked out. The harem he kept for Lucas and his other counselors, were locked in their room until called for. The serving staff, a mix of humans and Nightwalkers, were either locked in their rooms or told to go out for a while.

I practically ran to the bathroom to relieve myself. I swear I peed a lot more lately. It was probably all the water Curtis insisted I drink every day. It was annoying. After washing my hands, I figured I would brush my teeth, since I was already there. I wasn't far into it when the nausea hit. And it hit hard.

I dropped the toothbrush and ran back to the small closet-like room with the toilet. It took nearly ten minutes to expel everything from my stomach. Another round of brushing was definitely called for. After rinsing my mouth, I threw the water on my face.

The cold water felt nice against my heated skin. I was tempted to shower, but those were no fun alone anymore.

Just the thought of Curtis and the shower had my skin heating back up again. I closed my eyes and moaned as I pulled up a vision of what I knew would be happening later tonight. There were times when the new strength to my visions was awesome. Ever since Curtis froze time - when he started feeding me his blood, so my witch blood could keep healing him from the side effects of the long spell - my visions had been more realistic. As in, I felt in real life, what I would feel in the future.

It really sucked when I felt the pain of losing my son if Lucas fed me his blood during conception instead of Curtis. But times like this? Oh no, times like this were the best.

The vision came without much calling, I rarely had to work for them anymore. It started with Curtis washing my hair, his hands massaging my head. Then slowly, he washed my body. The moment I got pregnant he started doing as much as he could for me. He wanted all my energy focused on baking his son.

Well, when I wasn't using it on him anyway.

My skin burned hot as the vision played through, my need for him grew with intensity. I wanted nothing more than to run down that hall, the stairs, fly through the conference room door, and jump on his lap. He didn't care if the others were around. And I got over it a long time ago. But I wasn't currently allowed to leave the room.

I didn't know how long he was going to be either, so I let the vision keep going, my hands moving in real life to what the vision Curtis was doing.

I saw him lifting my leg onto his shoulder, in real life I laid it on the counter. One of my hands gripped the back of his head, which was actually the counter, for support. The other hand slid over me from the side and started making its way down. I moved back and forth, my body having already been reacting to the vision, my eyes rolling. About then, my logical brain caught up to me, and I froze. I had been too involved in the vision to notice what my hand had felt in reality, on its way across.

The vision vanished and my eyes shot open. I quickly dropped my leg and turned to my side, staring at my profile. That wasn't right. That bump was not there last night. It wasn't all that big, but big enough that I could see it. And so would Curtis. And probably Lucas. He'd seen me naked enough times by now.

What the hell? It had only been two weeks since he knocked me up! I gasped and covered my mouth, jumping back from the counter.

I threw up! I rarely did that. I'd been sleeping a lot too. And peeing a lot.

No, no, no. It was too soon for all of this. *Way* too soon.

Something was wrong with my baby. We did something wrong! I was going to lose him! Not again, no. I couldn't take that pain again. I didn't want to know how bad it would feel in real life. I didn't want to lose him for real either.

With tears racing down my cheeks, I ran to our shared closet and grabbed the first dress I could find. I didn't want to see what would happen if I tried to put any of my tight pants on. I ripped a set of underwear from the top drawer of our dresser, my fingers brushing over Curtis' boxers.

An image flashed through my mind of me sticking my tongue through the opening. The heat flared through my skin again, what I hadn't finished in the bathroom picked right back up, both terrifying me and turning me on more. I couldn't move as the vision took control of my legs. Before I knew what I was doing, my hand was back where it had been in the bathroom and my legs were shaking.

Feeling slightly relieved of the heat, I slid into the lacey underwear he bought me, whimpering at the roughness against my skin. I cried out in both pleasure and pain when I snapped the matching bra on. I ran my hand over the sensitive area, feeling them out. My eyes rolled back, and parts of me spiked through the lacey holes. I was tempted to relieve myself again, but I was too terrified about why they were so sore and sensitive already.

Shakily, the tears coming harder now, I pulled the dark purple dress on, wrapped it around me, and tied it on my right side. I didn't bother with shoes or trying to fix my hair. I ran out the door and headed straight for Curtis' conference room.

I slowed as I grew closer, the worry of leaving the room without permission beginning to settle in. Was Curtis going to be mad?

But would it be because I interrupted or because I somehow missed something in my visions and our child was in danger?

I jumped and squeaked when the door to his office flew open in front of me.

"I can smell your fear through the door. What happened?" Curtis didn't seem mad. No, he seemed more worried about me than anything else. He lifted a hand and started wiping the tears from my face, but they were coming too fast now.

He pulled me into the room and sat me in a chair, dropping to his knees in front of me.

"Grace. What happened? Did you see something?"

I turned my head enough to look at the half dozen men in the room. None of them looked surprised by what he asked, only wary.

“I already told them about you and our son. You can speak freely.”

Awe, so he kept his promise and told them. He wasn’t going to keep me hidden forever. I wasn’t going to have to pretend to be his pet forever. And a whole new round of tears started, which freaked him out.

“Grace.” His growl wasn’t angry or impatient, I was scaring him.

There was only one other time I got this upset over a vision. It was when I looked to see if Lucas feeding me instead of Curtis would work.

“I think we messed up somehow. There is something wrong, but I don’t know what it is.” It was hard to vocalize the words, it made them more real.

Curtis swallowed and waited to get his own emotions in check, probably trying to stay calm for me. He wanted this baby as badly as I did.

“What did you see?”

I blushed and my skin heated up again. I knew the others smelled my response when the soft chuckles started, and Lucas shifted his pants.

Curtis chuckled softly too. “Besides that, love.”

“I didn’t actually see anything. Not really. It’s just what made me realize something was wrong.”

He shook his head and put a palm on my cheek. “I’m not following. Start from the beginning.”

“I was brushing my teeth when I suddenly got sick. I barely made it to the toilet. The cold water on my face felt good afterwards, so I debated a shower. That’s when the vision kicked in, but it wasn’t much, just us in the shower." My skin prickled and I closed my eyes, he chuckled again.

"Obviously we won't be stopping that one. What happened next?"

Now I blushed because of embarrassment. "Well, you know how real they feel now." He nodded, a wicked grin on his face since he probably knew where this was going. "It made me… hungry. I knew I wasn't supposed to leave the room yet though. But I was aching really bad. So, I figured…" They all laughed again, I moved on. "I stopped though when I felt my stomach." My voice dropped to a whisper.

"What's wrong with it?" He reached in and started desperately untying my dress. Once it was open, he pulled me to stand.

I waited until he dropped to his knees again. He frantically felt out my stomach, his touch slowed and softened over the bump. When his glowing eyes came back to me, I finished the rest of the story in a panic. When I got to the part about the bra, he moved one hand up to double check that as well. I stuttered until he slid it back to my stomach.

"It's too early for all of this. I'm only two weeks along. The nausea alone shouldn't be here for another month or so." I hiccupped. "I don't know what's going on. I had to come to see you. I'm so scared, Curtis."

The top of his forehead leaned against my stomach. My panic spiked when I felt him shaking.

Holy Hufflepuff, I was so screwed.

Curtis pushed to stand up, a grin on his face. He kissed my confused face hard, and the whole room broke out into laughter. Well, now that just ticked me off. Lucas even fell out of his chair because he was laughing so hard.

Why was my pain and the danger of our unborn son so funny to them?

I pushed Curtis away from me, which made him laugh harder. Then I lifted one bare foot and kicked Lucas in the shoulder. I really just ended up rolling him over. They all thought that was the best yet.

Curtis dropped into the chair and pulled me onto his lap. His hand held my bare thigh tight, quickly zapping out my frustration. He massaged my leg until I was on the verge of begging him to end this freaking misery.

His laughter softened and he kissed the side of my head, pulling me against his chest.

"There is nothing wrong, love. But this was a good example to them about how little you know of our world. Some of them had worried that you were pretending to be so naive to get close to me."

I jumped to sit up straight, fear taking over me. How the hell did they know? Not the naïve part, obviously I hardly knew anything about the magical world.

Curtis' other hand rubbed softly on my back. "Do not fear, my Queen. This proved to them all how little you know."

I nibbled on my lip, willing myself to get under control. "I don't understand. How do you know nothing is wrong with our son? How does that prove they can trust me?"

Curtis moved his hand forward, pulling out my lip, and kissed me softly. "Magical babies do not use the same time frame as human ones, love. The stronger the child will be, the faster they develop. You only have a little bit of witch's blood, yet you are more powerful than most pure bloods. I was born to rule the Vampires. Our son will be a force to be reckoned with."

I sniffled and hiccupped again. "So, all of this is normal then?" I had to be sure.

He huffed a small laugh, kissing me again. I swear he was heating me up on purpose. "Yes, my love." His hand finally moved from my thigh but overshot the place I wanted by a few inches. Instead, he rubbed my baby bump. "Better than normal. Everything came fast, including the hormones. I'm sure that is why it scared you so much." He hummed and lowered his hand, finally! And started nibbling on my neck.

I gripped his lower arm as my hips started moving. The moment his teeth sank in, my eyes closed, and I finally got what I'd been needing. I forgot all about the others in the room, until I heard more than one zipper lower. The idea that they were getting off on what he did to me, somehow pushed me over. Again.

Curtis growled as he released my neck and moved his hand. Barely a second passed before I was facing him, my dress completely gone, and something much better took his hand's place. That hand kept me going with that other ultra-sensitive spot I had up top now. Looked like I wasn't the only one getting off on everyone watching.

I laid my head on his shoulder, his hand rubbing down the back of my head. I slowed my breathing or tried to. I caught a new scent. Something that had me wanting more.

"Already, love?" I felt him chuckling, which added to the smell.

"What's that smell?" My voice squeaked.

He sniffed a few times then laughed. "The smell of arousal and dopamine. Do you like it?"

I licked my lips and then started kissing his jaw, in response. "Does it affect everyone like this?"

"Yes. That's why our people don't care about doing things in public. If we feel it, why not enjoy it? And why not help others enjoy it? It's also why we don't care about who gets us there. As you experienced earlier, when you have a need, sometimes it can't wait." He lifted his wrist and bit into it. "Want to taste it?"

I eagerly took it, the craving hitting me as soon as I smelled his blood. I focused on getting all I could, knowing Curtis would make sure my other needs were met.

He took his wrist away, far too soon in my opinion. Still, I settled against his chest, feeling exhausted again, licking the remaining drops off my lips.

"Did you like it?" He didn't need to ask, he just wanted to hear me say it.

I couldn't speak, so I just hummed. He laughed.

"It's the same for me. With your hormones everywhere right now, your blood is fantastic. The perfect mix of sweet and spicy. I am going to enjoy them the most I think."

I closed my eyes feeling content and satiated. In more ways than one. I only looked up because I grew curious why Curtis wasn't continuing the meeting. I heard lots of grunts and growls, but I knew the harem wasn't in there. The scent was getting stronger too.

I turned just in time to see Lucas get spanked. I grinned. He was on his hands and knees in front of a guy who looked like Legolas from Lord of the Rings, while a man who looked like GI Joe was on his knees behind him, doing the spanking. They were using Lucas, but I knew he was enjoying every minute of it.

I couldn't turn my eyes away. Not until Curtis rubbed my cheek with his thumb again. I blushed and leaned on him. He just chuckled.

"Did you need me to leave, so you all could keep talking?" I asked softly. There had to be a reason the harem wasn't there.

"No. You can stay. They need to burn this off so they can focus. Besides, we are nearly done. Do you need to go rest?" I couldn't resist the smile. He sounded like he didn't want me to leave, and his grip had tightened around me.

"I can rest right here. I miss you when I am alone." And I probably should see what I could hear. I hadn't passed anything on for a while. In all honesty, I hadn't even thought about it in a while. It was the comment about them thinking I might be a spy that reminded me.

Curtis kissed my head softly, humming his approval.

It was only a few more minutes before the others started redressing. Lucas didn't bother. He just plopped back into his chair, a satisfied grin on his face. I couldn't help the giggle when he winked at me. Especially since it surprised him. It wasn't my normal response to him.

Curtis was right, my hormones were everywhere. Not helpful.

"Timothy, continue what you were saying. What did your father have to say? Did he pass anything on again, without realizing it?"

The others all laughed.

"Yes, actually. It was why I requested a meeting without your harem. Or rather, Lucas' harem. I guess you aren't using them anymore."

I'd recognize Lucas' deep chuckle anywhere. "Kitty's got claws."

The others laughed again, remembering the time I ripped a man off Curtis and took his place. I tensed up, remembering how little Curtis liked them laughing at him. He felt it and rubbed my back, laughing with them.

"She does, at that. She is worthy of her title."

I blushed again, hearing the pride in his comment. Some time ago, I stopped having to fake a blush, or fake anything really. It terrified me at first. Now, I had accepted it. I would do what I could to protect the people outside, but this was my life now. I might as well get used to it.

I ignored the flash of a sad looking Hill, or at least I assumed it was him. The shifter in charge of the shifter prisoners said it was, but I could have described him wrong. I wished those flashes would stop. They always made me feel guilty. They gave me a glimpse of a peace that I would never know.

"What did he say?" Curtis repeated, getting them back on track.

"He said he heard mention of a spy in your house. No one will say the name, or even a description. They are only referred to as "our little spy."

I tensed up again, holding tighter to Curtis. He rubbed my arms and back, trying to reassure me.

"Do we have anyone new to our number?"

"Only the harem, my Lord." Lucas responded in a flat voice. "You haven't been with anyone but Grace in weeks. They've hardly left their room."

I didn't like what he was insinuating, mostly because it was true. I lifted off Curtis enough to turn and snarl at him. He winced. Such a pansy.

Curtis put both hands on my cheeks and turned me to face him again. "He's not saying it was you. You have no way to contact the outside. Your things were thoroughly searched before they were moved to my room."

I frowned in confusion. If they searched through my things, then why didn't they find my phone?

"Why?" I croaked out.

He shrugged. "You were new, you were more obedient than most. I needed to know." His thumb worked to smooth out the still formed frown lines on my forehead. "No one doubts you, love. I had to know before I could let you get too close. They sent me a message while we were shopping, saying you were clear. Everything since then has been honest, I promise."

I was only partially listening. I was thinking back to where I last had my phone. I remembered searching for it when we got back from the wall. I relaxed on his chest again when I remembered it was still tucked in between the mattress and box spring of my old bed, in the room attached to mine and Curtis' room. It wasn't even in my things.

"What else did Bryant say?"

"Mostly just trying to motivate me to move back faster. He still believes that I am living in Spain. I told him I am working on it. I have many business interests over there. They need to be looked after. All things I did of course, before we moved on with our plans here."

A few chuckles sprinkled throughout the room.

"He is getting more insistent. It seems most of the clan are flocking in when they call."

"Tell them about Grace, my Lord. They will come here instead. It's all because of Deacon's heir." I didn't know who that was, and I didn't care.

Timothy cleared his throat awkwardly. "I'm not sure if it will matter anymore."

“Why?” Curtis half snarled.

“My father said the crowned Queen carries not one, but two heirs. That is why the others are responding so quickly. He was rather excited. Even in the prime of our rule, twins were unheard of.”

Curtis was the tense one now. Calming him was second nature to me by this point. I rubbed my hand up and down his chest soothingly, leaving soft kisses on his neck.

“They will not be happy if harm comes to her or those babies. If she survives, and it's looking like she will, they hope she can continue bearing children.”

Curtis tightened his grip on me. “Then we take her, before the children are born. When they are, we raise them here. Then one of you can try to breed her. Grace’s vision showed that the blood fed to them needs to be from a Vampire Born, it cannot be a Nightwalker.”

“How do we do that, my Lord? Father says she has bound herself to Colton as well. No one will be able to get to her. We would have to kill one of them, which would kill her.”

Curtis’ head snapped up, from kissing my head, to look at Timothy. “She cannot bind herself to more than one vampire. That would have put her and the children at risk.”

I heard a few people shifting awkwardly. They were afraid of Curtis. It actually made me a little proud. He commanded so many others. People quaked in their boots when he looked them dead in the eye like that. I moved my hand between us, lifting on my knees just enough for a small bit of him to slip out of me. Then I played with both of us.

Lucas whimpered, probably remembering when Curtis let him do that.

“She, uh, she used a witch spell to bind herself to Colton.”

I bit down on Curtis' chest to keep from screaming out and interrupting when his body shook with anger. That was… oh boy.

"I know that spell. It's why I can freeze time. Which means Colton can tell lies and intent now. But that also means we might be able to rid ourselves of one or both of them without affecting her. Otherwise, we will just have to lock them up somewhere. In time, their bonds will fade." His hand landed on top of mine and finished us both off. Then went back to my chest, enjoying the enlarged mountains.

Why did this bra feel tighter than it had in the bedroom?

"Pull the majority back to this side of the wall. We need to prepare for the larger war now. I had hoped to do this without taking the lives of our own clan members, but so be it. We will strengthen our hold here, first. Let the others see that we have a functioning society. Deacon is ill prepared to do that. Maybe we can lock him and his mate up together, since they have such success in the bedroom. They can make the babies, and we can raise them. Either way, if we can prove to the others who the better leader is, they may come quietly."

"Does that mean you are going to resume your visits through the regions again?" Lucas asked.

I could still feel his eyes, and I was apparently losing my mind. I chose to blame it on the hormones and pregnancy brain.

I braced myself on my knees again, my hand holding Curtis in place. I slowly moved up, giving my hand more room. I explored a bit, knowing full well that Lucas could see it all now. He even pushed his chair away from the table and leaned to the side. He obviously wanted a better view. I hissed when Curtis' teeth grazed that extra sensitive part, nibbling on the tip.

"Yes. I will give you all a few days to prepare. We will start in the South. Lucas, I will need you to keep an eye on things here again."

Lucas didn't answer, he was too busy whimpering. Oddly, that little sound set me off. My knees nearly gave out on me.

Curtis' head nodded and I heard the chairs push back. All but one left the room. Lucas was beyond hearing anything but his own blood pumping.

Curtis laughed, pushing me back closer to him, so he could kiss me. My hands forgot what they were doing and went to his hair. I sank down completely, practically dropping to his lap.

"Is my kitty having fun?" He growled playfully between kisses.

"Maybe." I giggled as he growled again and dug into my lower cheeks with his fingernails.

Chapter 10

Grace

"You are torturing my most loyal companion. The man has been by my side for more than ten centuries. He was the only one to support me when everything fell apart." He mumbled against my lips.

"And I'm sure you have rewarded him multiple times over." Holy crap, they were both old. I'd really like to know what happened, but so not going to ask.

"Hmm, I have. What has he done… recently, to deserve this?" He wasn't irritated by me torturing his best friend, the opposite actually.

"Maybe I just want to play. He makes it so easy."

Curtis fell away, laughing. "Whatever my Queen wants. Are you feeling better now?" He put a palm on my cheek and I leaned into it.

"Yes."

"Are you still worried about losing our son?"

I swallowed and nodded my head. He knew me so well. It was scary and yet pleasant at the same time.

Curtis sighed and kissed my forehead. "I won't let anything happen to either of you. You trust me on that, don't you?"

I nodded again, a small tear falling. "Yes." I whispered. It was true. I knew it was.

I sighed happily as he kissed a trail down my neck. I shivered when he licked the small teeth marks left over from when I got pregnant. I came to this place, planning to be in his harem, planning to spy on him. I failed the night I became his mate and the mother of his child.

Curtis didn't stop there, he kept going, until my back was arched, and my head was falling back. Lucas just sat there, watching everything. I stopped acting for him though. I nearly collapsed on Curtis; my energy completely zapped. To make matters worse, my stomach growled embarrassingly loud.

"Food?"

I sighed in annoyance. "Yes, please." They both helped me slide the dress back on, Curtis gently tied it around my waist.

Lucas went another direction, probably to the harem rooms, Curtis led me toward the Kitchen.

As soon as he pushed the door open, I smelled the frying meat.

"Steak. Mm. Yes." I closed my eyes and inhaled the mouthwatering scent. When they opened again, it was to a set of glowing eyes. I gulped.

"And how would you like them cooked?" Charles asked from the side, ignoring the *hungry* vampire next to me.

I kept my eyes on Curtis, biting the edge of my lip again, knowing how this next part was going to affect him. I blamed it on being pregnant with a vampire baby.

"Bloody." I squeaked.

"Bring it to the room when it is done. Lots of broccoli, potatoes, and a large piece of chocolate cake." Curtis commanded. I grinned. That all sounded divine. I may have closed my eyes and moaned again. "Your Queen is pregnant, make sure we have plenty of naturally grown fruits and vegetables. And anything else she craves."

My eyes shot back open. He just announced it. Charles wasn't the only one in the room. And they were all sure to talk.

Charles bowed, a small smile on his face. Obviously happy over the news.

Curtis took my hand and spun me around, quickly guiding me out of the kitchen. The door closed and he picked me up, a moment later he was closing our new bedroom door. I laughed when he dropped me on the bed.

Eventually, Curtis left to deal with the possible spy issue with Lucas. I pretended to be on the verge of falling asleep, knowing that would mean he would stay gone longer. I counted to one hundred before sliding off the bed and picking up my dress. I hastily walked to the room I had originally stayed in, through the connected bathroom. I held my breath when I reached under the mattress for my phone.

I sighed with relief when I pulled it out. Thankfully, it still had some battery on it as well. The perks of it never being on for long. As soon as I turned it on, the notifications light popped on.

Hill: Hey, it's me, your, uh, sister. The owner of this phone is currently away right now. He didn't want to risk losing this or breaking it. I don't know how this works. I don't know what I can say and not say, in case this gets seen. Maybe I shouldn't be saying that either. Screw it. I'd suck at being a spy. We got your gift. And we heard what you said. Well, here is what I have to say to that. WHAT THE HELL, GIRL? DO YOU REALLY THINK I AM JUST GOING TO SIT BACK AND LEAVE YOU THERE? And yes, I did know the caps was on. I did that so you would know I was yelling. I am getting you out of there. I don't care if you think you are too far gone. Family doesn't leave family behind. And you are family. Don't believe me? Ask that weird lady in my dreams! Lol. That was a trip, right? Look, sweetie. I love you. We all do. Rachel and the twins are antsy to get you home. Sigh. I wish I could talk to you. We didn't get much time together. But I felt a connection. Maybe it was the witch blood, or maybe it was just being a girl stuck in a bad situation. Do what you need to do. But know, no matter what, we are all rooting for you. And we will be here to drag your brain back from whatever acid induced trip it's on. I've learned a lot since we got free. A lot about who I am. Who WE are. I know the addiction of the ACID that you are probably experiencing. I will be here for you all the way. You know we have your back. Just don't give up, sister.

Hill: Oh, and because I know it's probably been bugging you. They are all safe. The one you left behind got comforted by an unexpected source. They, uh, sealed the deal, kind of. Just FYI. Love you, tons!

Hill: Final one, promise. Deacon is about to take this from me if I don't stop. He has ants in his pants since Colton is with you know who right now, stopping what you hinted. Anyway, I just wanted to let you know I am deleting this side of things. I promised you know who I wouldn't contact you. He worries too much. I know you better. Your phone is off and hidden well. Love you!

I laughed and wiped the tears that were silently falling from my face. Carrie must have gotten that weird lady in that dream place too. Man, I missed her. When the twins talked about this Bad A chick who baited the vampire so they could be safe, I was impressed. When I met her as Deacon's girlfriend, I looked up to her in a way. She was living the life she wanted and didn't care about anyone else. Then I heard both those women were her, and she was a witch. I thirsted for anything she could tell me. She knew my power. She knew how it worked. And she didn't look down on me, at all.

I remembered thinking one night that I would have loved a big sister like her. And here she was, saying she was that already. She didn't know what all I'd done. She didn't know about my baby. But she said she didn't care. They would take me anyway.

I sank down onto the bed, then curled up on the pillow. The cool sheets felt good on my warm skin. Nervously, not sure he'd want to hear from me after being silent for so long, I hit reply.

Me: Hey.

Oh, yeah, real smooth, Gracey. Still, his answer was immediate, as though he was sitting there staring at his phone too.

Hill: Hey.
Hill: How are you?

I smiled and sniffed back the tears again.

Me: I'm ok. How are you? Did anyone get hurt?
Hill: No. Well, two human soldiers didn't make it. One of the vamps bit one of my wolves for a boost then took off, but my wolf is fine.
Hill: We stopped them though. Because of you, we saved hundreds of lives that night.

I breathed a sigh of relief. Then I tensed when I saw his next message.

Hill: What did it cost you? And don't say "nothing." You've been silent for weeks. And no one came to help them. What did you have to do?

Yeah… I wasn't telling him that. Not yet at least.

Me: I followed the vision I was given. I don't have time to get into all that. Curtis knows there is a spy here. But they think it is someone in the harem. Good thing that's not where I am anymore, huh?
Hill: Where are you?
Me: Closer than we ever expected. Close enough to hear that they have a mole close to Deacon. Only thing is, the mole doesn't know he is one.
Hill: What?
Me: Tell Deacon that Bryant needs to stop talking to his son. Timothy isn't in Spain. He's here. In fact, he is running the Northern Region.
Me: They now know about her twins. They aim to capture and keep Carrie. They want her boys, and then they want to make her carry more of their kids. C made it sound like more than one of his councilors is a VB. Said one of them could try with her.

I heard heavy footsteps walking my way. I looked toward the window and saw the first signs of the sun coming up.

Me: Gotta go. Tell Carrie thank you.

I turned off the phone and slid it back in its hiding spot just in time. The door to the other room opened. I took a breath and tried to get comfortable.

I heard Curtis' chuckle from the doorway. "What are you doing in here?"

I gave a frustrated grunt, tossing to my other side. "I couldn't get comfortable. I thought I would try in here, but it doesn't seem to be working either."

Curtis walked over and sat next to me. He placed his hand on my stomach gently. I stopped moving and looked up at him. His other hand moved the hair off my face.

"I've heard that about pregnant women. You were plenty comfortable before I left though."

I huffed. "That's the problem. I get comfortable, start falling asleep, and then I'm not anymore. It's quite aggravating."

"Hmm. And this dress? Did it help?"

I pouted. "I got cold walking over here. It was helping, then it stopped."

He started untying the dress, pushing it to my sides. At least it was cold enough that goosebumps appeared, and other things, when the cool air hit my bare body. He frowned.

"I guess the weather is getting too cold for you to walk around without clothes. Soon, we will be heading south, it's a bit warmer there." He leaned down and scooped me into his arms, carrying me back to our room. "In the meantime, I think I know how to get you warm, and comfortable."

I kissed his neck. "You take such good care of me."

"I promised to always take care of my mate. I'm a man that learns from his mistakes." He set me on my feet again and pushed the dress off my shoulders.

I sat on the bed, slowly scooting back and laying down. I groaned in approval as he returned to me. "And what mistake was that?" I gripped his hair, already flying. Thanks to these extra hormones riding around in me, it didn't take much.

"I learned to take action instead of sitting back and twiddling my thumbs. I no longer care about the violence. If something needs to be done, I will do it. To hell with the consequences. I learned to think ahead to the end game, while not waiting on the sidelines for a miracle. I learned how to not be played any more."

I had a feeling asking any more questions, especially the clarity ones, would not be good for me. So, I changed gears. "And you are so good with your actions."

His serious tone fell away as he dropped with laughter. He kissed me softly. "I'm glad you approve. They all belong to you now."

I grinned and pushed enough to tell him to roll over. As soon as I was on top, I leaned down and kissed him. "Just as mine only belong to you."

I slept long and deep, comfortable in his arms. When the sun went down, he tried to move. I growled at him.

"I am comfortable, ruin it and you will pay." He laughed and snuggled back into me.

He was still gone when I woke up. The butthead. At least he had left a tray of fresh food since I had fallen asleep without eating.

Chapter 11

Andrew

As soon as I saw Grace's name pop up, I felt my wolf come to life in me. I may not have known her well, but I could hear the sadness in that one word. *Hey*. I wanted to dance for joy that she was messaging me though. Unfortunately, I knew she didn't have time for that.

What was her vision? What did Carrie do that required thanks? Why did she get off so quickly?

I guess that last one was kind of obvious. Still, Grace contacted me. I dialed Colton's number and waited impatiently.

"Hey. What's going on?" He answered. Somewhat out of breath.

I laughed. "Please tell me I am not interrupting something?"

He laughed. "No. I went out for a run. Well, I should say *we* did. Deacon lapped me. Happily, I might add. Then said first one back gets the first kiss. I think it's payback for when I dusted him in the truck, when we got the kids back."

I barked out laughter. I remembered that. Deacon was irritated with him because of it. I agreed with Colton, this was his revenge.

"You sound better."

And there went my amusement. "I heard from Grace."

"What did she say? Is she okay?"

"I think so. Physically anyway. It's hard to get a proper read through a message. She seems tired and a little sad."

I heard Colton open a door, probably entering wherever they were staying. A second later I heard another door open and close, a teasing voice in the background. Then they all got louder.

"Continue, Andrew. I've got you on speakerphone now. Thought it would be easier than having to repeat it all."

"Repeat all, what?" I heard Carrie. "Did you hear from Grace? Is that what's going on?"

"Calm down, angel. Let the mutt talk."

I then heard what I thought was Deacon getting slapped on the back of the head, most likely by Colton. I needed to get on with it before they forgot I was on the phone.

"Yes, I heard from Grace." That stopped them all. "She says she is okay. When I asked what she had to do in order to help us, all she said was that she followed the vision. I don't know what that means. She changed the subject. She heard something today."

"What did she hear?" Colton asked.

I could hear sniffles in the back, and whispered words. Deacon was probably trying to soothe his mate. How I wish I could do the same thing.

"It seems someone at your place has been talking, only they didn't know it. Do you guys know someone called Bryant?"

Colton had the tone of one on guard and wary. "Yes, he is our head of household and is like a grandfather to most of us. Why?"

I sighed sadly. This was going to hurt then. "Grace said to tell him not to talk to Timothy anymore. His son, I guess. Timothy isn't in Spain. He's in Cali. He's in charge of the Northern region."

Colton cursed. Quite a few times.

"It sounds like Bryant didn't know his son had turned. We have everybody spreading the news about Carrie and the babies, trying to get them to come back. Over half are on their way." Deacon reasoned.

"Yeah, about that." The other side went deathly silent. "She also said that they now want Carrie. They will raise the twins, then pass her around. Grace thinks more than one on his council is a Vampire Born. You guys need to be careful."

This time it was Carrie responding. "We will be. Thank you. Did she say anything else?"

I scratched the edge of my jaw. When was the last time I shaved?

"Yes, but it didn't really make any sense. She said to thank you, Carrie. No explanation as to why. Do you know?"

Carrie giggled. Deacon mumbled incoherently.

"No reason. Again, thank you for letting us know. We will take it from here. I know you don't want to hear what comes next, but I've got two mates about to lose their brown crayons. I'll have Colton call you back tomorrow."

I laughed as I said goodbye and hung up. I kind of missed them being around. A kindergarten teacher came up with the most interesting phrases to get around cursing. Heaven help that clan of vampires. They hadn't had a female to monitor them in some time, and they got *her*.

I wiped a tear from under my eye, the good kind this time, right as Morris came in. He gave me an odd look.

"Brown Crayons. She actually said they were about to lose their *brown crayons*."

He chuckled. "Carrie?"

I nodded and told him about both my conversations. I hadn't had much for a Beta to do, since we were both kind of in limbo about our positions with the U.S. Army. But it was nice to have someone to talk to again. The place had been eerily quiet before Grace released my pack from their prison. It was comforting to not be alone anymore.

With no word from the humans yet, we were all kind of in limbo. I got desperate enough to watch CNN earlier, all they said was that the Senate was called to an emergency meeting with the Acting President a few days ago, and they were still there. I wasn't sure if it was a good thing or a bad thing. I was hoping for the former.

Chapter 12

Grace

"Are you ready?" Curtis asked from the door to our walk-in closet.

"No." I scoffed. "Do I look ready?" I lifted both hands to Curtis, he looked at my body appreciatively. "Keep in mind that it is about 30 degrees outside right now, and I am carrying your child."

I had a feeling that would deflate him. Although nothing ever fully deflated what he was packing. I swear, we could go for hours, and he would still be ready to pop an eye out with that sucker. All vampires seemed to be like that. No wonder they were little horn dogs.

"What is it that is frustrating you this time, love?"

I frowned. "What do you mean *this* time?"

He lifted both hands as he walked to me, slowly, like he was approaching a hungry lion.

“I meant nothing by it. You are just a little touchy lately.”

“Ya huh, and you’re always touchy. What’s your point? Because I’m a girl I’m not allowed to get cranky? Or is it because I am not a vampire? Maybe that’s it. I’m a witch, but only by a *little* bit.” I turned away from him and went back to digging through my clothes again. “Which also means that I am mostly human. And we all know how you feel about them.” I groaned and threw the jeans on the floor. “Seriously! This is all your fault, you know.”

He chuckled, wrapping his arms around me from behind, softly kissing my shoulder. I hated it when he did that when I was upset. Him being sweet made it hard to be mad when I wanted to be. This was payback for all the times I calmed him down, I knew it.

“What is my fault… love?”

I heard the stutter. He wanted to say “this time” again. I knew he did. I scowled at him over my shoulder, he gave me that innocent “I didn’t do anything” smile.

“You ripped all my leggings. Every time I wore a pair, you ripped them.”

He growled in a way that had my mood beginning to shift. Not cool. I pulled away from him. Or tried to anyway. Behemoth.

“It’s not funny, Curtis! My stomach is the size of a freaking beach ball! I can’t wear any of my jeans, and it’s too freaking cold to wear a skirt! I figured I could at least wear leggings, they are stretchy, but *noooo*, you can’t wait the five seconds to actually take a clothing item off. Which of course is how I became a beach ball in the first place!” I was on a roll throwing fireballs, and I didn’t care.

I tried to pull away again, knowing he was going to come in for the kill shot, but I didn’t care. Those stupid anaconda arms tightened around me. I squirmed, they got tighter, just like any snake.

"Grace," he kissed my shoulder, "my love," he moved up to my neck, "my mate," he moved my loose hair, and kissed right next to my ear before adding in a whisper, "my Queen."

Dang it, and there went the strength in my arms.

"Have I told you yet today how absolutely stunning you are?"

I shook my head and sniffled.

"Allow me to remedy that, then. You are, without a doubt, the most beautiful creature to walk this earth. You can take my word on that. I've been all over. I've seen more than my share. I've even bedded most of them."

I growled at that comment.

"No one has kept my attention the way you have in nearly a thousand years. You are exactly what I needed. What I have been missing." One of his hands slid down to the silk boy shorts I was wearing. "You were made for me. Designed to fit me perfectly, in every way. You are made of just enough fire to keep me on my toes. And just enough sugar to make me high off a small taste of you. I can never seem to get enough of you. Just looking at the artwork you are would be enough. How incredibly blessed I am to look at you every day and get to *touch* you." I gasped, as his fingers went in with that.

It wasn't long before he spun me around, lifted me up, and pressed my back against the wall.

"I love you, every inch of you." He confessed as he released everything he had into me. Which generally took a minute or two, the man didn't do anything by halves.

"Even though I'm as big as a house?" I pouted, not able to let that go.

He dropped his head to my shoulder, laughing. His hand rubbed my larger than normal stomach softly.

"You are *not* as big as a house. Not yet anyway."

I gasped in complete shock that he said that. He laughed and then kissed me before I could curse him out. I may have done that a time or two over the last few days. Always hungry for more, his hand moved upwards.

"These are much larger today. I don't hear you whining about them."

I snorted. "You weren't in here when I tried to put that bra on. Why do you think I chose the sports bra? I'm going to need another one of those by the way. And the boy shorts. In silk. They were the first thing to feel good against my skin in days." I was convinced that I jinxed myself with that whole uncomfortable bit.

Curtis roughly pulled out, then closed enough distance to let it hang against me. He moved just enough to tease me with it, while rubbing the backs of his fingers on the globes sitting on my chest.

"Care to reevaluate that last statement?"

I'm sorry did he say something?

He chuckled at my silence, and possibly at my hands reaching for him. "Uh, uh, uh. Answer the question, love."

I groaned, refusing to give in.

He stepped away from the wall, holding me tight to him. He turned, and something new hit my chest, and my bare butt. I felt two hands hold my sides, a little high if you ask me, balancing me on Curtis. I whimpered with my eyes still closed. I knew who it was, I knew his scent by now. It always smelled a bit too cinnamony to me.

I had two pieces my body was craving, pushing against me from both sides. I was dying. This was pure torture.

Curtis leaned far enough away that he was able to start teasing me like he was going to give me what I wanted. I reached down to grab him, but he caught my arm and wrapped it behind my back, low. I felt and heard the hiss from Lucas when my fingertips brushed him. He then pressed into me harder.

I whimpered again, as Curtis leaned down and took me in his mouth. His tongue bent down and lifted one of Lucas' fingers up on top, soon Lucas was holding that part of me up to him. Both men were enjoying it.

Sadly, so was I.

Curtis' teasing became more intense, and just plain mean. Soon, his mouth moved to the other side. Lucas' hand did not.

"Gracey." Curtis sang, his lips tracing up my collarbone. Lucas pulled his waist away from me as I tried to encircle him with my palm.

"Material. I was only referring to material." I gasped desperately.

Curtis chuckled. And slammed back inside, the same time Lucas slammed me from the back. Curtis was still holding my hand back there. Lucas lifted enough to his toes and barely set it in my palm. Before it fell back out, I caught it.

I was going to claim reflex in trying not to drop something. At least I would later. I wasn't thinking about logical reasonings yet.

My skin heated up with both of them rubbing against me, my need was worse than ever before. Curtis stepped forward, while Lucas stepped back, until he was against the wall now. The hand not holding my top, as he refused to relinquish that, slowly moved down. Little by little, Curtis moved out, giving Lucas room to work.

My legs shook to the point that I could no longer hold on to Curtis' waist, and they dropped to the ground, releasing their grip on Curtis. He stepped back, watching his friend keeping me going. Which got him going. I watched him work himself, while Lucas worked me. I unconsciously licked my lips, and Curtis laughed.

"What do you want, little kitty? Say the words."

I wanted him back where he had been, but I also wanted something else. Seeing my frustrations, Curtis smashed me between the two of them, kissing me hard.

"I know what will help you. But I need you to trust me. Do you trust me, kitty?"

I moaned out as Lucas wasn't the only one in there anymore. It hurt, but in an oh so good kind of way. I screeched and shot my eyes open when I felt Curtis' hand slap down on my thigh.

"Come on, Gracey. Tell me you trust me."

"I, tr… trust…" I couldn't finish. I couldn't even think straight.

"Good enough for me." He said, then stepped away and sat on the floor. He curled a finger at me, and I dropped like the good little pet I really was.

Lucas' hands slid down my sides, and down to my waist. One smacked me, right as I latched onto Curtis. Curtis was the one to yell out when Lucas took it one step further. He wasn't just using hands anymore. And it wasn't just my tongue hitting Curtis.

I shot out of bed a minute later, gasping for air.

"Grace? What's wrong? Are you okay?" Curtis was behind me, holding me against his chest, wrapping his arms around my waist.

"Is it the baby? Did you see something?"

I breathed deeply, over, and over again, shaking my head. "No," I choked out. "Just a dream. A very weird dream." A very good, but very *bad* dream.

He slowly coaxed me to lay back down, holding me tight against him. He wasn't there when I fell asleep. I bet his bare chest hitting my back was what started it all. Mix that with what I saw Lucas doing in the office the other day, and let's not forget completely insane hormones, and you get warped, unrealistic dreams.

Ones that would not leave my head, no matter how hard I try.

"Want to talk about it? Might help you relax."

I chuckled, on the verge of hysteria. "Doubt it. It was just you and me in the closet. I was saying I looked like a beach ball again."

He stifled his laugh with my shoulder. His large hand spread over my stomach. At one point in time, his hand would nearly cover it like this, not anymore.

"Not a beach ball. More like a molehill."

"Are you saying I'm fat now?" I whined, not even faking it.

He frantically moved and pushed me to my back so he could lean over me. "Not even close. No one in their right mind would call you fat. Your body is perfect. You are nourishing my son, who, let's face it, is going to be one big baby."

I couldn't help laughing at that. "Great, I'm going to be as big as this house, and then he is going to stretch me to new limits on his way out. He's going to leave me looking saggy everywhere, and you won't ever want to touch me again!" I was full out crying now. Curtis looked like he wasn't sure if he should laugh or cry.

"My beautiful Queen, that will never happen. Your body will heal, especially with my blood helping it. And I am going to love you, no matter how your body changes, especially because I will always love how you gave me a son when no one else could. I can't imagine a reality where I am not entranced by your beauty. Your laughter, your light, your darkness. It's all part of who you are."

I let him distract me for a few minutes, it worked better than his words. I was relaxed and falling back to sleep, safely in his arms again, when he decided to try his luck.

"What did you dream about?"

I closed my eyes tighter. "It's already beginning to fade away." Not in the slightest, but I knew he would use it against me.

"Gracey." He called softly. "Don't lie to me. You were talking in your sleep, love. That's how I know it wasn't a vision."

I let an irritated sigh out. "Can't you let this go?"

From the deep chuckle, I knew what he was going to say. "You called out my best friend's name, mixed with mine. Do you really believe I am going to let it go? I feel you should know me better than that by now."

"I do. Which is why I would like to forget it ever happened and not talk about it." I grumped.

He laughed and held me tight, leaning into my ear, just like he did in the dream. "It's *going* to happen. You *want* it to happen. Just *let* it happen. Stop fighting it. Your hormones push you from one extreme to the next, there is no shame in trying to give them what they want."

"I don't know what you are talking about. It was just you and me in the closet. Lucas watched like he always does. Nothing more."

"Oh, I think there was a lot more." He rubbed the side of my arm with the back of his knuckles. "We are leaving for San Diego tomorrow. Lucas is staying here. We won't be seeing him for a week or more. I am leaving him without a harem. He's already been without for days. And you've stayed in here since my council meeting. I have refrained from helping him, out of respect for you. We are punishing him, and he did nothing wrong."

"What happened to his harem?"

"We could not chance that one or more of them was a spy. They needed to be removed. No changing the subject."

Fear like I had never known crept into me. They killed them all. Part of me knew that they would, but I hadn't wanted to think about it. They killed them and it was my fault. I was the spy, yet those innocent people took the blame. I choked on the sob as it came out.

"Hey. What's wrong? I'm not trying to push you, I swear."

I turned and rolled into his chest, hugging him tight. "I don't know why I'm crying! It's not about the crap with Lucas. So, I had a dream about the three of us, so what! But all those people are dead, and they may not have done anything wrong." I sobbed out, not caring what spewed out of my mouth.

There was nothing he could say that would make that part better. I mean, he could lie and say he sent them to a farm in the country, but it was too late for that. Instead, he just held me until I cried myself to sleep. And he was still there when I woke up in the morning. The only thing that changed was his position. He was sitting up now, my head just above his thigh instead of his chest.

He brushed my hair back as I tilted my head up to look at him.

"Morning, beautiful. How are you feeling?" He seemed a little worried. Considering the mess I had been in when I fell asleep, it was understandable.

I snuggled into his thigh again, closing my eyes against the sunlight coming through. "Better. I don't know what happened last night. I'm sorry. Like you said, these hormones are really messing with me. There is no middle ground with them. They are getting very difficult to manage."

He combed his fingers down the back of my head, I sighed contentedly. His leg clinched under me. I opened my eyes to see what was wrong, but I didn't tilt my head up this time. I looked straight to the flagpole standing in front of me. I giggled and blew softly. His leg clinched under me again when my warm breath hit him just right.

Curtis didn't say anything, just sat there and watched me. I lifted my hand and poked it. He hissed. So, I poked it again, then giggled. He growled and tightened his grip in my hair. I lifted up just enough to poke it with something else, something wet, teasing him.

When I laughed and moved away, I landed in someone else's arms.

Chapter 13

Grace

I screeched in surprise, but the arms that caught me didn't let go.

"What the hell?" I whispered, looking up at Curtis. His eyes were glowing. "Curtis?"

"Nothing happened while you slept. I promise. He came in this afternoon to tell me about a call he got from down south. Nothing really all that important, seeing as we are headed there today. But he looked so lonely. I told him he could sleep with us. I mean, over half the bed was empty." Curtis shrugged, putting on the air like none of this was a big deal.

Lucas, on the hand, started rubbing against me. My dream wasn't far from my mind still, and my hormones were already up from messing with Curtis. My eyes closed and I pressed my lips together, trying to keep the sounds back. But, of course, they have great hearing, and could also smell what it was doing to me.

My fingers were itching to fly back and smack him, but I still remembered the feel of it in my dreams. I didn't trust these stupid hormones to let me stay logical. Lucas' hand slid up higher, holding me right under something heavy and hanging free.

I looked up when I felt Curtis' hand on my head again. His knuckle blazed a path down my cheek. The heat in my skin flamed up higher. I closed my eyes as his fingers slid further down. My focus was all on him, not on my own hands, and certainly not on Lucas.

Curtis massaged my aching chest. His hand somehow grew more fingers the more it moved. I didn't try to hide my moan this time. My hand slid back to grab what was rubbing against me, the corresponding teeth bit into my shoulder enough to suck on my skin.

"Curtis." I whimpered. His fingers were great and all, but they were nowhere near what I needed down there. Before I could say more his finger entered my mouth, but it wasn't just me I was tasting. He had pricked his finger and was feeding me his blood. I wasn't the only one moaning as I sucked harder to get my favorite drink out.

Curtis growled as he ripped it out of my mouth a few minutes later. My eyes immediately landed on something I wanted even more. I whimpered. I knew where this was going. Would it be as good as it was in my dream?

"What do you want, my Queen? I live to serve you both. You are my masters. Command me."

I whimpered harder at Lucas' words. His fingers had taken up where Curtis had been before he started feeding me his blood.

"Feed the hormones, love. Take what you need. That is all that matters. There is no shame in giving your body what it needs."

I was so tired of fighting it. I rolled over onto Curtis' legs, keeping a firm grip on Lucas. Curtis moaned appreciatively as I took him in. I slowly released Lucas, while he pushed my legs further apart.

I knew what was coming, and I wasn't disappointed. I was pretty sure my butt was bruised by the time he was done, but I wasn't complaining. Curtis didn't either, over the number of times my teeth went into him.

I dropped my forehead to Curtis lap, since my legs were barely holding me up. Lucas was shaking and pushing the last of him out.

"Better?" Curtis asked.

I bit his leg playfully. Lucas smacked me halfheartedly. My skin flared up.

I gulped. They laughed.

"Seriously?" Lucas actually whined about it. He sounded tired.

I fell off him, laughing.

"I told you. She fits her title." Curtis told him proudly, sliding down to lay next to me. His mouth took over mine, his hand pushed me in line with him.

Within minutes, I was good.

"See why I called you?" Curtis looked over my head to his friend.

"Thought you said he came in here on his own." I mumbled. I was in a Zen moment and didn't want to lose it.

Curtis chuckled. "He did. I called him to come in and give me some message from someone. I knew you hadn't forgotten that dream, and I knew what you needed." He kissed me, not letting me scowl at him. "We need to get moving. Our flight leaves in two hours."

I gave him a dramatic sigh and sat up. "Fine. But nothing fits. You tore all my leggings, and my jeans don't fit anymore. That means a dress. And it's cold."

Lucas tentatively ran a finger down my legs. "They are such pretty legs, why cover them up?" It was nice to see that somethings would never change, he still sounded like a psycho to me.

I slapped his hand out of habit. He looked up at me like a sad puppy. I was starting to see why Curtis tended to give him what he wanted. I sighed and waved my hand for him to continue. Curtis' eyes were laughing when I looked at him.

"What?" He shook his head, the grin popping out. "It's hard to say no to him when he looks at me like that."

Curtis barked out a laugh before kissing me again. "I'll pick you out something to wear. I will buy you new clothes when we get there." He kissed my head and pushed me back down to the bed with the pressure of it. "Why don't you reward him for helping you out this morning?"

I gave him a confused look. "Wasn't that reward enough?"

Curtis stepped away, still laughing, and shaking his head. Whatever. I closed my eyes, preparing to enjoy lying in bed longer. I opened one back up when I felt my leg being slowly pushed away by the same hand.

I couldn't help but watch in fascination as Lucas was off in his own little world. When my back arched, I forgot about watching him.

Both my legs were over his shoulders when Curtis returned, his hands gliding over my spikes.

Lucas came away like a man finally coming up for air, his eyes glowing darkly. "Man, I love my job."

Curtis barked out a laugh before petting the back of his head. "We need to get you some new toys."

"Yes, please, master." I giggled at the begging tone. "I do miss playing every morning before bed."

"Hmm. Well, you better finish what you started with the Queen, or she may never reward you herself again."

"Yes, my King. Should I serve you, as well."

"No. My Queen doesn't like to share. She will take care of me. But thank you."

One of my legs was set back down on the bed, at the same time Curtis lifted a leg over my shoulders.

I was calmer than I had been for days by the time we left that house. My hormones had evened out, leaving me to believe that Curtis was right, I just needed more.

Lucas drove us to a small airport, where we boarded onto a small jet plane. The two Nightwalkers that had been standing at the foot of the stairs when we arrived, joined us on the plane. They closed all the doors, preparing for the flight.

My stomach did not like take-off. Or the flight, in general. I didn't care much for the turbulence either.

"Have you never been on a plane, love?"

I shook my head, afraid to open my mouth and lose the breakfast Curtis had forced me to eat before we left. He brushed his fingers through my hair, ending at the purple tips, lifting them up.

"Your color is fading. Did you want to have it redone soon? We can make an appointment at your salon, when we return, if you want?"

"I did it myself. The color came out of a box. My foster mother went off the rails when she saw the sink. I didn't realize the dye would taint her precious sink. I paid for it later. Especially when she realized I stole money from her wallet to pay for the dye." I smirked, laid my head on his shoulder, and held tight to his arm.

"I'm sorry you had to go through all that. Do you know where she is now? I can give her to Lucas. She can spend her days being punished by him and watching you have more than her."

I laughed. "Lucas wouldn't touch her. She looked like a rat, and I have no doubts she would taste like rat poison." Curtis and the other vampires laughed. "Besides, they snuck out in the middle of the night, after the first wave of attacks. Todd and I were pretty sure they were on the freeway when you bombed it."

"Todd?"

"My foster brother." I grinned. "When we heard Ryley and his friend coming, we got busy, thanks to ay uh, dream that I had. That's why Ryley didn't kill us and wanted to keep us instead." I had told him pieces of that before, so I figured it was still safe information to share.

One of the vampires cursed and laughed harder. Curtis looked at him and lifted an eyebrow.

"Sorry, my liege, but you don't know how many times I have heard Ryley complain about his missing pets. Recently it has shifted from whining to cursing his luck, and now I know why."

Curtis hummed thoughtfully. I put one hand on the cheek furthest from me, holding his head while I kissed the one on my side.

"You are a much better master." He rolled his eyes at me, then leaned in for a kiss. I quickly backed away. "Hold that thought." And ran for the bathroom.

We spent a good portion of the flight in that bathroom, and not always because I was throwing up. It was a nice bathroom, with good, sturdy counters.

When the plane started landing procedures, Curtis picked me up and set me on his lap. He lifted my skirt, and locked himself in. The bump when we hit the ground pushed me over the edge.

“We will have to remember that for our return trip.”

“What?” I asked, breathlessly.

“Your stomach didn’t register the movement this time since you were distracted. And we both know how easily you are distracted by me.”

I blushed and leaned in to kiss his neck. “I can’t help it. There's just something about you.”

He chuckled and stood up, setting me on my feet. I looked down at what was still hanging out. He was coated in fluid from me. And that made me want it more. He sighed like I was putting him out.

“Fine but make it quick.”

I wanted to sass him back, but those stupid hormones always got the best of me. Before the first words could form on my lips, my mouth was full.

“Where can I find me a kitty like that?” One of the guards asked the other.

“You can’t. She is one of a kind. Which is why she will be your Queen when I get the crown back from Deacon.” Curtis hissed.

I may have liked that comment a little more than I should have. Or was it the fact that he was sticking to the promise of not hiding who I was to him anymore? I was shedding the persona of the pet and being given the mantle of a Queen.

Twenty minutes later, we pulled up to another large estate on the ocean. Two men stepped out to greet us. Both bowing slightly. One was GI Joe. I didn’t recognize the other. He did look a little like that guy who was in *Twilight*. Not the main character. Gah. I couldn't remember his name. I just remembered him being like a big kid and mated to that snobby blonde chick.

"Mark," Curtis shook hands with GI Joe. His other hand was on my lower back, making the ownership statement. Might as well have peed on my leg.

"Welcome, my Lord. My Lady." Mark bowed a bit to me, surprising me.

I glanced at Curtis, he smiled and rubbed his hand on my back.

Curtis frowned when he looked at the next one. "Ryder. What happened?"

Ryder gulped and looked at his feet. "I'm not sure, sir. I watched the news before leaving for the ports, they continued with the same spiel about the storm. But when I looked at the waves, it seemed to be moving in faster. I trust my instincts with the ocean more than I do with human knowledge. Without the shifters, I thought it safer to divide and conquer. I divided my fighters into smaller groups. They were told to start where they were and move South. One way or another, we would be covered."

Curtis nodded that he agreed with that plan, Ryder relaxed a bit more before continuing.

"My team was the one closer to Washington's south border. Right in the middle. I hid them in containers the night before, so we would be in position the minute the storm came over us." He stopped to lick his lips. Curtis nodded again, getting slightly impatient. "I don't know what happened. Just minutes after we stepped out, I smelled shifters and Vampire Borns. They ran right at us. Looked like human soldiers too. I took one of them out easily. But my team was dying out fast. I jumped on the back of a wolf and drank what I could in the short time I had. Then I ran out of there. I went back to the safe house we were staying in. I called Lucas to see what I should do. He said you were busy."

Ryder's eyes glanced at me, and I felt Curtis' fist form on my back, pulling my shirt in with it.

"Lucas told me to wait there for a couple days, see if anyone came back later. No one ever did. I watched the human news, waiting for them to report about the attacks. Not a word was ever said. It was like nothing ever happened. I came through the Southern gate yesterday. I was going to make my way up to see you, but Mark told me you were on your way."

Curtis was so angry he was struggling to form words. I needed this to move along, so I could start planning how to see that gate. I curled into his side, and his arm encased me. His free hand lifted to hold my head against his chest.

"Has Mark told you my plans from here?"

"Only a little bit, sir. He said you were calling most of us back behind the wall. You know you can count on me." He bowed again, still casting glances at me curiously.

"You are a good soldier. Those are hard to come by. Now, let's go inside. It's too cold for Grace out here. We can't have her getting sick."

Huh, I hadn't even noticed that I was shaking. Now that he mentioned it though, I was freezing my metaphorical balls off.

Mark directed us to our room, the master suite of the house. Curtis took me right in and closed the door in their faces. I laughed. He then took me straight to the bathroom, nicely took my dress off, and shoved me in a hot shower. Once he deemed me clean and warm enough, he carried me to the bed and held me under the blankets.

"This afternoon I will take you shopping. We will buy you warmer clothes. I have another stop to make as well. We can do it all while we are out. First you need to rest."

"Why during the day? All your men will be locked inside."

"They will, but the drones still monitor the streets. Mark and Ryder will come with us. I want to see how the city is thriving with all the changes. Over the next few days, we will visit the surrounding areas as well. I haven't checked this part of the wall yet, either."

"What's on the other side of this one? Arizona?" It was a stupid question, but the only one I could think of to lead him in the right direction.

He tried to smother the laugh by kissing my head. "No, love. It is Mexico. Tijuana, to be exact." I bit my lip, trying to hide a shy smile. He rolled his eyes, which always looked ridiculous in that giant body. "You want to go now, don't you?"

I quickly rubbed my lips together. "No. I'm good. You have a lot to do. I can wait to explore outside of my little bubble another time. I've never been to San Diego before either. Mexico can wait until next time. Maybe when our son is older, we can leave him with someone else. I won't want to leave him for a while. And I do plan on nursing for as long as I can. I've heard breast milk is the healthiest thing for a baby." I snorted. "Let's face it, my body is gearing up to have a lot. I only want what's best…"

He cut me off with a kiss, which I quickly turned into more.

He held me tight to him as he pulled away. "I love you. I love how you care more about me and our son, then you do about you. But that wasn't what I asked. I asked if *you* wanted to go."

I looked down shyly. "You know I'm not used to that though."

"I know. Which is why I want to give you everything. I am creating a whole new world, just for you. If you want to go visit Mexico for a day or two, we can do that. You and our son are my most important responsibilities."

I kissed him this time, and he didn't pull away.

Chapter 14

Grace

A few hours later, we loaded into the back of a large SUV. It was plain black, no bling, no extra lights. It had more of a mom-van feel to it. Mark drove, and Ryder rode shotgun. The sun was high in the sky, so they were probably the only vamps out right now.

I leaned over to whisper in Curtis' ear, even though I was sure they could all hear me. "I thought the Vampire Borns were against us." I made sure to include me in that. Since we were supposed to be a team now.

Curtis chuckled, while the other two watched me warily in their mirrors. "Technically, they are. But the magical people have been hiding for too long. We are stronger, we hold the magic. Why should we be the ones hiding in the sewers and running for our lives?" He looked down at me. "We are the top of the food chain, which is our rightful place. I am not the only one who sees that. The rest will come around in time. I was born to be the King. Deacon and his father stole it while I was out of the country. I am taking what is mine back, and righting past wrongs. Humans are simple creatures. They fear what they do not understand. They desire a simple life. *We* will give that back to them. What we are doing seems drastic right now, but in time, everyone will see it was necessary and for the best."

His tone, his conviction that he was doing what was right, went right through me. Given that didn't take much these days. I grabbed the back of his head and pulled him down to me. He didn't fight me on it. Nor did he let me stay down long. I was on his lap in no time. And I was the one shifting clothes around. I was even starting to like making the others whimper. Those poor suckers were whimpering like toddlers from the front seats.

"I can't decide if I like these extra hormones or not." I confessed, falling onto this chest.

He just laughed. "I'm loving them. But we are at the mall now. I hate to say it, but you need to get dressed, love."

I whined, just to make him laugh, then kissed him one more time as he slid my sweater dress back over my head.

We walked into the mall, hand in hand. The place looked deserted.

"Where is everyone?" I asked.

"This is one of the three cities that are reserved for our people. The humans have already been moved to the outer lying towns. The only ones remaining are the donors. For now, they are sequestered in an apartment building. As they learn the rules, they will get more privileges." Mark answered me.

I had many questions but wasn't sure I could ask them. I gave Curtis a curious and slightly painful look. He chuckled and waved for me to go ahead.

"How many vampires are in the area?"

Mark didn't even bother looking at Curtis for permission, but Ryder did look at us both with confusion.

"At last count, we have 100 in residence here. They check in with their supervisors every night, receiving orders, getting updates, things like that. I meet with the supervisors once a week. I have divided them all into 5 groups, 20 vampires per group."

"And how many donors? Are they all volunteers or were some assigned?" I felt Curtis rubbing his thumb on my back, like he was supporting me and happy I was asking.

"We started with the bars and clubs, offering higher positions to the donors already working. They would not require training. Those who accepted are in charge of the others. If they had families, then they were given their choice of houses. They report to the feeding center every day for work. Whether it be to feed someone, or to monitor the others. They are paid handsomely of course. We did have to assign some donors to the job. We currently have 30 donors. Some will be staying until they can learn their place, others will serve for a few months before trading off with the next shift. They are not paid as much."

"Are they getting to choose what they are willing to do?"

"Mostly, yes. The rebellious, no."

I nodded. I wasn't completely sure I was good with that, but at least the majority got to pick.

"How do you separate who is available for what, and the families of the higher up donors?"

"The families wear wristbands. They have freedom to move about the city. As for those who have not earned that freedom yet, it depends on where they live. As with all the areas, they were given a large apartment building. The lower floors are just for feeding. The higher floors, with the penthouse suites, are for more."

I snorted. “Room to either be in private or public.”

Mark stopped and opened the door to a maternity store. He bowed slightly with a small smile on his face. “Exactly, yes. Plus, we hope the others will see the benefits and change their minds.” He winked at me and waved us through.

I stopped inside and looked around. Curtis kissed my head.

“Anything you need, love. Whatever makes you comfortable and happy, will make me happy.”

I laughed and pinched his side. “You are just hoping I’ll stop snarking at you.”

He grabbed the hand I used to pinch him and kissed the back of it. “Snark at me all you want. I know the trick to calming you now.”

I blushed, they all laughed.

All buttheads. All of them.

I walked around the room, pulling various items out. When I had a decent pile, I pulled my dress off and tried them on right there, in the middle of the store. I didn’t care about all the windows, or the three vampires watching me. More than one set glowed from time to time. But only one set came up from behind me after I took off the fourth outfit.

I hummed as his hands rubbed my bare stomach. “So beautiful.” He whispered in my ear.

I screeched, then cackled when he roughly bent me over and kicked my right leg to the side. The laughing didn’t last long. When the smell from the others hit me, I glanced up to my side. Mark had Ryder by the hair on his knees. His eyes were on us. When he saw me looking, he winked.

It was official, vampire pregnancy hormones were the absolute worst.

Fifteen minutes later, I was searching through the t-shirt section again. I stopped and laughed when I got to some graphic ones. I pulled two off and walked over to my mate. I lifted one up to him, holding it against his chest.

"What will it take to get you to wear this?" Up to now, I'd only seen him wearing slacks and either plain t-shirts, or button downs. Or just plain boxers.

Curtis looked down to the shirt I was holding up. When he looked back up at me, one eyebrow was raised in a "you're joking, right?" fashion.

I pushed out my bottom lip into a mock pout. "For me?"

"How badly do you want me to wear this?" His voice was deep and gravelly. At one time I didn't understand why Todd always tried to do that. I got it now. Todd just didn't have the voice for it yet. Curtis grinned when he smelled my response. "Mark."

I gave him that "huh?" look.

He stepped forward and wrapped his arms around me. "You asked what it would take to get me to wear that. I saw you watching him earlier."

Mark came up behind me, and suddenly I was dropped back into my dream. I whimpered. Curtis leaned down to my ear, slowly pushing the maternity pants I was wearing down.

"How badly do you want me to wear that shirt, love? What are *you* willing to do for it? Or is it no longer about that?"

"Using the pregnancy hormones against me is playing dirty." I mumbled, as Mark's hands were already sliding up and down my sides, my shirt going up with it.

"I'm a vampire, little kitty. We don't play clean. That's for the witches."

I huffed softly, on the verge of hysteria. "I am a witch."

"Yes, but you are so much more than that now." His hand held my molehill again. "You are not only mated to a vampire, but a born King. And you are carrying his son. You are Queen of the Vampires, love. Indulge yourself."

I was pretty sure that wasn't his hands pushing the bra off, and I didn't care. If I had stayed on the path of the favorite pet, worse than this would have happened. Technically, I had a choice here. At least, I'd like to think that I did.

By the time we left that store, Mark was whistling, Ryder looked somewhat confused, and Curtis and I were wearing matching shirts. They were both a light gray color. Curtis' shirt said "My humpin put the bump in." A baby bottle stood in the middle of the words. Mine was "I'm here for the sex." On both sides of the last word were baby footprints. One pink, and one blue. They were cute.

Curtis looked slightly more human wearing it. The triumphant grin matched it perfectly. He got what he wanted. And I got what I wanted. It was a fair trade.

As we drove to wherever it was that Curtis needed to go to next, he asked Mark questions about food, resources, how many rebellions he had to put down in the beginning, and such like that. I was surprised to learn that a few human groups had risen up and tried to fight back during the initial attacks. Neighborhoods gathered together in one place, protecting the young, and trying to fight back.

All they managed to do was make it easier for the Nightwalkers to kill them all. Mark, however, was different from Lucas. He told them not to attack the children. So far, Mark didn't seem as much like a psycho as Lucas.

Months ago, Deacon and Todd took a trip to get supplies. It was right after the twins ratted out my visions to Carrie - I was so glad they didn't let my pride get in the way. Deacon used that time to give Todd a little history lesson, which he then shared with us.

According to Deacon, Nightwalkers lost their souls when they were changed. Vampire Borns were born with half of one. Which was why they were nicer than the Nightwalkers, but also not as frigid as the rest of us.

Knowing Mark wasn't as evil, and psychotic made me feel a little better about what happened in the maternity store.

Half an hour later, we pulled into a parking lot. There was a large building with smaller ones around it. All the smaller ones had broken windows. This one did not.

I waited while Ryder opened my door and helped me out. He gave me a soft smile, almost like he was trying to give me courage for something. Ryder looked like a big kid. He was too sweet to be caught up in all of this.

Curtis put his arm around me, drawing my attention. His stare was attentive. He thought something was wrong. I went on my toes enough to kiss the bottom of his jaw and gave him a smile that said I was fine. He looked up at Ryder, who quickly looked at the ground. Curtis found that funny for some reason.

"Where are we?"

"This used to be a private bank. For over a century, it has served only those with money. The rich, the famous, the untouchables."

"So, people like you." I teased.

He chuckled. "Exactly. They have the strongest safes, filled with safety deposit boxes. There are smaller safes, for those with more, who need more room and security."

“So, it’s Gringotts. Got it.” I laughed at the confused looks from two of the three. Ryder just blushed. “Gringotts Wizarding Bank?” Duh.

Still blank and confused. I groaned and dropped my head back. “You guys are too old and too out of touch. Gringotts is a bank for wizards in Harry Potter. The further down you went, the safes were harder to get into. And more dangerous to get there. They were for the families that were wealthier and been around longer. And more powerful.”

“This is a book or movie, yes?” Mark asked. He seemed to be a bit more relaxed around me now. Unlike Lucas though, he wasn’t already begging for more treats.

I gave them a duh nod, then shook my head. Muggles. “Forget it. What are we doing here?”

Curtis blinked, like he was trying to come back to himself. “I need to get something out of my safe.”

“Ah. So that's why this is the only building on the street without broken windows.”

“Yes, all my counselors know the locations of places not to let their soldiers destroy. I have many safes and safe houses all over the world.”

Mark opened the door again, waving me through. He didn’t wink this time, instead he smacked my butt. I squeaked and jumped. They all laughed. Guess I was wrong. Mark did want more. He just wasn’t as pathetic as Lucas about it.

My heart raced when I saw that familiar hunger in his eyes. “You all suck. I might just have to lock myself in a room for the duration of this pregnancy.”

Mark stalked closer, Curtis closing the door for him, watching with amusement. “Yes. And how well did that work out for you the other day? I do believe you said your visions were what set you off then. Are they going to stop suddenly because you are alone? Or are you going to be so desperate for release that you try, and fail, to handle business yourself. As is, one vampire is not enough for you."

My lip quivered. It quivered! I tried stepping backward and ran into Ryder. Who was more than happy to hold my waist. Just leaning against a man had my eyes closing.

"My Queen has needs. Let us serve you. Let us worship the body that carries the heir to the throne." Mark's voice was reverent and polite. His breath coating my neck.

Ryder held my waist, while Mark went to his knees, sliding my pants with them. Curtis leaned over him, his lips meeting mine the same time Mark's lips met my skin. Neither let up until I was done.

"What was your excuse this time?" I asked Curtis when we started walking again.

Curtis just shrugged. "The more often you are satiated, the less you suffer from the not so fun hormones."

"In other words, you keep firing up the fun ones so that I won't cuss you out anymore or cry on your shoulder."

He shrugged while putting in a code, then letting a bright green light scan his eyes. He didn't answer until he was pulling on a small lever and turned to look at me.

"The others stress your body out. This one does not. This one gives you a way to release it and helps you to stay calm. Is it more fun? Yes." He pulled me into his free arm and lowered his voice. "I don't mind the other ones. I will hold you anytime you need to cry it out. I will become your verbal punching bag if that is what you need. I will always do what is best for you. Understand?"

I nodded, purring like a kitten, and rubbed against his chest.

He chuckled. "Still my sweet little kitty, aren't you?"

"Tasty little kitty, too." Mark added in a side comment.

Curtis and I both laughed, stepping apart after one more kiss. We followed him into the room. There were about two dozen safe deposit boxes of various shapes and sizes.

"This is all mine. I bought it out when they first opened. While I may not use them all, all of the time, I did not want anyone having access to my vault."

Curtis walked over to a medium sized drawer shaped one, and pressed his thumb on the black, two-inch, screen.

"As technology increased, so did their safety measures. Even if my men had broken into this bank, they never would have been able to access any of the vaults." He waved his hand, and I stepped over to him. The others waited at the door entry.

"What I am about to show you, has not been seen by anyone else in over a thousand years. I've taken precautions to preserve them. They were made from the finest natural resources, and they have withstood the test of time. I come here every few years and clean them myself. Not long before the curse hit, and our world crumbled around us, my mother came to me, and gave these to me. I had an arrangement with another family. I was to mate with their daughter. She was one of those killed the night the witches attacked. No one knows this, but a month before she joined us at the castle, my mother brought these to me. She had a feeling something was going to go wrong, that she may not be there at my coronation. She didn't want to risk them getting lost."

I watched in fascination as Curtis lifted up a wooden box. It was engraved with a symbol on the outside of the lid. It was a large V, formed with daggers, with a crown on top. I tentatively ran my finger over the top of it, feeling it out. Curtis' hand slid under mine and folded our fingers together. When I looked up, I saw something I never expected to see in his eyes. Misery, a deep foreboding sadness.

With his other hand, he pushed his fingers through my black hair, cupping the back of my head. His lips met mine softer than ever before. It almost felt like he wasn't kissing me, but someone else. Someone who he once held dear.

Was it the arranged mate he had lost? Did he care for her?

Was that why he turned against the world?

Did the pain and the anger darken his soul?

Curtis rested his forehead on mine, working to regain control of his emotions. I pulled my hand out of his and cupped both sides of his cheek.

"You are a good leader. A good King. A good mate. You are going to be a great father. I love you."

"And I love you, my mate." He cleared his throat and stepped back. "And now, it is time to make you the rightful Queen. In time, I will get my crown back from Deacon, but for now…" He lifted the lid and turned the box.

Inside was the most exquisite tiara I had ever seen. I may or may not have had a thing for them once upon a time. I mean, what little girl didn't want to be a princess?

I often dreamed of a limo pulling up in front of our rundown apartment and a man in a suit telling me that my father just found out about me and wanted me to come home. The man would hand mom an envelope with court papers, and probably money, and we would leave.

Alas, such did not happen.

The sides of the crown were made of some type of black medal, half a dozen thin rods flowed in out of each other like waves. The sides were adorned with small ivy leaves. In the center, was a V, supporting a large blood red oval ruby.

Curtis lifted the tiara up with two hands, and carefully placed it on my head. It didn't rest on the top though. It hugged my head, with two long end pieces circling around the sides. The ruby sat in the middle of my forehead, supported by a V shape.

"Long live the Queen." Curtis whispered in awe, dropping to his knee in front of me.

I vaguely heard the others dropping down as well. My attention was on Curtis. His eyes never left mine, as he inched my shirt up and kissed my stomach.

Chapter 15

Grace

I was still in a bit of awe as we drove back to Mark's house. Curtis had placed the tiara back in the box, pulled something small out, then locked the box with a key, to keep it safe. He said it would only be coming out for special occasions. For all other times, he put the smaller item on my finger. It was a ring that matched the tiara perfectly.

We drove in silence, Curtis' arm around me. I played with the ring on my finger, watching the way the sunlight reflected on it. Curtis rubbed his thumb on the back of my arm, watching me and the ring.

"You will rest tonight, tomorrow we will check out the human cities."

"What about you? Won't you be resting with me?" I looked up to meet his eyes, nervously. New place, new vamps, I did not want to be alone.

He shook his head sadly. “This is the best time for me to go meet with the Nightwalkers and check out the feeding centers. They run on the same clock as the Nightwalkers.”

Was I hyperventilating? It sure felt like it.

“I won’t be gone long. And you won’t be alone. Mark will be staying to guard the house, and you. If you have a need, ask him. As long as you are taken care of, that is all that matters. You will be perfectly safe. I promise.”

“But you promised to take me everywhere with you.”

“I will stay with you until you fall asleep. Will that help?”

I sniffled, nodded my head, and burrowed myself into his side.

When we reached the house, a cook had a meal ready for me in the dining room. I laughed softly. Another bloody steak. Curtis winked at me as he lifted a bite into my mouth. I let him feed me every bite, dramatically moaning. I was only partially messing with the other vampires walking around the house. It was fun.

“It seems I am not the only one who likes to play dirty.”

I blushed and turned to take a drink of water.

“Don’t stop. I love it when you play dirty.” His eyes were glowing, and his voice had taken on a slight growl. I blushed again.

Curtis insisted his *dirty* mate needed a shower before bed. So, I let him pull me into a hot shower. He massaged every one of my muscles, until I was no more than putty in his hands. He carried me to the bed, still wrapped in the towel, and laid me down.

Curtis picked a knife up from the bedside table and sliced a line down his pointer finger. “You will get more this way.”

“What happened to your wrist?” I teased him.

"I think we both like this way better. Now be a good little kitty and open those perfect lips."

"Which ones?" I purred, pulling my knees up and apart. He chuckled and settled between them.

"Such a good little kitty." He licked his finger, catching the drops of blood escaping. I licked my lips in anticipation. "You have been so good lately, letting my men and I take care of you. Does my kitty want a treat?"

His finger outlined my lips and I pathetically tried to catch it. Curtis laughed as I made a grab for it. He caught my hand instead and held it above my head with his nonbleeding hand.

"Tsk, tsk. Kitty needs to learn some patience."

I gave him a seductive grin and slid my other hand down my chest, his eyes followed the lower I went. I waited until he was thoroughly distracted with what I was doing, then jumped up and grabbed his finger with my teeth. He growled but didn't back away. Instead, he took over, proving he earned the right to wear that ridiculous t-shirt.

I snuggled into him nearly an hour later, not sure who was more exhausted, me or him. "Admit it, you keep pushing your friends on me because you can't keep up."

He barked out a laugh and held me tight. "Is that a challenge, love?"

"Hmmm, maybe."

"Are you complaining?" I didn't answer, I couldn't. I just held him tighter. "That's what I thought." He was smug now. Jerk.

I was fading into blessed unconsciousness when I felt him turn to look at the clock.

"Don't go. Please. I can't sleep alone. I need you." Sadly, it was true. I always tossed and turned until he came to bed.

He sighed deeply. "I have to go, love. I would take you with me, but you need to rest. It has been a long day. I need you to stay strong."

I sniffled. "And I need you." I was pathetic, and addicted.

"I'm right here, Gracey. Rest. I've got you."

I sighed, feeling like I won.

I woke up a few hours later, smiling about the thick chest behind me, and the large arms around my waist. I glanced up to the clock on the bed side table, it had only been a few hours. Either he made it very fast, or he stayed. I grinned, then remembered why I woke up.

This kid needed to move off my bladder.

I tapped the hands softly, and they moved, slowly dragging along my skin until I was whimpering. I groaned and shot out of bed. The laughter was soft but made me smile. I took my time washing my hands and catching my breath.

He stayed. For me.

Because I asked him too.

With a stupid, lovesick grin on my face, I walked back out to the bedroom. And froze. I looked at the bed, then at the bedroom door.

"Where did Curtis go?" I walked slowly back to the bed, ignoring how good his focus on my body felt. Personally, I felt fat, misshapen, and ugly. It was nice that none of the others seemed to agree.

Mark stayed in his position, lying on his side, and pulled the covers back for me to lay back down. He also pulled them back enough for me to see I wasn't the only one not wearing any covering. I swear he did that on purpose.

"Curtis had to go meet with the Nightwalkers. He promised to be back soon."

I frowned and sat on the edge of the bed, keeping a distance between us.

"When did he leave? And why are you in here?" And how long had he been there? Was that him holding me when I woke up?

Mark didn't seem phased in the least bit. "He left two hours ago. He messaged me and had me come in before he got out of bed. He made me promise to hold you until he got back. Apparently you can't sleep unless you are being held. He didn't want you to suffer and hoped you would sleep through it. You were sleeping fine too." He lifted the blanket a tad higher. "Come lay back down. I promise not to bite. Unless you ask me too." He winked at me, something I was starting to think he liked to do. Something they all liked to do.

My skin flushed. Which apparently *it* liked to do.

I chewed on my bottom lip, my eyes taking every inch of him in, carefully.

"Would it make you feel better if I put a blanket between us?"

Embarrassed - since I let him do all sorts of stuff to me, in public, just hours ago, and yet still couldn't lie next to him naked - I nodded my head.

I was trying not to laugh as he dramatically groaned and stood up, showing me all of his glory. I watched as he spread the sheet back down on his side, then laid on top of it, pulling the comforter on top of him. He lifted both again for me.

"Better?" He was still trying not to laugh at me. I was a living, breathing oxymoron.

"Yes, thank you." It was slightly high pitched and barely more than a whisper.

Carefully, I laid back down, and he set the covers on top of me. He then proceeded to wrap his arms around me again, holding me tight to him. Just the way we were when I woke up. It didn't feel right though.

I twisted my body back and forth, probably looking like a cat trying to get comfortable. Giving up after a few minutes, I grumbled and turned to face him. I tried to keep a few inches from him, but every time I moved, still trying to get comfortable, he inched closer.

I growled and started crying. Which freaked him out a bit.

"What's wrong, my Queen?"

"I can't get comfortable." My body shook and I sobbed into his chest. I sobbed harder when he moved away. I was crying hard enough not to realize what he was doing,

He was gone only seconds before he was back again. His arms wrapped around me, and I grabbed him desperately, needing to be held. Oddly, I was more comfortable now. I hiccupped a few times and pulled myself together.

I wiped my eyes and sniffed. "I'm sorry. It's just really aggravating when I am tired and can't get comfortable. One minute something feels fine, then the next it irritates the hell out of me."

Mark rubbed a hand up and down my back, further helping me relax. "And now?"

I sighed and laid my head against his chest, throwing my leg over his. "Much better. What did you do?'

His chest bounced against my head with silent laughter. “I removed the problem. You really can’t tell?” He rocked his hips, which were somewhat between my legs now, and something wonderful brushed against me.

The sound that came out of me was a weird mix of a moan, a purr, and a whimper. I pushed back enough to look down at what hit me. The moonlight wasn’t helping much. I blinked and waited until my eyes adjusted. Which meant I was staring at him for a solid two minutes straight. He liked my stare too.

My hand flinched, like it wanted to touch it. He chuckled and grabbed my hand, moving it for me.

“My Queen is welcome to inspect any part of me she desires. I live to serve thee.”

My head snapped up at him. Did he really just say *thee*?

Mark rolled his eyes, which made me giggle. “Yes, I’m old. I know.”

I giggled some more and watched his eyes as he wrapped my fingers around what I had been inspecting with my eyes. His face was fun to watch, he was very expressive. He didn’t ask to serve me this time. He just rolled me to my back and gave me what I needed.

I was flying high, enjoying the ride when I heard the door open.

“Welcome home, my Lord. Your Queen woke up to use the bathroom and couldn’t get comfortable.” Mark didn’t even stop what he was doing.

“Yes, I had a feeling that would happen. Let me guess, she insisted on you being covered.”

Mark laughed. I ignored them both. Well, their words anyway. Curtis undressed, his eyes on mine, until mine rolled back anyway.

"Yes. She was crying, I had no choice but to remove the sheet. She calmed down but didn't even notice until I said something."

Curtis walked over to me, the back of his hands caressing the side of my face before moving down. As soon as he hit gold, Mark leaned down, and they worked on the same side together.

I reached to grab Curtis, but my hands were slow. He picked them up and kissed them. "You are tired, my love. Let us do all the work?"

I watched as he put a hand to the back of Mark's head, still holding my other one. I fell asleep not much later, when I woke up, my head was against Curtis' chest, but I felt a warm body behind me. I looked up at my mate when he brushed my hair with his fingers.

"I take it last night was not a dream, then? You snuck out and left another man in your place?"

His fingers kept moving, top to bottom, then back again. "I had to leave. But I did not want you to suffer from it."

"I had to share you." I accused him.

"You were tired. Besides, I share you all the time lately." He smirked.

"Don't care."

"Are you saying you didn't enjoy watching it?"

I scoffed and changed the subject. "He's still here."

"Yes, you wore him out last night. And you were comfortable. You know I hate seeing you uncomfortable."

I placed a soft kiss on his chest. "You do so much for me. But I'm still greedy. I won't share."

He laughed and kissed my head. "I will always seek your permission first. How's that?"

I scoffed. "Fine."

I felt soft kisses on my back, trailing down my spine. Soon, my upper leg went up, and Curtis grabbed it, holding it up. I didn't complain. I didn't ask questions. At this point, there was nothing I could say. I had no firm ground to stand on anymore.

Chapter 16

Grace

After breakfast, we loaded into a car again, this time driving to the middle of nowhere. Eventually, we came to Curtis' large wall.

Curtis played with the hem of my dress, still not happy that I wasn't covered more. But every pair of pants I tried to put on felt awful against my skin, like they were choking the life out of me. I ended up in a sundress of all things. It was cute and I had to have it. The material was soft and smooth. Everything else felt itchy. I at least agreed on a jacket and a blanket.

The jacket was fleece, as was the blanket. Curtis was trying to keep things soft for my indecisive body.

I waited against the car, while Curtis ran up and down the wall. Mark stayed by my side. Ryder hadn't come with us this time. It was peaceful. There was no awkwardness, no pushing for something while we waited. I was finding that I kind of liked Mark. He was easy to be around. Much easier than Lucas.

Originally we were supposed to be checking out other cities and areas today. Curtis made a last-minute change of plans. For me.

Curtis was only gone for twenty minutes, and barely out of breath when he got back.

"You're getting faster, my Lord."

"Yes, feeding from a mate will do that to you. Especially when they are also a witch. Just as my blood is keeping her healthy and strong, she is strengthening me. It's not by much, not like a fated mate would be, but the longer we go, the stronger it will get. Same as for her. Her powers have gotten stronger too."

Mark elbowed me playfully. "Hence the realistic shower vision."

I rolled my eyes as they laughed. "Are you guys ever going to let that go?"

"No." They both scoffed at the same time.

Curtis put a hand up for me. "Are you ready for your first international trip?"

I squealed and jumped on him, hugging him tight, forgetting my irritation with them a moment ago. He laughed as he hugged me back. I turned to Mark.

"Are you coming with us?"

Curtis chuckled as he kissed my head.

Mark seemed happy that I was asking. "Yes, my Lady. I am the King's back up."

A twinge of fear hit me, and I looked at Curtis. His eyes softened, wanting to soothe my fears.

"We are going outside the wall. I have no control over there. Not really. Anything could happen. I do not want to take chances with you or our son. Mark is going to come so he can watch our backs." He winked this time. "And in case your hormones get the best of you again."

I punched him lightly in the shoulder. I didn't want to hurt myself.

Curtis gently set me back on my feet and took my hand to pull me forward. We walked along a dirt path, Mark behind us. I turned and looked at him.

"Why are you back there?"

"So, I can watch your backs better. And I have a *great* view." He winked. I blushed and turned back around.

"Mark always was a lady's man. Even in our youth." Curtis mused.

"Did you two know each other back then?"

"Yes. He lived in a village on our Southern borders. Very close to the border dividing our kingdom from the witches. It was my responsibility to travel to our border towns and check on them. We had fun each time."

I hmphed. "Yeah, I bet."

They both laughed harder as we approached the large wall.

I raised my hand and slid it along the shaved stone. The wall was smooth, with no chance of holding onto anything rough in order to climb. Curtis placed his much larger hand over mine, holding it flat against it. He stood behind me, holding us just as tightly together.

"This wall will protect our family. This is the wall that will keep you safe from all those that would mean you harm. Only peace will reside on this side of the wall. It will block out the horrors of war from the other side."

"What war?" I whispered, hoping it would disguise my shaking voice.

I didn't need him to answer my question. My power did it for me. I saw kids screaming as fires flamed around them. I saw Vampires laughing as they circled wolves. I saw drones flying down the streets, shooting everyone in their path. I saw mothers holding their dying children, husbands holding their wives who had torn clothing and ripped out necks. Lastly, I saw Carrie. Chained in a basement, bloodied, and bruised. Her stomach swollen, while Curtis taunted her from the other side, two toddlers holding his hands. They looked scared and confused.

I gasped and cried out, not registering the arm supporting me as I crumpled to the ground. Frantically I searched with my mind, begging the fates to tell me another way. A better way.

Mercifully it came quickly. Responding to my pleas faster than before.

I saw Hill and the shifter in charge, standing near the wall. I saw them opening a doorway into the wall. They listened before tiptoeing and opening another door, which led them here, to this spot. They looked around, then went back in. Small devices were placed inside. They ran and hid behind trucks, waiting. Then the wall blew. The vision shifted, I saw Carrie sitting happily on a front porch, her kids running and playing. I saw people walking around. Witches, shifters, vampires. All bowing slightly when they passed her. I saw communities of people, living life like normal. Things weren't perfect, but life never was.

I blinked my eyes open, gasping for air. "I don't think I like this new strength to my powers." I repeated the lines I said after seeing my unborn son die. They only ever seemed to get worse. This time, I felt not only my pain, but the pain, fear, anger, and sorrow of every person I saw.

Curtis held me tight on his lap, keeping me off the ground, kissing my head over and over again. Mark rubbed his hand on my arm, as he sat on his heels.

“What did you see, Grace?” Curtis whispered to me.

I choked on the sob trying to come out. “I saw death. Destruction. War. Violence. Everywhere. I felt the pain of the mourning. It was horrible. Why Curtis? Why must we go through all of that?”

“The humans only learn from violence, from destruction. They fight like toddlers over a doll, until one is the winner. Only when tribulation comes do they band together. We must weed out the rebellious, those with a thirst for violence. The naysayers that will bring contention. When farming, fields are often burned and left to rest and cleanse the land. Only from complete destruction can healing begin. As I said, this wall will keep it out of our home. You will feel none of it. With your visions, you can help me target only those who will rise up against us. I will try to keep my army aimed at them and save the innocent. But I will never lie to you. There will be casualties.” His words were harsh and deadly, condemning people to death - people who didn’t deserve it - but his voice and his touch were soothing.

It made my head and heart ache. I missed the days when things made sense. I missed the days when I knew what to expect. Cold showers in the morning, followed by a bowl of cold cereal. Six hours sitting in classrooms. If I was lucky, I would find someone to hide in a closet with to ditch a class. Then home, where I was locked in my room until dinner.

It was a sad and meaningless existence, but at least I knew what to expect from life.

I wrapped my arms around Curtis’ neck and pulled myself up to hold him tight. I wrapped my legs around his waist next, and he held me.

"Let us take these thoughts and feelings away, my Queen. Let us help you." Mark begged, his tone was more of someone begging to help, not begging for a reward.

"My love, the stress isn't good for the baby. When you have these visions that stress your body, let us do what we can to take it away." Curtis added the fuel to the fire.

Mark started inching my dress up, while Curtis unzipped it enough to push the straps down. I let go of his neck and leaned back on Mark. I did need to get that memory and that feeling out of me. I did want to escape that pain, at least for a few minutes.

Mark stood up and held me with an arm around my waist, one hand much higher. Curtis kept my legs around his waist, connecting our bodies. Soon we were replaying the dream from the closet, only with the border wall instead of the closet wall. Mark was a much better addition than Lucas, too.

It took some time, and I wore out two vampires, but eventually my hormones leveled out again.

"I thank you for your assistance, gentlemen." I said breathlessly, still mostly laying on Mark. They'd tried hard to keep me out of the dirt.

Both men huffed laughs and gave me thumbs up.

"Was it like this for the female vampires when they were pregnant?"

"Not exactly. I do remember my mother being highly emotional when she was pregnant with my brother. But never to this extent. I think it is because she herself was a vampire. Whereas any other species typically weakens and struggles with our seed, she did not. My blood is keeping your body strong enough to handle my son, and ensure you survive, it might also be strengthening the hormones. I don't want to test it though, I will not risk your life."

I rolled my head across Mark's very large and firm chest, to get a better look at Curtis. "You have a brother? How old were you when he was born?" I felt Mark tense and saw the darkening of Curtis' eyes. "I'm sorry. Did I say something wrong?"

Curtis pushed himself to stand up, then pulled me off Mark and began cleaning me off. "Not at all. It's just a sensitive subject. I was already nearing my ninth decade when he was born. He was hitting his teen years when our mother died. She and my father had been thinking about trying for a girl. I loved my brother very much. But, as with most things, life changed after the curse hit."

I lowered my hand and ran my fingers through his soft brown hair. He was on his heels pulling the boy shorts back on me. At least he remembered I preferred these lately.

"Where is he? Maybe he will join our cause. He is a tad older now."

Curtis scoffed and stood up. Mark shifted uncomfortably. Curtis kissed me swiftly. "I appreciate the thought, but no. I tried many times to get him to see sense. I failed. He died not that long ago. Enough with talking about the past." Curtis nodded and Mark touched the wall and a door cracked open.

"How did you do that?" I asked him in a bit of a gasp, I was amazed and curious. As long as they didn't question my motives for that curiosity, we would be good.

"Simple. Look right here." Mark took the hand Curtis was not holding and lifted it to the wall. I leaned in closer. "Do you see that, my Queen?"

"Yes. Is that the Royal Crest?"

Mark smiled proudly. "Yes, my Lady. If you push that, a door will open."

"How many doors are there?"

"Three. One for each region. But they are very well hidden. We had planned more, but time was of the essence after the others blew out the one in Mojave." Mark pulled my hand down, covered my eyes with his free one for two seconds, then let go. "Do you still see it?"

I gasped in shock this time and stepped closer. I didn't so much as bat an eye when he folded our fingers together. "It's gone!"

They both chuckled. Mark kissed my knuckles, then released them so he could push the door open further, with both hands. It looked a little heavy.

"No, it is just that hard to see."

I followed him inside and lost sight of both of them. I gripped Curtis' hand tighter.

"Do not fear, love. I am right here."

I heard the scrape of a match moving along bricks and fire flashed in my eyes.

"What, no flashlights?" I laughed at both their grimaces.

"Sometimes the old ways are better. We don't need to worry about dead batteries and broken bulbs." Mark sounded like he had a bad taste in his mouth.

I laughed hard. "Now you are both starting to sound old. You're like the little old guys trying to figure out their cell phones."

I could tell they wanted to say something snarky back, but they were also trying not to laugh with me. For some reason, they liked it when I was happy. It was even funnier when my laugh echoed around the inside of the wall.

Curtis settled for huffing and shaking his head, then pinched my butt.

"Dirty old man." I mumbled. His grin cracked then. "Where are we now?" I asked, trying to change the subject. I would no doubt lose my underwear in this place.

"Inside the wall, my Lady."

I looked around, it was wide enough for the three of us to stand side by side. I couldn't even see the end of it.

"Is it hollow all the way around?"

"Yes. My men are able to guard the walls from the inside, protecting them from the sun. And even if pests decide to try and break down the wall from the other side, they won't take down the whole thing. By the time they made it this far, someone would have discovered them."

Curtis moved behind me and wrapped his arms around my waist. "You left your jacket in the car."

"I got hot."

"But now you are not. You are shaking."

"I'm not cold. I'm just not overly fond of so much darkness. I can't see past our little bubble. I can't hear anything either. How can they protect the outside of the wall if we can't hear or see anyone?"

"We can hear out there fine. Our side is quiet, the Mexican side has traffic moving smoothly."

His breath brushed over my skin, making goosebumps pop up.

"How often do you have guards here?"

"I excused the shift for today. The Nightwalkers don't know where the doors are. I didn't want them to see us pass through. They are brought in by someone else at the beginning of each shift." Mark stepped into my light more and started rubbing my arms lightly. “Are you sure I shouldn’t go back and get your jacket?”

“You two are evil. I hope you know that.” My lips trembled, just not from the cold.

“It's a dark room, with a beautiful woman. Your hormones are running so strong through you at all times, the scent is driving me absolutely mad.” Mark sniffed deeply, then his eyes lit up brighter than the torch that sat on the wall.

I was right. I lost my underwear. But I was fairly certain they ended up in Mark’s pocket, not lost on the floor somewhere.

I had to cover my eyes when we emerged onto the Mexican side. The brightness of the sun was a severe contrast to the pitch-black tunnel in the wall. I saw a small brick wall, the kind that kept people from falling into a ditch. It was directly in front of us, blocking the view of people coming in and out.

Pretending to be curious, I ran my hand over the edge of Curtis’ wall, a few inches from where the door closed. Mark softly laid his hand on mine and moved it over to the right spot. He left his hand over mine as I traced the engraving with my finger.

I turned my eyes to his and we stared at each other. I had one shot at this, and I needed to do it right. I pulled the corners of my lips up just a touch and he smirked. I put my hand on his chest, his hand still on mine. He pushed it further down. I curled my fingers enough to drag my nails with it. He held on as I slid his zipper down, all the way until I started going down on my knees.

I pushed his pants and boxers down with me as I went. Both men soon joined me on their knees, my dress flying onto my back. I dug back and forth in the dirt, trying to get the holes as deep as I could and yet look like I was just holding on.

I felt them both starting to fall, but I wasn’t done yet. The holes were still too shallow. I lifted a hand and smacked Mark’s butt.

Then jumped when Curtis retaliated. They both sped up, all I could do was grip the dirt harder. I pleaded for them not to stop, over and over again. By the time the holes were deep enough for my palms to sit flat on the ground, my fingers gone from sight, I wasn't sure they would be able to walk again. I made them shake five times! I lost count on mine. At different points, they had to lift their legs off the ground, rotating which knee they were on.

I laughed at the way they fell. Personally, I couldn't move.

"I never cared for Tijuana much before. Now it might be my favorite place." Mark mumbled, not having the energy to move his lips more.

"What the hell, woman?" Curtis tried to smack my butt, which I was sure was still in his face.

"I should apologize, but I won't. I can't. I think you're right about this kid. Um, can someone help me? I can't seem to move." I carefully pulled my fingers out, placing my palms over the holes.

They both laughed, then groaned as they tried to get up. Very carefully, they helped me stand, then caught me when my legs couldn't hold my weight. We walked slowly at first, getting the feeling back in their legs. I kept a careful eye around our surroundings, wanting to give as detailed directions as I could.

We walked down a small dirt hill, both of them holding my arms to support me. At the bottom was a wide road, kind of like a freeway. Curtis lifted me up, then after a second of tornado-like winds hitting my face, he put me down again. Mark stepped up behind him.

"I miss the days of being able to beat you." Mark griped.

Curtis laughed. We were now on the opposite side of the road.

I took a deep breath, trying to push away the panic about having just run across a freeway with cars moving a hundred miles an hour. I took a breath again and closed my eyes.

"In all my 1500 years, I've never said this to a woman, but can we please take a break. I'm too tired."

I nearly fell over laughing, landing on them both. I patted Mark's chest, then teased him by sliding it down. He whimpered.

"I'm just messing with you. I'm too tired. And hungry." I closed my eyes and breathed deeply again. "That smells divine." I moaned out the last word.

"Please stop doing that."

I opened my eyes and looked at both their glowing eyes. "I thought you said you were too tired?"

"We are, but if you keep that up, I'm going to find myself a large man to drink, then make you pay for it." Mark growled.

I giggled. "Feed me. Then we'll see about feeding you. But you might want to cool down your eyes a bit. You're going to freak people out, then blow up our chances of staying incognito."

They did as I said and took me into a small place called *Mama Rosita's*. It was a good thing my mate was so well traveled. I didn't understand a lick of Spanish. I took two years of it in school but didn't pay attention to any of it.

My teacher had wandering eyes, I had low cut shirts. We both knew what we were doing. I sat in the back of the class, typically with my shirt lower, like low enough for darker pieces of skin to be on the edge low. I got a passing grade, he got to look all he wanted without losing his job.

I only discovered that little secret weapon after spilling water on myself during a test, while wearing a white shirt and pink bra. I knew I failed the test when he asked me to stay after class to talk about it. He spent the whole time staring at my chest. I cleared my throat, and he guiltily scribbled an A on the top of my paper.

Frequently he dropped a pencil at my feet, usually on days I wore a mini skirt. I spread my legs just a touch, giving him a show. And then got extra credit.

It worked for me. It worked for him.

After a while, I got bored, so I started playing with my collar. It was always funny when he lost his train of thought mid-lecture. I may have gotten a few closet dates with football players on those days.

I let Curtis order my lunch for me, not caring as long as I got food. He ordered me steak tacos and asked them to not cook the meat all the way through. That's what he told me anyway when I asked why he pointed at my stomach. The waitress giggled and nodded her head.

Even they ate. I must have really wiped them out. I also stole food off their plates. I must have downed like four bowls of chips and salsa on my own, before getting my food. Eventually Mark just pushed his plate to me. He only ate the tacos. I polished off his beans and rice.

They watched me carefully when I licked my fork clean of all the beans I had mixed with guacamole. It was so good. I went through three bottles of water, and their two. When I finished the whole thing, I sat back with a sigh, patting my overly full, and growing belly.

"I don't think I can fit anything else in there." I groaned, grateful I had worn the dress and not pants.

"You sure about that?" Curtis asked with a small laugh.

I looked him up and down and licked my lips. “Maybe after my stomach settles.” They laughed as I closed my eyes and leaned on him.

“Sopapillas?” The waitress asked, setting down a tray of something that smelled heavenly and made my mouth water.

I somehow found room for them.

Two hours after we entered the restaurant, we finally left. Curtis had a small, compact car waiting in the parking lot. A man handed us the keys, bowed slightly, and then vanished.

“You have people everywhere, don’t you?”

“Yes. I have been planning all this for nearly a hundred years now. The only thing that wasn’t planned was you.” He wrapped an arm around my waist as we settled into the back seat. He turned my chin so he could kiss me softly. “You were the best surprise.”

I hummed and kissed him again. His lips still tasted like honey from when I forced him to try a sopapilla. He said I tasted sweeter.

They both laughed as I climbed on his lap in the backseat, practically eating his face. “You taste like honey.” I mumbled as my excuse.

“Guess you have a reason to eat food more often then.” Mark teased from the front.

“Didn’t think I needed one.” He groaned as I slid down to my knees. I was too tired to ride him. “Remind me to tell Charles to pick up some honey.”

I ended up collapsing onto the floor of the car, I was too full to take him all in again. He didn’t seem to mind, he pumped it all onto my chest. Then picked me up and laid me on the back seat.

Mark drove us further south, deeper into Mexico. I slept for most of it, mentally kicking myself later for all the scenery I missed. Mark pulled up to a small, one bedroom cottage in Ensenada, not far from the Beach.

It was the most beautiful thing I had ever seen. And so much quieter. The sounds of the city had nearly given me a headache.

We spent two days there. During the day, we walked through the nearby town, finding hidden alcoves to make out in. I even ended up making out with Mark a few times. Curtis had to take some calls from back home. Those may have been some of my favorite times. Mark backed me into a shadowed wall the first time, then slowly put his lips to mine. It was sweet and loving. And soothed me more than anything else ever did.

Neither of them seemed to care about my consistent needs. My crying and cranky hormones stayed leveled out, as long as the beast stayed fed.

Was it possible I was pregnant with a demon? I mean, technically he was the devil's spawn.

We made love on the beach, in the ocean, on the hood of the car, against the side of the cottage, and of course, in the bed the three of us shared. The only place I was alone was in the shower. The only time Curtis and I were alone was when Mark had to go hunting. He said he needed an energy boost. It wasn't always all three of us. There were times they took turns, tagging each other in. I scowled at them when they did that. Then they distracted me.

I was a little nervous when we went back to the hidden door in the wall, worried the holes somehow had closed. They hadn't. They were still there. We spent two more nights at Mark's house and spent the days driving to nearby towns and cities.

Once that was done, we returned to LA. Mark and I had a long, intense session, the last morning, while Curtis was talking to Ryder again before he went off somewhere else.

By the time we boarded the plane again, we had been gone for nearly a week.

Chapter 17

Grace

"My Lord, my Lady. Welcome home." Charles greeted us, holding the front door open.

Lucas had met us at the airport with the car and drove us back. He grabbed all my bags out of the car, and Curtis' one bag.

"Thank you, Charles. How have things been here?" Curtis asked, one hand on my back.

Charles bowed slightly. "Just fine, my Lord. No problems."

"And the changes I asked for you to make?"

I looked at him, curious what that was. He winked at me.

Charles chuckled softly. "Ready and waiting for your inspection, sir."

"Good. The Queen needs to eat and rest. Will you bring something up to the room in about an hour, please?" Curtis softly pushed on my back, signaling me to start walking again.

Charles bowed again as we passed. "As you wish, your highness."

Lucas was already up the stairs, putting my things away. Guess I now knew who moved my things before then. And here I thought it had been Curtis.

"How was the trip, sir?" Lucas asked, walking back out of the closet.

"Perfect. San Diego is thriving, and Mexico was peaceful. I see now why humans enjoy their vacations so much." He winked at me again and I blushed.

"I see something else is flourishing." Lucas pointedly looked at my stomach. "I assume that's why all the bags."

I scowled at him. "Yes. My stomach grows an inch a day, thanks for pointing that out."

"Careful, my friend. She is still touchy about that." Curtis' warning was weakened by his amusement.

"You may grow bigger every day, my Queen," Lucas stalked closer, slowly lowering to his knees in front of me, "but you grow more beautiful as well. Very few are strong enough to carry a royal heir. They are the strongest and most powerful creatures out there. You are a unique woman to be able to carry this child, and still be as active as you are."

Well, crap. Who knew Lucas had it in him?

"Allow me to alleviate your fears, my Lady?"

I nodded, feeling totally out of sorts. Curtis centered behind me, as balance was not a friend of mine these days. This kid was growing so fast, my body never had enough time to adjust to the new weight before gaining more. Lucas gently lifted my leg onto his shoulder, pushing my dress up and my silky boy shorts down. I gripped Curtis' hands, which were protectively resting on my stomach.

Lucas moved back a few minutes later, smacking his lips. "Thank you, my Queen. As always, it is a pleasure to serve you."

I laughed quietly at his passionate gratitude. "The pleasure was definitely all mine."

Lucas stood up again and bowed.

"Have you refilled your pets yet?" Curtis asked.

"Not as of yet. There were more important issues that needed to be handled first. As we spoke of on the phone the other day."

"What happened?" I asked warily.

"Nothing much, a Nightwalker got a little overzealous in the feeding center. The donor had a silver dagger hidden in her apartment. She stabbed him in the chest rather than let him stab her below." Lucas explained, while reaching over to rub me, in case I didn't catch his meaning. He didn't stop either. "Do not stress yourself, my Queen. She was not harmed. Her floor was not for that type of activity. He should have known better."

I whimpered out an "okay." It was quiet, all except for me. He didn't stop until I was far from quiet. I promptly walked to the bed to sit down.

"She is much more sensitive now, isn't she?" He asked Curtis, a tone of concern lacing his words.

"In very many ways, yes. We will have to be careful. Have you been using the feeding center?"

"Yes. I thought of taking a few from there, but then I'd have to restock the center. So, time consuming." Lucas grumbled.

"Who did you put in charge?"

"Lou. He is old enough to have control."

"I don't remember him. Have I met him?"

"I don't think so, my Lord. He mostly stuck to the Southern regions before. It was his home."

"Ah, yes. Quite common after a time. If our home was still around, I'd visit it too. Civilization nearly wiped it out though. Warn him that I am coming, please. I'm too tired to deal with surprises tonight."

"Are you leaving me again?" I had fallen to my back, feeling tired myself, but I popped back up again when he said that. Okay, so pop may have been the wrong verb to use there, but I did sit back up. It just took a second or two longer than normal. No sit ups for me, then.

Curtis walked over and knelt in front of me. "Only for an hour or two. You can relax and wait for me." I pouted and he lifted my leg to start taking off my shoes. My feet were swollen, and it made me scowl. He rubbed them softly. "You need to rest. You can go with me next time. While I am there, I will see if I can find someone who does hair for you. Would you like that?"

I smiled down at him. "I'd love it. I've never had my hair professionally done before. Thank you."

He came back up, kissing me on his way. "I have a surprise for you." He took my hands and pulled me to stand again. Lucas had snuck out while I wasn't paying attention.

We walked with me in front, and him behind me with his hand over my eyes. "Are these the changes you asked Charles to make?"

"Yes. I wanted to surprise you. We can change anything you don't like, but it's a start. Most of the phone calls I had to take were concerning this."

We patted through the bathroom, the tile felt cool beneath my bare feet. We stopped at what I assumed was the door to the extra bedroom. I was buzzing with excitement. No one had ever given me a surprise before, not the good kind, or something actually for me, anyway.

"Are you ready?" He whispered right above my ear.

I nodded.

He lifted my hand and placed it on the doorknob. I turned it carefully and pushed it open. We took two careful steps inside, then he removed his hands.

I gasped and covered my mouth.

Charles had wiped the room clean and turned it into the most perfect nursery anyone could ask for. It looked like it fell out of a magazine. The walls were mostly painted a creamy color. One wall was painted dark purple. Against it was a black crib, with a purple blanket hanging over the edge. Hanging over the top of the little bed was one of those turning things, with trees, stars, and little animals.

Diagonal from there was a matching dresser and changing table. The knobs were the same dark purple. The pad on the table had a purple sheet on it. Under the changing table were shelves filled with diapers of different sizes and wipes. There was even one of those trash things that you put dirty diapers in to keep the smell out of the room.

"Do you like it? I circled items in pictures, things I thought you might like, but I wasn't sure. We've never talked about it before."

I spun around, getting slightly dizzy, and interrupted him with a kiss. "Thank you so much. It's absolutely perfect!"

"Yeah?" He said, a bit croaky.

I giggled. "Yeah. I love you, thank you for doing all this for me."

He lifted me up and laid me on our bed. His speed really was handy to have around. He told me he loved me over and over again as he proved it.

"I need to get going. If you want to sleep, but can't, call for Lucas." Curtis practically pleaded with me. "He will hold you while you sleep until I return."

I snorted. "Lucas will not just hold me. He will give me that puppy dog look that he knows I can't say no too. Was he like that as a human?"

Curtis threw his head back and laughed. "No. He was loyal, and he was devoted. I may have spoiled him a bit though, since then."

"Gee, ya think." I sighed. "As much as I don't want you to go, the sooner you leave, the sooner you come back. While I can get comfortable in the arms of another, it's still not you. I prefer your arms."

He growled and kissed me again. "Leaving. I'm leaving. Heading for the door, right now."

I cackled as his words and actions were saying two very different things. He didn't leave for ten more minutes.

I heard a knock on the door not much later, grabbed my dress, and went to open it. I could smell the food through the door, and I was starving.

"Evening, your highness. I have your dinner. Would you like me to put it on the bed for you?" Charles asked politely.

"Yes, thank you. I can't tell you how much I appreciate your help."

"No worries, miss. You should probably close the door, though."

Confused, I pushed it closed behind him and followed him to the bed.

"Master Lucas' hearing isn't quite as good as the Lord's, but it picks up through open doors." Uh, okay. "Did the master show you the other room?" He set the tray down on the foot of the bed, then carefully started tucking the sheet and blanket back in.

"Uh, yeah, he did. It is perfect, thank you." I watched him, wondering how to nicely ask him to leave so I could inhale my food in peace, and in the nude. The waistband on this dress was beginning to itch.

"Good. I am happy to hear that. Don't worry about anything you left behind in there. I cleaned it all out and made sure everything was put in a safe place."

I tilted my head, confused by what he meant. He turned to look at me, bent to his side, and lifted the corner of the mattress up. My eyes widened in shock when the small black rectangle registered in my mind. I started frantically trying to think of an excuse.

"I… I… uh."

He cut me off with a wave, lowering it back down, and continued fixing the sheet.

"Before the master moved in, I served another family. Believe it or not, some humans are worse than vampires. When they offered me more money to stay," he shrugged, "I figured this was the best option. I've seen some awful things happen in this house. I've heard awful things. I've lost countless hours of sleep, wringing my hands, as I heard the sounds of screaming from above me. Male and female alikec . I'm sure your plans weren't far different from mine when you came. These men act like we are mud under their shoes. I know what has been troubling them, and it all started when you arrived."

Charles walked over and patted both my arms, then my stomach. "Your plan got twisted, I get that. Don't give up on yourself though. There are better things out there. A better way of life." He kissed my cheek, not having far to go since we were about the same height and walked toward the door. "Oh, I charged it for you as well."

With that, he was gone. Locking the door behind him.

I sank onto the bed, lost for a moment. Charles was not very big, he obviously had help moving the bed out. What would have happened had someone else seen the phone first?

I'd be dead, that's what.

I put a hand to my stomach. No. I wouldn't, at least not until my son was born. But life would not be so great until then.

A memory came to me, one from the vision I had at the wall. I saw a mother, holding her child, crying. One mother to another. I couldn't let that happen.

I reached down and pulled out the phone. No missed messages. Carrie hadn't gotten hold of the phone again then.

Me: Miss me?
Hill: This may sound odd, but yes, very much so. How are you?

My heart warmed. I closed my eyes and let the expected flash of a man, roughly the same size as Mark, fill my mind. He was sitting on the porch of a cabin, wearing only break away pants. He had no shirt on.

Me: Better now. You always walk around without a shirt on?

In my mind, I saw a spit take, and laughed as he jumped and tried to wipe himself off.

Me: Do you need a bib?

If I was not seeing him in real time right now, then I probably sounded very stupid.

Hill: Please tell me you are around here somewhere?
Hill: And no, I rarely wear a shirt when I've been running. These pants fall away faster and don't need replacing. Plus… a shirt would have just been ruined.

I laughed and absentmindedly picked up the lid to my dinner. Fried chicken and mashed potatoes. Yum.

Me: I wish I was there. Still in my gilded cage.
Hill: ???
Me: My powers are getting better.
Me: You've always been easy to see though. Every time we talk, I get a flash of you. I didn't know if they were real time or not. I wasn't sure but thought I would test it out.

His response took longer this time. But I saw the dots start and stop many times.

Hill: I've had dreams of you, but by the time I wake up, I can't remember your face, or your laugh.
Me: Why do you think this is happening? I've tried to check in on my friends. I see the future, nothing else.
Hill: Morris has a theory. One I am beginning to believe.

I waited, eventually I decided he needed some prodding.

Me: Which is?
Hill: It might make your job harder. I know it is mine.
Me: Maybe I need to know. Maybe I need a reason to get out of here.

I closed my eyes and swallowed a sob. He punched a hole in the wall. Guess that was my answer. He was probably right, knowing would make it that much harder.

Me: Get someone to fix your hand. I have a better wall for you to put a hole in.

I forced a few more bites down, feeling pretty confident that he was getting his bloodied hand fixed.

Hill: There, happy?
Me: Good to know you can follow orders.
Hill: I prefer to give them. But your orders I will follow for an eternity.

And there went the last of my appetite. I worked to control the sobs beginning. He must have known I was struggling.

Hill: Nothing that has happened matters to me. From the beginning, my wolf and I both agreed, you were the bravest woman we have ever - sort of - met. There is nothing that you could have done that will change that. I know vampires. I know what they are like. My imagination has told me a lot. Please don't give up. One day, I will come for you. If Morris doesn't beat me to it. He is dead set on bringing you home.

I smirked. I didn't know who he meant at first, but now I had an idea.

Me: Is Morris a big cranky dude that fell out of the sky?

I could practically hear his deep laughter, and it filled my heart.

Hill: That would be him. Seems to believe he has a promise to keep.

Well, that did me in, right there. They hardly knew me, but they were willing to rescue me anyway.

Hill: What wall?

Feeling grateful for the subject change, and reminder I had a purpose in messaging, I wiped away my tears and started to type.

Me: In Tijuana, along the border with San Diego, there is an awesome little restaurant called Mama Rosita's. Across the highway, is a small brick wall, it looks like it should be keeping people from falling into a ravine. Only, there is no ravine. No purpose that others can see. Behind there, look in the dirt. There should be eight small holes, like someone was holding onto the dirt for dear life. Straight up from there, you will have to look carefully. The VB crest is hidden. Push it. The wall is a hollow, pitch-black tunnel, and guards patrol inside. Take it down. The vision with it up is not a future we want to live in. Most won't.
Hill: Do I want to ask how those holes got there?
Me: Probably not. It's just one more reason you are probably better off forgetting about me.
Hill: Not a chance in hell.

I felt the tears coming again, this time they needed a release.

Me: Goodbye, be safe. Send my love to my family.

I turned off my phone and slid it deep between the mattresses. It being in the same room as Curtis worried me.

Forcing all the food down took a great deal of effort while crying. But I managed. I pushed my mind to other things, refusing to think of the two words trying to force their way to my mind.

I fell into a fit of sobs when the vision came anyway.

Hill jumped off the porch, his pants falling away. His black wolf took off running, my scene skipped ahead a few hours. He was running to the wall. Howling at it. I shook when he ran headfirst into it, as though he could bust through it on his own.

Mine. I heard it clear as day. I felt the possession and determination in his voice. I felt the love behind it.

Thankfully, I cried myself to sleep long before Curtis got back. When he questioned the dried streaks down my face, I told him I missed him. I didn't want Lucas. I wanted him.

Chapter 18

Andrew

“Alpha, nice of you to join us.” Deacon teased me when I walked back into the cabin the next morning. His smile dropped when he saw me. I was sure I looked like hell. I sure felt like it.

They arrived last night. The humans were finally ready to sign an agreement and were coming today.

Carrie jumped out of her seat, well she tried to, anyway. She had nearly doubled in size again since I saw them three weeks ago.

“Grace?”

“She’s fine. At least she says she is.”

“You don’t believe her?”

“Physically? Yes. Mentally? No. She still doesn’t think she’s worth saving. Her powers are getting stronger though. She was watching me somehow.”

"How do you know?" Colton asked, pulling Carrie to sit back down between them on the couch.

I dropped into a sofa chair. Morris brought me a bottle of water. It wasn't as fresh as the stream my wolf had found during our pitiful walk home from the wall, but it would do.

"She asked if I ever wore a shirt. I had just taken a drink of a beer when I read that and ended up spitting it all over me. She then asked if I needed a bib. At one point in our conversation, I punched the wall. She told me to get it fixed, then said she had a better wall for me to put a hole in. Grace gave me the location for one of the hidden doors. She left holes in the ground, so we can't take long to get there."

Carrie looked at me with pity.

"Where is the door?" Morris asked.

"Between Tijuana and San Diego."

"We can charter a flight for this evening, which gives us plenty of time to deal with the human government. They might want to help. It would be good for us to work together again." Colton stated, one hand behind his mate, rubbing her neck.

"Sounds good." I pushed to stand up, crushing the now empty bottle in my hand. "I need a shower."

"Did she say anything else? Did you ask about what happened when you were in Seattle?" Carrie turned as I walked, begging me.

"Seattle, no. But I don't really want to talk about the other stuff."

She opened her mouth to ask another question, but then closed it. She was a powerful little witch herself. I was sure she could feel my evasive intent and need to walk away. If she didn't, her mates did. They called her attention to something else, giving me a reprieve.

An hour later, we stood on the front porch as the American President and General Brooks pulled in. The secret service piled out of the car first, surrounding it. I rolled my eyes. This was all a little over the top.

"Gentlemen, welcome back. You've been gone longer than we expected."

"Democracy takes time, son. You should know that." The General spat on the ground, obviously still not happy with the news that he had shifters in his Army.

I put a hand on Morris' shoulder, patting him and reminding him to calm down. He was not impressed by the disrespectful attitude.

"It would behoove you to remember that you are on pack lands right now. Alpha Andrew is welcoming you politely. You should treat him with the same courtesy you treat all other dignitaries." Colton suggested.

The General's eyes came back to mine. I let my wolf push through enough for him to see mine darken and to feel the power of my wolf. He staggered back. The President stepped in front of him.

"Our apologies, Alpha. He's tired. We're all tired. The Senate took a long time to debate. We had to sit there the whole time. Shall we continue this in your conference room?"

I turned and walked in front of them. Morris ran ahead to hold the door for me, putting on a show. I let it slide. Technically, the humans started the measuring contest. Little did they know…

It took a few minutes to get everyone seated.

"You are coming along rather quickly, your majesty. When are you due?" The President continued to put the nicer foot forward. It worried me a little.

"We're not sure. Magical babies tend to come when they please. It all just depends on their power level. As I have two in there, we don't really know what we are working with. My healer, kind of like a midwife, is estimating another month. At the most. Frankly, I wouldn't mind if it were tomorrow."

They nodded from across the table as we sat down. Men didn't really know what to say in times like this. We weren't all that great with women stuff, no matter the species.

I wouldn't mind learning though.

"Well, good luck to you. Twins aren't easy."

"Thank you, shall we start?" They looked at each other, then back to us, nodding. "Great. Why don't you tell us what your Senate has decided, and we will start from there."

We unanimously decided after the last meeting that Carrie should run the show. They responded better to her.

The President snapped his fingers to the side, and an aid pulled papers out of a briefcase. He laid them on the table, with a pen.

"After weeks of deliberations. The Senate has agreed to your terms. The magical people living within our borders will be granted visas. They are welcome to continue their lives where they are, as long as they continue to pay their taxes and uphold our laws. If they break said laws, they will be given the same consequences and rights as any other citizen. We expect the same decency to be given to the humans remaining in California. We have heard a few rumors about the treatments in the feeding centers. We expect those to be remedied as soon as you are in power there. We would also like to keep the trades already in place, open. Import and export. It is important for both economies."

I pulled the paper toward us and picked it up. I directly handed it to Morris. At the confused expressions, I explained. "He was a lawyer before he was a soldier. His father has a thriving practice back home."

"How do we know our people will not be persecuted once they declare themselves to you?" Carrie asked.

Good question.

"If we could guarantee that didn't happen, we would. There have been more than enough riots over civil rights violations. We can't control the people. But we can say the government will treat them just the same. It's not like you can guarantee the same on your side of the wall." The General grumped.

It was obvious he was not at all okay with any of this.

"Just remember, we would like to remain allies. Don't try anything. It won't work. And it will come back to bite you in the butt." Carrie grimly told them.

I wondered if she felt the intent to deceive coming from him. It wouldn't surprise me.

"This is a viable treaty. All parties are getting what they agreed to. Nothing more nothing less. If they violate this treaty, it won't just be us they have to deal with. If they break ours, why wouldn't they break someone else's? And I must warn you. America is the only place where we do not have people in the government." Morris stated, placing the treaty down in front of me. "This will require a signature from King Deacon, representing the vampires. Queen Carrie, representing the Witches. Alpha Andrew, representing the shifters. And President Price for the humans. The American ones anyway."

The General huffed and crossed his arms as he leaned back in his chair. Carrie relaxed again. Colton and Deacon were still on edge though.

"We weren't sure how you all felt about publicity. Usually, we sign these in front of a camera, letting the world know what has happened and the measures we are taking." The President said a bit nervously.

"We don't mind. Our secrets out anyway. Why not let them know we are not all bad? I don't want to wait on signing this though, for all of our protection." Deacon was tense, but his body language and tone said otherwise. He was sitting back, one leg over the other, one hand holding Carrie's on the table. He looked like this was any other day, but the air around him said he was a vampire preparing to play defense.

"I agree. Let's sign this now. We have a mission we are planning, our little spy contacted me last night. We know where one of the hidden doors in the wall is. We can knock part of it down. Even if we don't use it, it will provide us with a better entryway."

"How do you know you can trust her? She's in deep and was silent for a long time." The General asked me.

I didn't need Carrie's power to tell me that he had something up his sleeve. all the same, Carrie snarled.

"She is putting herself at great risk. Do not doubt her."

The General lifted his hand, the same aid pulled another document out, this time a photograph.

"We commandeered access to any security camera we could when Curtis started blowing up buildings. We needed eyes. Alerts were set on ones that were inactive. Especially in private buildings with higher security. This was given to me a few days ago. I've never met the girl, or Curtis, but… well, you tell me." He pushed it across the table.

Carrie reached for it desperately, then started crying. Colton took the paper and held it up for Morris and me to see.

Four people were in the photo. Three men on one knee, a woman with black hair and purple tips was the only one standing. She was the most beautiful thing I had ever seen. Colton tapped the picture, right above her head.

“Now we know what happened to the Queen’s crown. Curtis had it all along.”

“How did a Nightwalker get my grandmother’s crown?” Deacon growled menacingly.

The humans backed up. The General only sat up straighter, trying to act like the tough General he normally was.

Colton cleared his throat somewhat nervously. Deacon’s gaze swung over to him, his voice showing betrayal.

“What have you been hiding from me?”

Colton grew desperate. I wasn’t sure this was the place for it, but it was probably something we all needed to hear.

“I didn’t keep it from you on purpose. The command came from your grandfather, at first. Curtis’ name was stricken from all records. We were forbidden to ever mention him. Your father insisted it remain that way, I was forbidden from ever telling you.”

“I became King months ago.”

Colton looked down in shame. “I didn’t know how to tell you. I was afraid of your reaction.” His head came back up. “You were already going through a lot. I was afraid we would lose you to your revenge.”

Deacon’s teeth were grinding. “What secret does everyone but me know?”

Colton sighed reluctantly. “Curtis was once known by a different name. He had a family that loved him. Hell, I loved him. I was only a child, but he was kind when he came to our village. He had a younger brother, nearly a century younger than him, he doted on him." Colton cleared his throat, the sign the hammer was about to fall. "Crown Prince Conrad was loved all over the land. Until the curse hit, then he became a curse word in the wind."

Carrie put a hand on both her mates' arms, torn on who she was supposed to be comforting.

"He was the one?" Deacon whispered.

Colton shook his head. "I wasn't even a full decade. No one was saying anything. I do know a week or so before the curse hit, I followed Conrad into the woods. He had been checking our Southern borders. I wanted to pop out and scare him, like I did in the village. I lost him for a time, I was getting worried because we were no longer in our own lands. Then I saw him swimming out to a woman bathing under the waterfall. I was too far away to see much, but I had seen mates meet for the first time before. I left, leaving them be. A week later I woke to the screaming. My mother and older sister were dead."

His voice shook and Carrie squeezed his hand harder. Deacon was the one torn now, he wanted to comfort him, but was still hurt himself.

"Things were a crazy mess over the next few days. People were cursing out the witches. A shield went over their lands. No one could get in. A message went through the kingdom. Conrad was never to be mentioned again. Centuries went by, and Conrad finally came to visit your father in the caves. It was right after he took your mother. Conrad had an army, he wanted to get our lands back. Some of the others wanted to support him in that, until Dominic reminded them of the curse. I was much older then, so I started putting the pieces together. I don't know what happened when they argued on the mountain, but I do know, from that day forward, the name Curtis was banned as well. It was drilled into us for centuries to not talk about him, Deac. I'm so sorry."

The whole room was quiet, with the exception of Carrie crying softly. I waited for the sign that Deacon put it all together, the last piece. The reason Colton would fear losing him to revenge.

When it came, he was soft before it turned into a roar. "He was my uncle. I had an uncle…my father's older brother." His breathing increased. "He killed his own brother!"

Deacon jumped out of his seat and started pacing, his eyes glowing darker than ever before. Carrie jumped up and grabbed onto him, trying to hold him and calm him. Colton sat there, knowing a fated mate was different. She had powers over him that Colton never would.

Carrie lifted her hand to Deacon's cheek. His eyes were unfocused through their glow as they habitually went to her.

"Deacon, baby, please. Look at me. I need you to breathe, baby. Please. I know you want to find that door and kill him now."

Deacon growled, this time it was softer, but it still went through the nerve of every man in that room. Even Morris quivered and stepped back.

Carrie grabbed his fist and placed it on her stomach.

Good move.

"Deacon, I need you. We need you. I cannot survive these babies without you. Nor am I sure I want to." The sadness in her voice, and her words, shocked him enough that he blinked and visibly sagged into her.

Colton jumped up and helped her hold his weight. Soon, he was whispering reassuring words into his mate's ear, further calming him down. Morris and I turned, pretending we could not hear. I picked up the picture and began studying the woman I knew was mine. A woman I had yet to meet in person. I had yet to hear her laugh or hear her voice.

I dragged a finger over her face, and down her stomach. And then I paused. I brought the picture up closer, I had to be seeing things. I startled when another picture hit my elbow. When I looked up, the General was watching me.

"It didn't seem like the right time yet for the close up." He was more reverent and respectful this time. He lost his brother in the Twin Towers. Which had served to fuel his need to protect our country. He understood the power of anger and the need for revenge.

I picked up the new picture and choked back the lump in my throat. It was of the two of them standing together on the way out. He was holding her hand. Not a big deal really. But we also had a good shot of what they were wearing. I picked up the first picture again, it had more of a profile shot of her and his hands on her bare stomach.

I pushed away from the table and made to run out the door.

I knew where that gate was. I could get over what was left of Trump's wall. I could be to her by morning.

Unfortunately, my Beta was not going to let that happen. He had one arm around my shoulders, one around my stomach, using all of his effort to keep me in place.

"Little help, please." He pushed through his teeth. Getting the other's attention.

"What happened?" Colton shouted, running over, and adding his strength to their battle.

"Mine." My wolf growled through my lengthening teeth. I was pretty sure one of the humans peed himself.

From the corner of my changing eyes, I saw Carrie pick up the paper. Deacon was calmer now, using my problem to distract himself.

"I wondered when I saw the first picture." Carrie sighed.

"Grace is pregnant." Deacon explained calmly to the men holding me.

My wolf shook with anger, hearing it verbally. Carrie stepped on a chair in front of me. Deacon was confused but supported her balance.

"Alpha Andrew Hill, I command you to knock this off at once!"

My wolf growled back at her. "Mine!"

Deacon flinched and tried to pull her down. She swatted him away.

"I know that. I've known for a while. I'm the only one with brains around here apparently." She put her fists on her waist and practically stomped her foot.

I wanted to laugh, but my human side was too far gone. The wolf was in control.

She softened her voice though and came closer. "Deac, ask Clarise to come in please."

Deacon disappeared and reappeared a second later. A blonde woman in his arms, screeching and hitting him.

"What the hell? I said ask her, not kidnap her! Clarise, I need some help here. His wolf is not letting him listen to reason."

Clarise straightened up, and suddenly a calm feeling coated the room. My wolf struggled to fight against it. So did the muscle behind me.

"Not everyone, Clarise." Carrie sighed.

Clarise huffed and walked over. "Fine, but this might be a bit too strong, I'm still working on it."

Her hands lifted to my chest, right over my heart. I tried to squirm and push all three of them off. Deacon joined in to hold me down.

"Ouch. He is in a ton of pain. Oh, sweetie. I am so sorry." Clarise whispered.

A warm feeling flooded through me, like a hot shower after running in the snow. One muscle at a time weakened. My wolf fell to the back of my mind, curling into a ball and falling asleep. I dropped to the floor myself, the sobs starting.

"Wow, Clarise. What did you do?" Carrie asked, worry pushing her to the floor in front of me.

"I think I knocked out his wolf. Should make it easier for you to talk to him now. Most of the anger was coming from the Alpha wolf inside him. He was one angry sucker. What happened?"

"He just found out that my sister is his fated mate, and she carries Curtis' child." Carrie got on her knees and wrapped her arms around my neck.

Clarise hissed through her teeth. "Yeah, that'll do it. I'm going back outside, let me know if you need me again. FYI, y'all have scared the daylights out of the humans. I'm thinking more than one of you went postal."

"Uh, yeah. We can rehash it all later."

Clarise nodded once to her friend and then left.

Carrie held my head like I was a pup again, and the tears came flooding out harder. So much for being the Alpha.

"Andrew, this isn't the end. Don't check-out yet. She needs you, now more than ever. I think we know what you felt in Seattle too. My bet, that is when this happened. She said she had to follow the vision for your mission to be successful. She must have known it was coming, that's why she said she wasn't worth saving anymore."

Well, hell. That made sense. My wolf was still sleeping but it was far from restful.

"I need you to be strong so you can help me save her. You are the best bet in helping her come back from this."

"What's a fated mate?" One of the humans whispered, leaning over the table just a bit.

Deacon stepped closer to him, giving Carrie and me some space. He was the most qualified.

"A fated mate is someone that was designed just for you. Think of it like a soul mate. In the case of vampires, our mate carries the other half of our soul."

"For shifters, it's similar. Our souls connect together like pieces of a puzzle." Morris added.

"And for witches, it is usually the power that matches. No matter which way though, when you find that one person, you are whole. They are your everything. Carrie is my fated mate. That's why she was able to calm me. If the little spy were here, she would have been able to do the same thing."

"What happens if you lose your mate?" The same human asked, it was the aid they brought with them. The only one not to prideful to ask.

"Curtis is an example of that. As well as what you just saw with the Alpha. Curtis found his mate, a long time ago. I don't know the details, but he somehow betrayed her trust. If I remember right, he was arranged to mate with a female with an influential family at the time. I remember my parents getting an invitation to the celebration ceremony. One can only guess what happened. The witches managed to cast a spell on our kingdom, sneak in, and kill all the women. A curse was also placed on us. No females have been born since. As for the Alpha, he nearly lost control over his wolf, thinking he lost her. Mates are cherished, they are protected." Colton explained, sitting back down.

"That's it." Carrie whispered. "His mate could freeze time. Curtis must have bound himself to her before the betrayal. He still has her power."

"Bound?" The General asked.

"Think of it like this. They eloped without telling anyone. When that happens witch mates share their powers. He got her power. Then he most likely cheated on her. A woman scorned gentlemen." Deacon dropped into a chair next to Colton. Who reached over and held his hand.

The humans saw but did not question. I guess that one they could figure out on their own.

After a few silent minutes, I patted Carrie's hand, letting her know I was good to get up. Then I had to help both of us stand up.

"My apologies. Now more than ever, we have to trust our little spy."

"Why? Look at these pictures! He put a crown on her head, and they knelt to her. It looks to me like they are making her their Queen, and she is carrying his heir." The General pointed at the pictures on the table, from a few feet away.

The humans were still keeping their distance from us. Good.

Carrie scoffed and shook her head. "That witch in my dream said this would happen. Look, you all can join us or not. We trust her. That is what matters. My sister is struggling with something that no one but me can understand right now. Carrying a vampire baby is not easy. If you've ever been around a hormonal pregnant woman, times that by a hundred. Our bodies were not exactly designed for this. And I'll tell you what, my mates are working for it to keep me happy and from bawling my eyes out every five minutes." The two idiots high fived each other. She was standing right behind them, and smacked both their heads.

"Beta Morris has told us himself that she doesn't think she is worthy of being saved. Well, now we know why. If we stop trusting her and listening to her now, then we *will* lose her." Carrie's voice cracked. "And I'm not willing to do that. I say, we sign this treaty now. Send a team to tear a giant freaking hole in that wall, proving the point to Curtis that he is *not* Mr. All Powerful. Then we broadcast a message to the world about us working together. Let those in California know that help is coming. Let the rest of our people know that they no longer have to hide. And if one word gets back to Curtis about my sister being a spy, I will personally turn everyone in this room into a toad! Do you understand me?"

I leaned down to Colton. "If my wolf was awake right now he would either be panting at your mate or curling up in a ball again."

"The humans are more scared of her than us." Morris added.

"Hottest thing ever. Man, I love my mate." Deacon whispered. Carrie pushed his head, struggling to keep her straight face.

Chapter 19

Grace

My dreams were chaotic. One minute, it was the vision with people screaming, running, bombs going off, the next minute I was laying on the conference table, Lucas on one side, Mark on the other, and Curtis crawling over me. Only he looked mean, and beyond evil.

Then the dream shifted, and I was standing on the beach at sunrise, Mark stood between me and a brown wolf. That scene repeated itself over and over again, but with different endings.

The first version had Mark lunging as the wolf jumped at him. The silver dagger went right into his gut. The wolf dropped to the ground, shaking. Soon the wolf was gone, and Morris was lying there. The shifter I risked my life to rescue and send back to Hill.

The second version was the one I preferred. I grabbed Mark's arm with the dagger and tried to run between them. His dagger dug into my upper arm and hurt like hell. The silver wasn't poisonous to me though, meaning I could live through the pain. Curtis' blood would heal me as soon as we got to him. Mark dropped the dagger in the sand, horrified by what he had done. While he was studying my arm, Morris shifted back and picked up the dagger. I tried to yell out for him to stop, but it was too late. He stabbed Mark in the heart, from the back. I apologized profusely to Mark, sobbing. Morris cradled me in his arms and ran.

Before I could grasp the meaning of this, I was back at the wall, watching it explode. A black wolf ran through in a fury. Colton had to stop him from running further down the dark hall. I couldn't hear what they were saying to each other, but it didn't take a genius.

The only part of the dream that didn't freak me out was me sitting on a porch swing with Hill, his arms wrapped around me as we watched the sunset together. It was peaceful, it was deep, it was simple.

I woke up with a start, feeling Curtis' hands all over my face and body. These weren't affectionate though. He was frantically searching for something.

"About the hell time, Gracey!" He yelled. He didn't sound angry. He sounded terrified. I had never heard him sound like that before. His face turned away from me. "She's awake! Where the hell is that ice water?"

"I'm coming! Calm down. You, freaking out, is not going to help her." Lucas' voice was only slightly calmer than Curtis'.

"Like hell I will, I am not losing another one right after I got them."

"My Lord, you need to take a breath. If you stay calm, she will stay calm." Lucas imitated deep breathing as he set a bowl with a towel hanging out of it, down on the bedside table.

My eyes shot around the room, trying to figure out what the problem was. I took mental stock of my body. My skin was burning so hot I was sweating through every pore. My eyes even burned. I could feel my heart aching and pounding so hard that I thought it was going to come right out of my chest.

"Curtis." My voice didn't sound all that great either. "What's happening to me?" I hiccupped and out the sobs came, the flashes of my dream coming back. I was the one freaking the hell out now.

"I don't know, love. You were asleep when I came in, but you were tossing and turning like you do. You were calling out different names. Mine, Lucas', Mark's. I thought it was funny at first. I tried to wake you up, but then I noticed how hot you were." Curtis grabbed a wringed out towel from Lucas and laid it across my head. He then placed more on my arms. "I've never seen you burn so hot. You started screaming for help. Then it got eerily quiet, and I thought it was over. Then it started all over again. What happened, Gracey?"

I'd never seen him so close to losing it before. I started crying more, and he rushed to put more towels on me.

"So many things. Most were memories from that vision at the wall. Mixed in with memories with you. Explosions, people crying. Then in bed with you. It was too much, too many emotions."

Curtis dropped to the floor, holding my hand in both of his, kissing it. "Tell me what to do, little witch. I can't lose you. I *won't* lose you."

"I… I don't know. Can't you get this out of me? I want to go back to small flashes. I don't want to feel this anymore."

"You could try feeding from her, my Lord. It might help." Lucas' voice was shaky. Whether for me or for what my dying would do to his friend, I didn't know.

I rolled to my side quickly, trying to grab Curtis' head. That idea sounded divine, on so many levels. "Yes. Please, Curtis. *Bite me.* I need you. I need your fangs." I moaned as a flash came through. Blood trade. "Feed me, Curtis. Feed me while you take from me.

Fill me with all of you." I moaned again, the feeling from the flash running through me.

"We weren't going to trade again." Curtis whispered.

"It's either that or prepare to lose her. You chose to keep her. You want to spend your life with her and your son, you need to suck it up and deal with it. Screw the power to freeze things. Angela's gone. If you don't act, Grace will be too. Your son along with her. At this point, he's baking inside."

Curtis snarled as he climbed on the bed and settled over me. All in a move that was softer and gentler than his sounds deemed possible.

"If you get worse, you need to stop me. Understand?"

I whimpered, clawing at his boxers to come off. Lucas chuckled. "As much as I'd like to stay and watch this, I'm thinking it's safer if I go."

"Lock the door." Curtis said, his only clothing item ripping out from under him. I was pretty much panting and doing the splits by the time he was ready. "I hope you know what this may cost me. But I love you, and I can't stand the idea of losing you. Not again. If I believed in reincarnation, I'd swear you were her."

"Less talking, more drinking."

Curtis chuckled deeply as he lowered to my lips. I practically attacked him.

We didn't even get to the blood part right away. We got a little distracted. But it was so good when he did. I screamed so loud that I expected the glass to break. He didn't go in gently, from either direction. But it was exactly what I needed. He gave me his wrist this time, which gave me more at once.

I spent ages in Heaven before he withdrew his fangs and his wrist.

"You're cooler now. Not quite back to normal." He chuckled and kissed me softly. "No hotter than you normally are for me and my men."

I wrapped my legs around the back of his thighs and shoved him back where I needed. He laughed happily, relieved that it was over. We spent the entire night in bed, alternating between sleeping and … other things. We didn't move the next day, not even when Lucas came to check. I sent him a way with one, specific, finger in the air. He laughed and walked back out.

Around sunrise, Curtis carried me to the shower, and helped me rinse all the dried sweat off. Then carried me back to bed and held me. Someone had changed our sheets and left a bowl of soup with a couple rolls for me. Curtis insisted I eat something, still with a bit of fear that he was going to lose me.

I felt an incredible amount of guilt that I betrayed him once again. Hardly anybody knew about the secret door. He trusted me enough to not only take me through it, but to allow his man to show me how to open it. And then I went and seduced both of them, in an effort to leave some type of mark for Hill to find.

I almost wished I could take it back. I couldn't contact Hill and tell him not to do it. Then I would be betraying my friends, and they would do it anyway.
Nm m,
Why did I do it? Curtis had been good to me. He loved me, or at least this woman, Angela, that I probably looked like.

Maybe I could curb his violent streak if I was here. I calmed him down. He listened to me. I could keep doing that. I could help the world that way and not have to hurt him. I was so tired of hurting people.

"Gracey?"

I turned in his arms just enough to look up at him. His arms were safe. I didn't have nightmares when I was in his arms.

"What's Hill?"

"What are you talking about?" Please tell me he didn't find the phone. If Lucas changed the sheets, he might have found it, and found a way to clue Curtis in.

"Hey, hey. It's okay. I'm not mad at you for anything. Why are you getting so scared?"

I shook my head, so do not want to talk about that.

He sighed, slightly aggravated. "Can you at least tell me what hill meant? You said it a few times when you were still under. I didn't know if it was a person or a place."

And now I started blushing and was still scared. What did I say?

Apparently my reaction was funny. Curtis turned to face me. "Tell me, please." He begged. He even tried taunting me by grabbing my butt and holding me against him the way I liked.

I moaned, like the failure of a spy that I was.

He started kissing down my neck, breaking down my willpower. "Tell me, love. What has you so embarrassed you are scared? I promise I won't be mad."

Yeah, that wasn't true.

"One of the, uh, good parts of the dream, was on that hill, on the Mexican side of the wall. With you, and uh…"

"You dreamt about being with Mark and me. You thought I would be mad that you dreamt about my friend?"

"Ya huh." I'm sorry, what did I just agree with?

"I told you that you would enjoy it. I can't tell you how happy I am that you finally caved. Multiple times. Lucas will be happy to hear it too. You know, he has been pacing out there for nearly 24 hours. He was worried about you too."

"Mm, huh." I loved what this man could do with his hands. And tongue, all the parts of him really.

"Shall I call him? You can reassure him that you are better now."

Curtis came back to my lips but stayed just far enough away that I couldn't kiss him. He didn't have to prompt me. I knew what I wanted.

I groaned. "Fine, but you better not stop."

He chuckled and kissed me again. "I would never dream of it."

With one hand, he didn't stop, but with the other, he picked up a pillow and threw it at the door. He wasn't kidding about Lucas being close by.

"Why did you throw a pillow at the door?" Lucas chuckled, walking over while unbuckling his pants.

Apparently he already knew the answer.

I woke up a few hours later, Curtis was gone, but arms were still around me. I looked around confused, half expecting to see Mark.

"The Master seems to think you sleep more peacefully if someone of the vampire nature is with you." Lucas shrugged. "I was happy to volunteer."

I laughed and sat up. "You're an idiot." I patted his face roughly. "But we love you anyway." He laughed as I got up. "I have to pee, keep the bed warm."

He saluted me, then made a point of panting as I walked away. It was sweet of Curtis to think of that. I didn't know how true it was, but I appreciated the thought anyway.

I replayed the last two days in my head as I washed my hands. Curtis was busy trying to take over a country, organize the one he had, and yet, still made time for me. I already had his son in me. I was a soft spot for him, whether it was because he loved me for me, or because I reminded him of Angela, it didn't matter. He still loved me. I could do more good here, with him. I just needed to fully step into my role as his Queen. Maybe I misinterpreted the visions. They only showed me how to get here. They didn't technically say that I had to spy. They said I would make the difference.

I cursed at myself. What did I do?

I couldn't message Hill anymore, no matter how much that pained me. Maybe that was the sacrifice the dream witch meant. I had to sacrifice what could have been for what was already there.

I steadied myself, resolving for this new mission, this new outlook. I stared at myself in the mirror, willing the resolve to come.

Instead, I felt like I was lying to myself. I was just making excuses to chicken out and hide in the hole I dug.

I deflated and walked back to the bedroom, where Lucas lifted the blanket, just like Mark had done before, only with a much cheesier grin. I giggled and shook my head with exasperation.

Lucas was off the bed and flying to me a second later when I stumbled and gasped. The vision came out of nowhere.

Hill found my marks. He lost it and had to be pulled away from the wall by Morris. Colton searched the wall until his fingers grazed across the crest. He reached into the dark abyss with one hand, grabbed a head of hair, and yanked it outside. The vampire burned to a crisp in less than a minute. There were more. Wolf-Hill ran inside, lots of screaming and tearing could be heard from the outside. When he came out again, his wolf was bloody and smug. The others laughed, he shifted into human form, letting me see a whole lot more.

I would be good with that for the next 50 or so years.

I was also beginning to think I had a thing for large men. No wonder Todd had not appealed to me much physically. He was too skinny.

Colton stepped through the other door. Someone was pulling up in a familiar black SUV. Colton spotted him, scowled, then stepped out of the wall to wave at him with a sardonic smirk. He then ran back through the wall. Mark was right behind him, trying to catch the intruder.

The tunnel exploded. Mark was inside.

"No!!!" I screamed and fell to my knees, Lucas caught me. Seconds later, Curtis was back.

"What the hell happened?"

"I think she had a vision. Her eyes went all white like they do. She nearly fell over, unbalanced, she was quiet, and then she wasn't." Lucas reported to his boss.

Curtis took me from his friend's hands, for once not wanting to share. I happily wrapped myself around him. Safe.

"Gracey, what happened? What did you see?"

"Mark. Wall. Bomb." I mumbled into his neck.

I could feel them trying to make sense of it without talking and disturbing me.

"Can you give me a little more to go on, love?"

I sighed and let go of his neck, sitting back enough to look down at my hands. He had sat us on the bed. Random stray thought. Yeah, I had checked out.

"Soldiers are going to be searching the wall. They are going to find the holes I made with my fingers. They have a Vampire Born with them, and a shifter. Somehow they find the crest. A Nightwalker will get pulled out of the wall and into the sun, then a black wolf will run inside. The Vampire Born will see Mark coming, they wait to blow their bombs until Mark is there."

"How do you know it's a Vampire Born, love?" Curtis kept his voice soft, and on the same level as mine. Probably trying not to startle me.

I shrugged. "I could be wrong. He seemed to recognize Mark. And I think he was in the flash of the Mojave wall when it got blown up. The black wolf too."

"Colton." Curtis growled. "Has to be. Bryant told Timothy he was working with the shifters. Deacon gave him the General title. I'm not surprised. His father was a good General to mine. I remember him liking to hunt in the woods when he was a kid." Curtis shook the thoughts off and kissed my head. "Can you give us a time, love? When will it happen?"

I shrugged and picked at my nail. Seeing all this death was really starting to mess with my psyche. "Sun was high, that's all I know."

Curtis shifted enough to pull his phone out of his pocket. "Mark. Grace had a vision." I only half listened as he retold it to Mark. When he hung up, he handed his phone to Lucas, who set it on the table.

"I'll get her some food. You try to bring her back to life." Lucas mumbled, walking out the door again, his pants still on my floor.

Curtis carefully moved me over, laying down with me. Surprisingly, his clothes were still on.

"It's going to be okay, love. Mark now has a warning. They will all be ready."

I barely nodded my head and moved to lay on his chest. I put my hand on him and played with his buttons, not really thinking about anything.

I needed a vacation. A real vacation.

Alone.

"Grace. He'll be alright. You told us and we will fix it. I promise. What did the alternate vision show?"

I shrugged again. "I didn't get one. That was it." My voice was flat. Flat as my stomach used to be.

Curtis lifted his head to look down at me. "What do you mean you didn't get one?"

I sighed and pushed to sit up. "Exactly what I said Curtis." Oh, goodie, there was one emotion left. Irritation. "I got one vision. For all I know, I just sent Mark and the others to their deaths. Maybe they wouldn't have been there, had I not told you. Maybe they would have been." I threw my arms up to my sides. "How the hell should I know? I don't determine these things. I am just cursed to watch them."

He tried to grab me again, but I pushed him away. He won. Butthead. The second my face hit his chest, the next emotion came, sadness.

I liked Mark. He was nice. He reminded me of Deacon. He just wanted to be free and have fun. It had been fun in Mexico.

I sat on the beach, while the two of them raced in the ocean, seeing who could swim faster. He got tired of losing and tried to grab a hold of Curtis' foot and drag him down. Curtis then held him under. I worried at first, but then realized it wasn't what I thought. Technically, we had already crossed that bridge together. And it was kind of funny to watch. I don't think Curtis knew Mark was going to do that when he first pushed his head down. Curtis' eyes nearly blended into his hair. I didn't fully catch on until Curtis started pumping.

A few minutes later, Mark crawled out of the ocean and right over me. None of us had bathing suits, nor were we in a public area. They wouldn't have cared, but I sure would have. No way I was doing that in front of kids!

I sobbed harder into Curtis' chest while he just held me. Lucas came back at some point, setting down a tray of whatever he brought me, then climbed in behind me and held me from behind.

Both of them were being oddly sweet.

Eventually, my sobs ran out, but we stayed there, with me hiccupping every few minutes. Pretty sure I met Lucas' max with lying next to a woman, naked, and not doing anything. He started kissing my shoulders and onto my spine.

"Can I try to cheer you up, my Lady? Let me help you. The only way I really know how."

Okay, that was sweet and pathetic. "Sometimes, just being with someone can help. Both of you lying with me helped. I'm not really in the mood for more. But thank you, Lucas."

I sniffed again and tried to sit up.

"If you feel up for it, I set an appointment for you with one of the donors, right after sunrise. She used to do hair for a living. I had Ryley help her move equipment into her room. She is thrilled with the idea of doing the Queen's hair." Curtis offered.

"Yeah, that would be fine, thank you. Can I eat now?"

"Of course, love." He reached over and grabbed the tray.

Charles had made me an omelet this time, loaded with lots of meat and veggies. On the side was a bowl of strawberries and yogurt. It all felt like lead in my stomach, but I knew my son needed me to eat.

Lucas left to do whatever it was that he needed to do, while I showered and got dressed. My boobs hurt, so I figured I'd skip the bra. But walking around with these hard freaking bowling balls free hurt more. I ended up in a tank top with a built-in bra. The bottom strap itched a little but didn't hurt like the other options. None of my pants felt comfortable, and every other shirt was annoying. It was too cold for any of the sundresses too.

Curtis came to me with a pair of his basketball shorts. They were soft, and sadly only had to be rolled twice to fit.

"How am I so big already? It's barely been over a month! I look more like 6 months!"

Curtis chuckled and stood behind me in front of the mirror, his hands on my stomach, both of them barely covering it now, and his chin on my shoulder.

"You still look like a goddess to me. As much of a dream as you were when I first saw you, standing under that waterfall."

I lifted my hand behind me and patted his face. "You can stop sucking up. You've already knocked me up and marked me as yours. Pretty sure you got me already." I teased.

He laughed and kissed my neck. "I will never stop showing you how much I love you or telling you. I find I enjoy doing both very much. And I also love the way you look in my clothes."

"They barely fit, even with the belly they are too big."

"Nah. They just have room for one more person."

"Dude. I'm already pregnant. You're gonna have to wait a while on another one."

He threw his head back and laughed. “No, that is not what I meant. But I will remind you that you agreed to a second son when you try to refuse later.”

I widened my eyes. That was so not what I meant to do. He laughed again, kissing my shoulder.

“I meant those shorts are big enough for me to join you.” Whoop, and his hand just went straight in there.

It wasn’t long before I was holding that counter for balance and those shorts were all the way on the floor. Along with the rest of both of our clothes.

“I miss all the fun.” Lucas whined from the bedroom door, looking into our open concept bathroom.

I laughed and dropped my sore chest onto the cold counter. I pretended to not see Curtis waving him over behind my back. I was right in front of a mirror, they weren’t very slick.

Except when they did that.

Lucas slid in smoothly, the way still wet from Curtis. Who moved to kneel under me, taking advantage of my extra sensitive areas.

He stayed on the same spot for a long time, his hand helping Lucas out more. When he finally released me, he licked it a few times.

“I can honestly say, my son is going to be eating well.”

“Huh?” My brain was fried, it had been a long morning.

“Your milk has come in, love. That is why you hurt so bad. If all milk tasted this good, I would partake in human food more.” He rubbed the one he had been attached to for the last few minutes.

“Feel better?”

I sighed. "Much. Thank you." I stumbled back with how fast Lucas let go of me and ran around.

"Can I try some?"

"Uh, sure. But I think I need to sit down first."

They both laughed as Curtis picked me up and set me on the counter. He dropped to his knees though while his friend relieved me of my discomfort. I may have held him on a little longer. I blamed it on what Curtis was doing to me.

After Curtis finished his part, he disappeared for a minute, then came back in with a regular bra and a long sleeve t-shirt.

"Care to try for something warmer now?"

"Yes, please. As soon as your greedy puppy releases his new toy."

Curtis laughed and spanked Lucas who then attacked me with more voracity. He took advantage of my position, connecting us once again. Before I knew it, Curtis was behind him, both rocking into me, but Lucas took the spankings. It took all my energy to keep from falling into the mirror.

"Thank you, your majesties. I can't imagine anything better."

I laughed as Lucas stumbled out of the bathroom a few minutes later. Curtis chuckled and hugged me to him.

"Did you pick out new toys for him, yet? I don't know if I have it in me to keep entertaining him."

Curtis laughed and shook his head. "Not yet. I think he is worried you will stop letting him play with us if he makes new friends."

I laughed then sighed. "Isn't it too early for my milk to come in?"

Curtis held my bra up for me and helped put it on. "No. I don't think so. Human women start lactating about halfway through their pregnancies. They don't usually have anything come out until later, but then, I doubt many of them actually try to pull it out."

I stared at him in shock. He shrugged and picked up my shirt. "That's where I was when your vision came in. I was in the library doing research online. The only real difference between our babies and human babies is the gestation period." I let him help me off the counter and slide on the shorts and underwear. Again. "So far, most things are normal. You are faster than what I remember, but I've never seen a pregnant witch, no matter who the father was."

I slipped the shirt over my head. I immediately grabbed his and pulled him in to kiss him. "Thank you for looking things up. I love you."

He smiled and kissed me again. "I love you, too. I would do anything for you, you know that. Now we better get out of here before I take you back to that bed. Alicia is waiting."

Chapter 20

Grace

Curtis drove us downtown, basically parking in the middle of a street. I had been locked up in his house for so long, I forgot how horrible it looked out there. Being up in the air, you only saw the crumpled buildings. Being on the ground, you saw the bricks, the broken windows, the charred remains of buildings unknown. There were even dark, dried puddles on the cement. I didn't want to think about where the stains came from.

"Are you going to leave the city like this forever?"

"No. When things settle down, we will have people start the clean-up. Right now, I am more concerned with making sure we have a working economy between the races, and stability in the outlying towns. People have been fighting over property, jobs, assets, even the dogs."

"People lash out when they are scared. I saw it many times in the shelter."

He lifted my hand and helped me step over a large brick. We walked around to the back of a large apartment building. It looked oddly like the one my friends and I had stayed in. That one was on the other side of the city, though. The lobby was filled with cream furniture and vases of tall fake flowers. The front door had been boarded up, hence us coming in from the side.

Curtis took us over to the elevator and pushed a button.

“Did you give the city power again?”

“Yes. Once most of the humans were gone, we flipped the switch.”

“I thought you had taken out the transformers or something.”

He chuckled and pulled me inside the now waiting elevator. My friends and I had to take five flights of stairs where we had stayed after we left the shelter.

“No, love. We turned it off at the power plant. I didn’t want it permanently gone, and there was no guarantee that engineers and electricians would survive.”

I nodded and kept my mouth shut. The elevator went up too fast and left my stomach on the first floor. Curtis recognized the signs and quickly got me to the penthouse suite on the far right. He knocked, and a minute later the door opened. I didn’t even have time to look at the beautiful blonde before pushing her aside and running for the bathroom.

Thankfully she had left the door wide open, so it was easy to find.

“You alright there, darling?”

Ugh. She even sounded like an overly peppy cheerleader. I hated peppy blondes.

“Yep. Right as rain. Vampire baby plus fast elevator equals me face down in the toilet. I’m surprised Curtis didn’t follow me in here. He's going to be the definition of a helicopter parent." I closed the toilet lid and pushed to stand up. I moved to the sink and started washing my face and rinsing my mouth.

My eyes floated up to my new hair stylist's reflection in the mirror, while I turned off the water and grabbed the hand towel.

"Have we met? You look really familiar." She asked, tipping her head, and sounding like she should be chewing gum while talking.

I cursed and flipped the water back on, closing the bathroom door at the same time. It was only a half bath. Just enough room for a toilet, a sink, and the two of us.

"Who all did you tell about working in Deac's bar?" I hissed.

She clapped excitedly and jumped up and down. Did I look that retarded when I did that?

"I knew you looked familiar. Grace, right?"

I sighed and nodded. "Look, I need you to keep your voice down so grumpy pants in there doesn't hear us. Who all did you tell about Deac's bar?"

"Oh, nobody, honey. I didn't need to. Lou, one of Deac's old buds, brought me here. Tell you what, I like it. I'm living in style, they come to me, and I get paid. Psh, who wants to live in some old town? Nah. I'm like you. I'm going to reel me in a big fish and keep him. Ain't nobody stacked like these boys, am I right?"

I sighed. "Lovely. Well, if you want to live long enough for that to happen, I'm going to let you in on a little secret."

She leaned in closer, eager to hear some secret tip to sleeping her way to the top.

"Whatever you do, do not mention Deac. Ever. He is enemy number 1 with these guys. Especially with the king of cranks out there, got it?"

She looked confused. "So, no matter what, act like I never met Deacon or worked in his bar?"

Maybe she did get it. I smiled and sighed. "Yes. Exactly. Deacon and Curtis have a very bad past. Plus, the whole, two sides of the same war thing and all."

"But…why? I figured Deacon and his girl got shipped off to some other place or what not."

How was she still alive?

"Alicia, sweetie. Deacon was a vampire. Just of a different breed. Everyone but the donors knew that. Well, I guess a few of us did. But I'm a witch, like Deacon's girl. So, I knew more."

She looked like a brainless twit the way her mouth opened and closed.

"Look, Curtis is going to freak out if we don't get out there soon. Just remember, you don't know Deac."

She scoffed. "Apparently not. And how do we know each other?"

"The shelter."

She nodded once and straightened up like she was preparing for battle. I tried to hide the eye roll as I turned the water off and opened the door again. I nearly slammed right into said cranky pants.

"Hi. What's up?" I asked carefully, how much did he hear?

The back of his hand went straight to my forehead. "Are you okay? You've been in there a long time, and you stopped throwing up a few minutes ago."

I laughed at myself for overreacting, then took his hand down and held it. "I'm fine, baby. I just had to rinse my mouth. A lot. The after taste made me want to hurl again. Alicia, can I get a bottle of water, please?"

"Oh yeah, sure darling. No problem. My chair is in the kitchen, anyway. Follow me and we can get started."

"You two got a chance to talk?" He was a bit wary for some reason.

"Only a little, I was a bit busy. We actually met in the shelter though. Alicia was kind enough to tell me more about being a donor, after we met Carter the first time. She likes doing it but would prefer to be a private pet someday."

Curtis lifted an eyebrow at me.

"Oh yes, I've always had a thing for vampires." She turned and winked at him before bending to reach into the fridge for water.

"If you bring her into our home, I will stab you with a silver dagger in your sleep and cut your balls off." I mumbled quietly to him, smiling at her as she came around.

Curtis didn't care what she saw or heard, he just laughed.

By the time my hair was trimmed, and my tips were redone, Curtis understood why I didn't want her around. She was so annoying. Then again, maybe it only bothered him because she kept dropping not so subtle hints and coming onto him. But he promised me that he would not touch another woman. The man thing he floundered on from time to time.

Like this morning. I did not give permission for him to do that. But it did move Lucas along so he would stop draining my boobs. I really hoped this kid did not have teeth when he was born.

We waved goodbye as we loaded back into the elevator. The second the doors closed, he lifted me against the wall and kissed me. The shorts fell off of course, and he took advantage of that the old-fashioned way. Someone joined us on the way down, not sure who. They just kept their back to us and got off on the next floor.

"We never would have been able to do that on the other side of the wall. We would have been arrested for public indecency." Curtis said, a big smile on his face as he lowered me down.

"Is that why you built a wall and invaded California? So, you could have an afternoon quickie in an elevator?"

He barked out a laugh and helped me redress. "I love your wit."

He tucked me into the car a few minutes later but didn't quite make it to his side. I turned and looked out the back window, trying to see what was keeping him. He was on his phone.

I waited anxiously for him to tell me. The few minutes dragged on before he opened my door again and squatted down to be on my level.

"Mark?" It barely came out in a squeak.

"He's okay. He called the guards working in that section and put them on alert. Problem is, they still don't know where the door is. Well, I guess that isn't a problem anymore."

I gasped and covered my mouth. He nodded.

"Oh, yeah. A tanker truck could get through there. Thankfully, it's not a convenient spot for that to happen. I think this was mostly a message for me."

"Mark wasn't in the explosion though?" That was all I really cared about.

"No." Curtis leaned forward to put his head against mine. "He would have been though. He was already planning on checking on the guards today. But not until later tonight. I think you were right. Your vision may have somehow sent him into the fire. But when he saw Colton, he didn't follow, he hid behind his car. So, no matter how it all worked out, you did save Mark. And I thank you for that. He has been a friend for a long time. One of the few who believed my side of the story."

I sniffed. "I'm glad he is okay. I was so worried."

"I know, which is why I approved for him to come visit us. He will be here in about an hour by chopper. He wanted to thank you for saving him, and I thought you would feel better if you saw him for yourself."

I nodded and wrapped my arms around his neck, holding him tight. My stomach grumbled and he laughed. "Come on, let's get you home and feed you." I bit the corner of my lip and he laughed. "Food first, love."

I waited until he was in the car and driving again before asking my next nagging question. "Are we rebuilding the wall?"

Curtis laid his hand on my stomach and rubbed softly. "Not until after our son is born. The humans can start building it, but I won't risk using a freezing spell. I'm… uh… not sure how well it still works anyway."

"Why not?"

He cleared his throat and rubbed my stomach again. "Because I was once mated to a witch with that power. When they mate in the way of the witches, they share the power with their mate. It was the only reason I didn't want to trade blood with you, mate you. I thought I still needed that power. I've had it for centuries. I was used to it. I tested it after we knocked you up." He winked and I blushed. "It was working fine. But I didn't keep it up for long because I didn't want to need you to heal me, not right now. Then the other night happened. I knew I had to choose between which would be easier to live without."

"You chose me? Over power?" I was flabbergasted. I heard him saying something about it to Lucas last night, but I hadn't exactly been in a good headspace.

Curtis swallowed uncomfortably, keeping his eyes on the road. "Yeah. You are more important to me than having the power to freeze things."

I couldn't believe it. The man was known for being power hungry. This whole thing started because he wanted to be King. He wanted to rule and hold the power. Now he gave part of that away. For me.

I had nothing to say to that. Part of me wanted to pick him, too. Even if he didn't know there had been an option for me. But I couldn't do that. Instead, I did something else. I reached over and unzipped his pants.

We both laughed over the fact that I couldn't do it. So, he did it. I cried. My belly was too big. He stopped the car right there, in the middle of the deserted road, and walked around to my side. When he opened my door, I got quite the eye full. His pants were still open, and he had pulled himself out for me. I sniffed and giggled.

Charles was walking out of the kitchen when we walked through the front door. He smiled, then turned and went back in. He already knew what we were going to ask. I barely sat on the bed before he was knocking on the door. Curtis moved out of the way and let him carry it to the bed for me.

"Mark will be here soon. Please make sure his room is ready. In case he needs it."

Charles bowed and walked back out.

"Why wouldn't he need it? Is he not planning on staying long?"

Curtis sat behind me, letting me lean against him while I ate my sandwich. "He shared a bed with us for three days. He could have died today but didn't because of you. I fully expect he will tie himself to our bed and let you have your wicked ways with him."

I snorted, then nearly choked on my food. Smooth move, Grace. "Please, I am too fat to have my way with anybody. It's more like I just lay here, and you all take turns playing with me."

His hands on my arms froze. I really put my foot in my mouth this time. "Does that mean I am inviting Lucas to come play too?"

I laughed. "Hell, no. How many holes do you all think I have?" He laughed and hugged me tight from behind. I went in for the kill shot. "Who knows, maybe I won't even let you stay tonight."

My giggles turned into full laughter when he started tickling me. They ended rather quickly though.

He ended up making me have to pee.

I brushed my teeth after I finished eating, I could still taste the lovely event from Alicia's apartment. I looked at my reflection for a few minutes. I had to admit, she did a really good job. You just had to get used to tuning out her psychobabble.

I squeaked and jumped when the bedroom door flew open. Curtis laughed from the bed. Mark came running over to where I still stood and knelt at my feet. Which he also kissed.

"You saved my life. I don't know how I will ever repay you for that. But I sure plan on spending hours trying."

I laughed at the ridiculousness of it. He wasn't kidding though, nor wasting time. He just kissed his way right up, removing things as he went.

Eventually he made it to my lips, which I happily accepted. He had been fun to kiss in Mexico. Especially when we were pretending to hide from Curtis.

"See, I don't know why your breeders complained." I stretched and yawned between the two thick bodies. "A bunch of gorgeous guys constantly wanting to do that to you. I'd be good with it."

Curtis kissed my back, his hand on my raised butt, rubbing it of course. "Why am I not surprised that you would be okay with it?"

"Because you are a smart man."

His hand came down hard before gripping me again. "I am at that. I was smart enough to bring you home and keep you."

I felt two more hands join him, rubbing up and down my back, keeping me from lowering back down. I groaned when it wasn't just hands anymore. I lifted to my arms, getting the hint from Curtis who pushed them up slightly. My eyes rolled back when he and Mark slid their heads under.

I was only confused for a split second before I realized who was behind me. I should have known they would find a way to do this. And Curtis was right, I was not complaining.

"Sorry if I stole your thunder there, my Lord. I just can't resist her in this position." Lucas purred, rubbing a hand up my back. "I came to tell you that I brought that kitty home from the feeding center. I wasn't sure she would want to leave, which is why I hadn't. Thank you. I will enjoy her immensely."

"Good. Just remember, she irritates your Queen. Either keep her muffled or locked in your room. I have a feeling she won't complain." Lucas kissed my rear and started walking away. "Oh, and Lucas. Try to make this one last for a few weeks, at least."

Lucas' chuckle reminded me of the psycho I hadn't seen in him for a while. "I make no promises, my Lord. I only go easy on the Queen, you know that."

Curtis sighed like he was disappointed. "I know. But we only have so many now."

Mark and I laughed at the frown on Lucas' face as he left.

"You are such a mean master." I mocked Curtis. Leaning over to kiss him.

"Good, I was afraid I was going soft there for a minute."

I laughed again and gripped him. "You are *never* soft, my King."

"I beg to differ. After that little stunt outside the wall, you pretty much took all the air out of our tires." Mark was lying back, one arm under his head, the other scratching his chest.

The reminder took the wind out of my sails, and I dropped down to the bed.

"What did I say?" He jumped up, worried.

Curtis put his arm under my head and pulled the blanket up. "In her vision, the nail marks she made in the dirt were near the door. She feels responsible."

Yeah, because I was.

"You have to remember how real they are for her too. She felt like she was there, watching you die."

Mark cursed softly and scooted over to hold me from the front. I leaned against him enough to hear his heartbeat. He wouldn't have deserved to die like that. Just because he was on Curtis' side didn't mean he was a bad guy.

"Do we know how they knew to look there in the first place?" Mark asked softly.

Curtis' hand was gently stroking my arm, but there was a dangerous feel to it. One that held the promise of pain for somebody.

"Not for sure, but I have my suspicions."

"Who?"

"Have you heard from Ryder since I spoke to him?"

Mark growled, I inwardly hissed. Once again someone was going to pay for what I did.

"No. I haven't."

Curtis grunted, like that was as he suspected.

Chapter 21

Grace

I was having another day of clothes being jerks. I ended up putting on one of Curtis' t-shirts, twisting it in the middle, and pushing it through the collar and down. I sighed with relief.

Somewhat supportive and did not rub against me.

Perfect.

I didn't even care if he got mad. That's what he deserved for leaving while I slept.

I mean, yes, I wasn't technically alone. I was never alone when I slept anymore. And it seemed to be helping. Even when I had weird dreams, they didn't get like they did the week before.

I searched through both our dressers until I gave up and grabbed a wraparound skirt. I didn't even want any kind of underwear anymore. Everything felt restrictive and my skin was extra sensitive.

Curtis kept the house at 74 degrees all the time. Unless I randomly got hot, then it dropped. I was maybe seven weeks along now. But I looked like I was closer to seven or eight months. I didn't even bother with shoes either since my feet were in a constant state of swollen.

It was like my body was having a competition to see what could get bigger the fastest. My boobs? My stomach? Or my feet?

Lucas wasn't coming in as often anymore since Curtis told him to bring Alicia home. I needn't have worried about her bugging me. She hadn't once left the harem suite.

Mark went home the day after he arrived. I bawled like a baby. Then Curtis distracted me.

I hated being pregnant. If I ever got out of this mess, I might just become celibate altogether. Absolutely no chance of pregnancy then.

I walked out of the room, needing to move around a bit. Lucas had left the bed not long after I woke up. He liked sleeping with me when Curtis had to leave before the sun went down. I usually let him have a reward after. Curtis was pretty sure he was addicted to the taste of me, something he himself had started during that first helicopter flight here from Mojave.

I honestly didn't care anymore. It was better than suffering from the fevers and hot flashes.

I walked down the hundred flights of stairs to the bottom, wishing we had an elevator, and then wondering why I ever left the room in the first place. Once I hit the main floor, I had to run into a guest bathroom to pee.

I hated being pregnant.

I could hear sounds coming from down the hall, so I followed them. They led me to Curtis' office. Gone were the signs of the humans who lived here before. Now there was just the basic furniture.

And a picture of me in the shower?

"Where the hell did you get that?"

Curtis turned to see where I was pointing, then laughed. "I took it when I tested the freezing power after we mated."

"You froze me in the shower? Why?"

He shrugged and put a hand up, silently telling me to come here. "I told you. You are the most beautiful creature. I enjoy being able to see you all the time." His eyes roved up and down my body. "If I had known I could get you to walk around mostly naked though, I wouldn't have bothered." He flicked the edge of his shirt on me. "Clothing an enemy again today, love?"

I pouted and sat on his leg. "Yes. It's a conspiracy, I swear. They are lazy and just don't want to be worn."

He laughed and kissed my head. "I see my clothes take after me, at least. They love being against your skin."

I sighed and looked at the tv on the wall. "Apparently. Why are you watching CNN?"

He leaned back into his chair, taking me with him. "I had a mole in Deacon's house, not that my mole knew he was a mole. He's been quiet lately."

I wondered if he was talking about Bryant.

"Do you think Deacon figured it out and took him out?"

"Hmph, doubtful. Deacon has a soft spot for the old man. Honestly, we all do. He's older than dirt, and probably looks like it by now."

I looked back to him, it was a commercial, anyway. "Vampires age?"

"Yes." He said slowly, as though questioning my sanity.

I pushed off his lap and folded my arms across my chest. I hissed, bad idea. I grimaced. "How was I supposed to know? You and Mark are the oldest vampires I know, and you don't look a day over 30!"

He mocked offense by covering his heart. I scowled and folded my arms again. I really needed to stop doing that!

Curtis chuckled and grabbed my waist with both hands. "Do you want me to help you? You know I don't mind." His eyes were literally glowing with excitement.

I kept my scowl firmly placed, even though I was pretty sure my scent was giving away my true feelings on that subject.

He sighed and slowly pulled me back onto his lap. "We age, it just takes a really long time. Roughly a decade in human aging for every millennium in ours. At least after we hit manhood. Before that, we age the same as everyone else."

He placed my knees on each side of his legs, pulling me closer. My stupid skirt came untied and fell off. He smirked when he looked down.

"So, your whole side of the closet was against you this evening?"

I pushed against his chest, trying to keep a straight face. "Shut up, you jerk. Are you going to help me, or not?"

His eyes relit and his chuckle was deep. At first he was gentle, but the more he took, the rougher he got. I felt his fight to not grab the other side, so he hadn't lost control completely. That hand went down instead.

Charles brought a dinner plate in a few minutes later. I had to close my eyes and pretend he wasn't there. Apparently there were still some audiences I did not want to have. Curtis laughed as he came up for air, catching the last drops.

"He's seen worse."

"Don't care. Didn't feel right."

He shook his head and moved to the other side. This time he was able to play with the deflated one, only the good kind of sensitivity was in there now.

"Ah, are we too full already? Feels like just yesterday." Lucas giggled, coming in and sitting on the couch, one foot resting on his other knee. His pants were already popping open so he could fully enjoy the show.

I flipped him off. "It *was* just yesterday. I think you guys are making it worse. It's refilling what you are taking."

He grunted out a growl and made a mess of the couch. I stupidly licked my lips. Lucas chuckled as he got back up and walked around the desk.

"Kitty wanna give me a bath?" He barely had to touch my head before I bent over and started licking him clean, then taking it all in. "Oh yeah, much better. Maybe you should be giving my new pet some lessons."

I grinned at him as he fell away from me. "I've done that, you know."

"What? Give lessons?" He sounded excited by this.

I nodded, Curtis released me and moved me forward to lay on his chest. This was probably one of my favorite spots. I closed my eyes and sighed with relief, now he felt good to wear. Or was he wearing me?

"Yes. When we were in the shelters. I knew I was supposed to get to Curtis somehow, the flashes said a harem. But we were a bunch of kids in a shelter. Alicia told me what they did, or what she thought they did anyway." I had to make sure I kept the story straight with all the little tidbits I'd accidentally dropped over the last few months.

How long had I been there now? 9 or 10 months?

Did the frozen time we spent building the wall count?

I worked to refocus my thoughts. "I'm sure by now you have shown her the error of her ways."

Lucas giggled like a teenage girl. I had to stop talking for a minute, Curtis was purposely making it difficult. He was pleased with himself.

"Anyway, I wasn't exactly innocent. Neither was Todd, my foster brother. We taught a different kind of lessons in the classrooms, preparing our new friends for the life they were joining us in."

"You mean the twins?" Awe, the puppy was pouting again.

I loved messing with him though. "Yep. And wouldn't you know it, they liked to play together too. They showed us. Just us girls, no one else around." I told him slowly, drawing it out.

He was whimpering big time.

"And you say, I'm the mean one." Curtis smirked, then tried, and failed to twist my shirt again. I laughed and took over.

"I take it you like this outfit?" I swung my leg over and got off his… uh… lap.

He waited until my skirt was tied again, then leaned in and kissed my growing watermelon farm. "Very much so. I love that you are showing off my son."

"Apparently your son is a showoff, because he does not like to be covered."

Curtis put one hand on my cheek and brought me down for a kiss. "I love you."

"I know." I winked at him and moved away.

He growled and stood up to stalk after me, like a lion chasing a gazelle, or a panda. I was too fat to be a gazelle.

Lucas interrupted us by turning the tv up. "It's starting, my Lord."

Curtis stopped teasing me and turned to the tv. Without a word, I stepped closer and let him hold me.

"What's starting?" I picked up a piece of bread from the tray Charles brought, having forgotten all about it already.

"An announcement was made this morning. The Acting President of the United States is going to address the nation regarding the recent events in California." I wasn't sure if Lucas was trying to do an impersonation of someone on the news, or if he was disgusted by it. "Since we haven't heard from our mole in a while, this is our only shot. We knew Deacon was meeting with the humans, that is all. Deacon is getting smarter about who he talks to. For some reason they have cut down on who's around when they talk."

A man who looked pale and weak stepped up to the microphone after being introduced.

"My fellow Americans. It is my pleasure to speak to you today, and to inform you that we have made large steps towards rectifying this situation with the vampires in California. I picked up where President Reynolds left off. I met with some unexpected allies. Ones that had been right under our noses this whole time."

Curtis cursed and held me tighter.

"As there always is with wars, sacrifices have had to be made. As you know, the Senate met nearly night and day for almost three weeks. But we have come to an agreement that we believe is the best for our people."

He looked down at his notes uncomfortably, then off to the side, new people walked into the room from a side door. My knees shook bad enough that Curtis sat down again, putting me on his lap.

"Before I get into the agreement, I would like you all to hear their story first, from them. I'm not known for my speaking ability." There were a few lighthearted chuckles from the newsroom. He stepped back but held a hand up for a *very* pregnant woman to step up to the microphones.

"I take it back, I'm not fat." I mumbled. But Carrie sure the hell was. She was only a few weeks ahead of me too. I turned to Curtis while they were fixing a microphone to come closer to Carrie, she was limited on space back there. "Please tell me I am not going to get that big,"

Curtis' chuckle fell flat. "No. She is pregnant with twins."

"Do you know her?"

He shook his head. "No, but I have a good idea who she is, and the line she descends from." His hand gripped my waist tighter, like he was afraid I would disappear.

"Good evening, sorry about that. These things were obviously not made for women about to pop. In all honesty, I would rather be home in sweats right now, with a tub of strawberry ice cream." The newsroom laughed harder this time.

I wanted to cry. I missed her.

"My name is Carrie Michaels. Previous to Labor Day weekend of this year, I was a Kindergarten teacher in Arizona. I wanted to spend the long weekend with friends in Los Angeles, but, well, we all know how that worked out." A few more people snickered. "Worst freakin weekend of my life. I know you are all wondering how I got out. Well, that's kind of a long story. I was running from a vampire on my second night there, he was toying with me of course. Evil little blood sucker. I stupidly found myself in an alley, blocked in. I frantically banged on every door. Thankfully, one opened. I was pulled into safety by that man back there. The one with longer hair than me. Best thing to ever happen to me. Deacon was a bar owner in LA. And believe it or not, he, like many other bars and clubs all over the world, served vampires at night." She waited through the shocked gasps and whisperings.

"They've been around for centuries. Many humans have made extra money acting as donors to them. With the vampires out in the open, humans stopped coming out at night. Deacon recruited more donors. I know, it sounds bad, it did to me at first too. The thing is, when vamps hunt, they are more likely to kill. Donors kept them off the streets. The donors were willing, and they got paid. Most people in the larger cities had no way to take care of their families, we gave them one. Not all the vamps were bad. Just like not all humans are. You just have to look through the history books or through our prison systems for proof. I'm not saying they are fluffy little creatures you want to feed and pet…although, I do know some people like that."

The snort came out on its own. Both men in the room looked at me. "Dude, she literally just called shifters fluffy little pets. That was funny." I scoffed at their blank looks. "Fine, whatever."

Curtis kissed my neck in apology or just trying to calm me down. Who knew anymore?

"But that is for later. My point is, we can't judge everybody based on a few bad apples. I mean, seriously, how many of you have family members you wish you weren't related to. Deacon, put that hand down!"

She didn't even turn around, but she knew it was there. Curtis couldn't help the smirk at that one. I was wrong on why though.

"Think he finally knows the truth?" Lucas asked.

"What truth?" My eyes caught on the half-naked man trying to hide in the back. He was right there, in real life. Well, realer than only in my head.

"I'm his uncle." Curtis said flatly.

I wanted to say something, but I already knew more than I should, so I kept my mouth shut. I just leaned into him, keeping my eyes on the screen.

Carrie gave an aggrieved sigh and mumbled something about boys never growing up. "With those family members in mind, I implore you to keep an open mind on everything you hear from here on out." She took a big breath. I held mine for her too. "My name is Carrie Michaels, and I am the Queen of the Witches. While once my people lived side by side with humans, that eventually came to an end. We have tried living in peace on our own. Most have hidden who they are. We all still carry scars passed down to us from the Witch Trials. Don't forget, those were run by humans, and more often than not, they captured their own people. I strayed from my family teachings when I was younger. Enough so, that my own mother, the Queen at the time, did not tell me of my status. My powers grew weak. Until I was 17, and both my parents were killed by vampires. The same as most of my ancestors. If anyone has a right to fear them, it's me. Being trapped in LA was a living nightmare for me. But during that time, I met the man I would, in human terms, marry. I got this lovely gift." She pointed at her belly. "Two of them actually. Stop grinning like an idiot on live tv Deacon."

Curtis hmphed. "I kind of like her."

I giggled. It was obvious he hated admitting that.

"I found my way back to my own people. And, if they are watching, I beg your eternal forgiveness for abandoning you the way I did. I'd like to say that if I had known, I wouldn't have left, but I don't know that." She gave a small smirk. "My mom was the clairvoyant one, not me. I am here today, doing what I promised to do, protect my people, and to guide them. The Nightwalkers saw fit to bring magical people into the light. They started this, it's time we finish it. And we will do that by cleaning up the mess they have made. My mate, my husband, Deacon, is not your typical bar owner either. Like his people, he was living in the shadows. A place they have been for thousands of years. Nightwalkers are vamps that can only come out at night. They are created. They have no souls. As they get older, they can learn control. At one point in time, they had a task master."

Curtis and Lucas both hissed at what was coming.

"Their creators, their masters, are not like them, not completely anyway. They are born vampires, but they have a soul, they live normal lives. They are stronger, faster, and they can love." She pointed at her pumpkin stomach. "And the biggest thing that sets them apart, they are not hindered by the sun."

She stopped and waited while cameras flashed, and shouting happened. Most of the shouts were from unbelievers. Carrie sighed.

"Can I get the camera to scroll over to the back of the room please?" She disappeared and we saw all the reporters. "Can I get someone to hold their badge up, please? Thank you. Deacon?" The woman standing with red hair, her badge in the air, screeched as it disappeared from her hand. The camera spun back to Carrie, who was now holding it. Deacon kissed her cheek and stood behind her, one hand on her back.

"Again, this is live footage. May I introduce my mate, Deacon." Carrie stepped away, waddling back to Colton. Someone brought a chair out and she sat down gratefully.

"As my mate said, I was a bar owner. I tried to get her to do all the talking but she insisted I suck it up and deal with it. I'd like to blame it all on the hormones, but she's always been a bit bossy." The newsroom chuckled nervously, still on edge from his little show. "In the early 1900s, I got tired of living in caves and ventured into the world. I was bored. I was spoiled and greedy, as my best friend likes to point out regularly. Eventually, I bought a bar and became a functional member of society. When we got word in LA that Curtis, a rebel Vampire, was making Los Angeles his home base, I freaked. Carrie was already pregnant. Which is not easily done for us. I knew my unborn son would be seen as a threat to the world Curtis was building. So, I grabbed her, and we ran. I jumped the old wall, with her on my back, and landed straight into government hands. As luck would have it, my father was in a meeting with President Reynolds at that very moment. It did not go so well. Certain individuals wanted to lock my pregnant mate and I up and use us to control my father. My father," Deacon had to stop and look down for a minute, then cleared his throat. "My father and I never saw eye to eye on things. The day we were chased from our homes, long before I was born mind you, my father became King. I knew he had done the best he could with what he had. I didn't know it at the time, but he wasn't meant to be King in the first place. He inherited the role when his beloved older brother was banished. I'll save you the family drama, let's just say, it wasn't pretty. When the government put a gun on my mate, trying to force us to leave with them, again, *pregnant* mate, we reacted. Again, not so pretty. My father pulled his offer to help. Curtis had my father killed that very night."

The reporters screamed when Deacon's eyes lit up like Christmas lights. Carrie was quickly behind him, a hand on his back. He blinked and looked down at her.

"I told you that you should be the one doing this."

"Suck it up, buttercup."

He huffed and turned back to the microphone. "I told you she's mean. I never wanted the mantle of being a prince. I wanted to live my life. Now, I proudly wear the mantle of King of the Vampire Borns, and I promise my people, our days of hiding are over. My father agreed, we would not go back into our holes. We will take up our posts once again of monitoring the Nightwalkers, and we will bring them to heel. And Curtis, I know you are watching this. I know the truth now. I know who you are. It took some time, but I understand why no one told me. I just don't know why you didn't. I probably would have followed you in my ignorance. I know what happened, and I know how that affected you, but this isn't the answer. I will come for you. And I will put you down for all the wrongs you have committed. For killing your own brother. By your hand or not. I will see you soon, *Uncle*." His lips tipped up in a snarl with that last word.

I hissed. "Yeah, I'd say he knows."

Curtis was tense behind me.

"Why didn't we tell him?" Lucas asked.

"Because Dom begged me not to. He had no one left. He didn't want to risk losing his only son."

"Maybe I will take over now." Carrie laughed nervously. "As I said, we all have bad apples. I know we are throwing a lot of new information at you, and I'm sure by now you have figured out why. We have come to an agreement with the U.S. Government, and we have worked together on a few things. We had a blended squad of magical people and human soldiers who blew up the first wall, allowing hundreds of California citizens to escape. We intervened on a plan to take out the ports in Washington and Oregon a few weeks ago. And, just the other day, blew up part of the wall between Tijuana and San Diego. There was a weakness there that we were able to exploit. I'm told it was very fun. By the same person I am introducing you all too next, and don't worry this is the last magical species coming out into the open. These are my fluffy little friends. To most of the U.S government, he has been known as Captain Andrew Hill of the U.S Army. But to our people, he is Alpha Andrew. Leader of the Grand Lupine wolf pack."

"Hill?" Curtis whispered. "How did you know that name?"

"I don't. I've never heard that name."

"I can smell your fear, Grace. Why?"

"I don't know. Maybe because your voice has that someone is about to die, tone?"

I felt his struggle to take a deep breath and reign it back in.

"Alpha Andrew is a special kind." Carrie rubbed the top of his black hair. "Aren't you, boy?"

Lucas chuckled. Curtis was still trying to decide if someone was going to die.

Hill raised an eyebrow at Carrie and the reporters laughed. "Gah. Fine. You are no fun. So grumpy lately. Explaining him is too hard."

"How about you tell us where his shirt is?" Someone yelled.

Carrie laughed with everyone else. "I've asked him that a few times and I always get the same answer. It's faster without it. And before you ask what *it* is, I'm just going to let him show you. Alpha?"

He rolled his eyes, like he was already put out as he stepped away from everyone.

"Well, Gracey, looks like you finally get to see a shifter shift." Curtis was trying too hard.

Andrew jumped and did a backflip, when he landed, he was on four black paws.

"Th…that's the wolf I saw."

"Which could be where she learned the name. Maybe someone said it in a vision. She doesn't exactly pay attention to the words. And that night, she dreamt about a *lot* of bad stuff. Things that still scare her, besides your big bad voice." Lucas told him.

I could have kissed him, but I'd rather refrain from that with him for as long as possible. I didn't know where that mouth had been.

"Again, I give you, Alpha Andrew Hill. And as this is live TV, he is going to stay in wolf form until we can get him behind the curtain again." Carrie bent down, stopped, spread her legs, then tried again. Colton was there in a blur, picking up the pants.

He bent down to her ear, which wasn't that far from the microphone. "We told you to stop doing that."

She stood back up and stuck her tongue out at him.

"Why are they acting like children?" I needed to sound like I was being critical of them.

"Because they are." Curtis grumped.

"It makes them seem more human. They are playing it up for the humans, trying to show they are no different. It's a good strategy." Lucas pointed out, earning a scowl from Curtis.

"Okay, I think that was all the hard stuff. We are not that different from you. Some sprout fangs and prefer their meat on the bloody side, some sprout fur, and some of us can tell when people are lying to them and what their intent is." Carrie giggled. "Can't wait until these two try to pull fast ones on me. I just have one more thing to say to my *sister* witches. I know the pain you have been through lately. I know your sorrows. I know you feel alone in a room surrounded by people. I *know* why you feel down. Don't give up. Help is coming. We haven't forgotten you." Carrie put a hand to her heart, her eyes bearing through the camera and into my soul.

How did she do that? “Anyway, I am going to hand you back over to President Price to tell you the rest. I’m pooped and hungry.”

Curtis lifted the remote and turned off the tv.

“Why did you do that? Don’t you want to know the rest?” I wanted to see my friends longer and hear them laugh again. I sniffled.

“Why are you crying?” Yay, my softer mate was back.

I huffed out a laugh. “I don’t know. I just am. That was sweet what she said there at the end. I don’t have any sister witches. I only have a bunch of egotistical men.”

Curtis turned to me so he could cradle me in his lap. “I’m sorry, I snapped at you. And soon, I will bring more witches in for you. You can have sisters. You can have women to talk to. If you want, I’m sure Lucas would let you visit Alicia.”

I elbowed him. He chuckled and kissed my head.

Chapter 22

Carrie

"Do you think she got my message? Do you think she was watching?" I paced back and forth in our hotel room in D.C.

"Angel, sit down, please." Deacon left where he was packing our bags and walked to me by the window.

We'd been there for three days, preparing for the announcement. I felt ridiculous doing most of the talking, but the others all agreed that I was supposed to be the one to unite us all. I had rolled my eyes when they said that. They were just using me as a cop out.

"Angel, my love, miracle of my life," I rolled my eyes at him, and he smirked. "I can almost guarantee that she did. Bryant has not spoken to Timothy in weeks. He was devastated to hear that his son turned on him. Curtis' only choice was to watch the broadcast to get information on us. I'm sure she was with him."

I hiccupped and pulled one of my hands back to cover my mouth, tears falling on them. "Did I make it worse for her? Do you think he figured it out?"

Deacon chuckled and pulled me against him, wrapping me in his arms. “No. I don’t. You said nothing that would give it away.”

I nodded into his chest and let him soothe me. “How are you doing? You got a little intense back there.”

Deacon gave a low growl then held me tighter. He’d been doing that frequently to both Colton and me.

“The demon inside me still wants revenge. But I'm better now. If I wasn’t, Colton never would have left with Andrew. He would have left the job to Clint and Steve.”

I sighed and pushed away, wiping my face. “That’s true. I wish there was a way we could know what was going on out there.”

Deacon picked up the remote and turned the hotel tv on, then went back to packing. “I’m willing to bet there is someone somewhere that will catch something.”

It took some work, but I managed to climb on the bed and scoot back to the headrest. These babies were getting ridiculous. They were either in my way or beating the crap out of each other. At least for right now, they were calm. Deacon just shook his head, silently laughing at me.

I threw a pillow at him. “Turn it up, I can’t hear anything.”

“As you wish, my Queen.”

I rolled my eyes at him again but didn’t bother hiding the smile. No point when he would feel it anyway.

For New Years, last week, the three of us laid in bed for two days watching movies. Well, sometimes we watched movies. We knew that would most likely be our last chill weekend for a while.

“I don’t know, Neil. I still think it’s all a bunch of smoke and mirrors.” A man with graying black hair said to a blonde.

"It wasn't, Rick. I was right there, in the same room. When that Deacon guy's eye glowed it was freaky as hell. I was close enough to Stephanie that I felt a gust of wind when he ran by. Those were not stunts."

"Yeah, but that witch Queen was too nice." Rick chuckled. "She reminded me of my wife when she was pregnant with our boys. She always insisted she could do things for herself. You've met both my boys, neither of them were tiny."

Neil laughed. "That's true enough. What they didn't get on camera was her using her powers. That would have been awesome to see, but they are all mental."

"What exactly are her supposed powers?"

"She can tell when people are lying and their intent. It's pretty crazy but we saw it."

Rick turned his chair to face Neil better. "What do you mean? What happened?"

Neil shook his head, almost in awe. "As they were getting ready to leave, she stopped, turned, and walked right up to this young reporter. Can't remember his name, Allan something, I think, from Fox news. Anyway, she goes right up to him and hugs him. We all froze, wondering if he was one of them or something. He stood stock still, completely confused. After about half a minute, she stepped back, put both hands on his face, and looked straight into his eyes. Then she tells him that she sees him. He is not alone, and people *will* miss him if he does it. She told him not to give up. Then she kicked him in the nuts and told him to man up."
Rick grimaced, and Neil chuckled. "That could have been staged though."

Neil waved him off. "Nah. The woman next to him sat down and just held him crying. Word is, she took him to a psych hospital after that. This wouldn't have been his first attempt at his own life."

Rick looked like he wasn't sure he should believe him. Part of him wanted to, part of him was afraid too. He opened his mouth to say something else but was cut off when someone spoke into his earpiece. His hand went up and he held it tighter, catching every word.

He cursed, very audibly. Neil's eyes widened.

"Rick," he hissed, "you can't say that on live television."

"Our email is being flooded with videos right now. Large wolves are being spotted in various cities all over the country. Beside them, are a variety of men and women." A small black screen appeared above his left shoulder and got bigger. "This one here was taken by a convenience store clerk in Billings, Montana."

The screen got larger and shaky video footage took over the screen. Walking down the street were two tan wolves, a tall man, a stocky man, and a woman with dark green hair braided down her back. They spread out to take up the whole street. The phone camera shifted to a rugged and somewhat scary looking dude inside the store. Another clerk stood not far from him.

"You all right, sir?" A thick accent I couldn't place asked.

The man looked at him with bright eyes, hissed, then ran out the back. The clerk didn't even hesitate, he ran out the front, waving his arms.

"One was just in here!" He pointed at his store frantically. "He ran out the back when he saw you coming."

The wolves and the tall man took off running, the man was a blur and gone. The other two followed, quite a bit slower. The camera jerked and jumped as the person with the phone followed.

I got a little queasy watching it.

By the time they rounded the corner, the Nightwalker was surrounded. The wolves were biting at his heels, the tall man - most likely one of our Vampire Borns - was taunting him.

"Alex always did like to play with his food." Deacon chuckled, sitting on the edge of the bed.

"Look, I ain't part of all that. I'm just trying to survive here, alright? I don't want no trouble from no one." The Nightwalker tried to reason.

"You smell of fresh blood." Alex spat on the ground.

"Donor, swear. There is a bar in town that has a bunch of 'em. Ask 'em, I paid. I always pay. And I only take what I need. Please."

"If we let you live, you will have to follow the rules, you have to live behind the wall."

"Sure, yeah, no problem. As long as I don't have to be in no army and hunting humans. I like humans. I just didn't want to die. The cancer was kicking my butt. I couldn't leave my family to fend for themselves."

Alex nodded and relaxed his stance. "How old are you?"

"It's been 50 years since I got turned. I watch my grandkids from a distance now. Drop money off when I can."

Alex nodded at the woman. She walked up to the Nightwalker.

"I'm going to put you to sleep. When you wake up, you will be with your own people behind the wall. No more running. No more hiding. And you can still send money to your family."

The Nightwalker sighed, like a weight had been lifted off his shoulders. The woman lifted a hand to his forehead, then he collapsed.

The screen shrank and moved to the corner again, bringing the two reporters back on screen. The video was still playing as Alex picked up the Nightwalker and threw him over his shoulder.

“Are we sure that wasn’t staged?” Rick asked, still refusing to believe.

Neil huffed. “No way. With how hard that big guy put him on his shoulder, he should have had some type of reflexive response. No way he was faking that. Tell you what though, when my Johnny was teething, we could have used that power.” They both laughed. “Don’t think I slept that entire year.”

“Well, for those of you at home, thinking the supernaturals are taking them all over the wall, you better think again. Videos are not only being sent to us, but they are already lighting up on Tik Tok and YouTube. The Producers here and KNYZ have been following them, and they found one here, in our own backyard.”

The screen appeared again and this time we got a close up of Colton and Andrew. Deacon moved the suitcase to the floor and crawled up next to me.

“If you watched the Live broadcast from the President and our new allies, just hours ago, you might recognize these two. The black wolf transformed right in front of reporters and cameras. The man next to him is the one who told the Queen Witch to stop trying to bend over.” Both men laughed. “Didn’t sound like it was the first time either. They promised to help clean up the streets before hiding behind their new wall, and they are proving that point right now.”

The screen grew and someone pushed play. A couple kids were on the screen now, running down the street.

“Dude, like, you're the guys from the news, right?” One with unruly curls of bronze on his head asked excitedly.

"Yes, you need to go inside. There is a group of Nightwalkers hiding out in that abandoned building." Colton told them, in his usual brusque attitude. Well, his usual *public* attitude.

"You two are taking them out? Just the two of you?" His bald-headed friend asked in awe.

"Yes, now please, for your own safety, go inside."

The first kid hit his friend, who was staring at Andrew with an open jaw, and pointed to the side with his head. They followed from a distance, not realizing both the men could smell and hear them back there.

They pulled back more but were still close enough for the camera to pick up their talking. Well, Colton's talking.

"What makes you think you get to call the shots?" Colton asked with a smirk. He was quiet for a second, then threw his head back in silent laughter. "You're never going to let that go, are you? Fine. I'll let you go in first this time. Save me a couple of them, please. You're not the only one who has steam to burn off… Jealous?" Colton's smile fell and he put a hand on the wolf now, giving him the lead. "Sorry, my friend. The time will come. And when it does, we will help you save her. Now, let's give them a real show."

Colton turned and winked at the camera, proving the kids weren't at all slick.

Andrew took off to one side. I counted to 10 and the snarling and screaming started. Soon, two Nightwalkers came running out the side. Colton sank into the shadows and waited. They knew he was there – probably smelling him - and slowed down, looking around. His back was to the camera, so we had a great view of him pulling two silver daggers from the back of his bullet proof vest. With speed only known to his kind, he jumped on the top of the dumpster he was behind, twisted in the air and landed right behind them.

The two turned in shock, he gave them a greeting head tip, then shoved a dagger in each of their chests. They gasped for a few seconds before slowly sliding to the ground, landing on their knees, out of the range of the camera. The kids ran forward and watched silently as Colton kicked the Nightwalkers over. He stared at them, watching their skin pale until they were nearly translucent. Then he ripped his daggers back out.

Colton cleaned the daggers off on their stomachs, spun them in his fingers, and slid them behind his back once again.

"Show off." Deacon chuckled. Repeating the line Colton always used when Andrew flips and shifts. I elbowed him to shut up. His chuckled deepened and his hand slid to my thigh. "You like seeing him fight."

No denying that.

"And you didn't? That was hot and you know it." He was already distracted, pushing my hair off my shoulder. and kissing my neck.

I did my best to ignore him while I watched Colton. He stalked closer to the building, then suddenly took off running, as though he was responding to a call. The kids cursed and chased after him. By the time they got to a broken window of the abandoned store, Colton was standing next to a human version of Andrew, a table blocking the fact that he was naked. Not far from him, but out of shot from the camera, was a booted foot on the ground.

On the table though was a girl, maybe sixteen, tied down, and sobbing uncontrollably.

"Hey. It's okay. We are going to get you out of here." Andrew told her softly, putting a hand to her forehead. "Deep breaths, the bad vamps are gone."

"Y…you…w…were…"

Andrew chuckled. "I am a wolf shifter, yes. But I will not harm you. Not all magical creatures are bad. Just like not all humans are bad. My friend and I are going to untie you now, and he is going to carry you out of here." Andrew carefully searched her body, most of her clothes were torn. "I don't see any bite marks, but they can cover those. Did they drink from you or do anything else to you?"

She shook her head. "I was leaving band practice late. They came out of nowhere. They had barely tied me down when someone said they smelled a mutt. Was that you?"

Andrew chuckled and nodded to Colton. Together they started untying her. "What's your name, sweetheart."

"Roxi."

"Nice to meet you, Roxi. My name is Captain Andrew Hill with the United States Army. This is my friend General Colton of the Royal Born Army."

She sat up and rubbed her wrists. Colton started working on her legs, being as gentle as he could.

"How are you a soldier and a wolf? The Army didn't care?"

He shrugged. "I didn't exactly tell them at the time. They know now, though. Witches, shifters, and even Vampires have been around for a long time. But we feared people wouldn't accept us for who we are. Humans don't exactly have a great history with being tolerant with those who are different. Magical creatures don't care as much. Take Colton here. He was born a vampire, over a thousand years ago. Now me, I'm only 29. And Nightwalkers - vamps that are created – the ones that brought you here, they have killed a lot of my family over the years. But Colton is still one of my best friends. And he killed the ones that tried to get away tonight. So, you see, Roxi. Before the Nightwalkers decided to be stupid and act out, we had to hide for our own safety. Now, what do you say, we get you out of here?"

Roxi nodded her head, still confused. She didn't know Hill was talking to more than just her right then.

"Good. There are two gentlemen outside with a phone that seems to be working pretty well, as long as they didn't kill their battery trying to film all of this. They are going to call 911, and have an ambulance check you out to make sure you are okay. Got it?"

She nodded, then her eyes widened, finally seeing why he wasn't walking around the table. He just laughed and blushed a little.

"Hazards of the life. Can't exactly carry clothes in my teeth when I am fighting bad guys." He winked, then shifted, without the flourish this time.

The kids holding the camera cheered him on like he scored a touchdown.

"Mind if I pick you up? Or would you rather me not touch you since I am a Vampire?"

"You're not going to bite me are you?"

Colton chuckled. "No, my wife would cut my balls off, while I was awake, if I did."

She laughed as she nodded, and he picked her up. "You're married?" He walked slowly to a broken window, closest to the camera kids.

"Yes, ma'am. To the most beautiful witch out there. She's expecting our first sons anytime now."

"So, you're like, not that different from humans then."

He shook his head, a small smile on his lips.

"Why the blood?"

"Well, for my people, the born ones, it's kind of like taking Vitamins. Our bodies produce all the same chemicals, but at a much slower rate. The Nightwalkers, the humans who chose to be turned, and yes it was a choice, no one can be turned without participating, their bodies are more than half dead. Their blood holds very little ability to create the chemicals. They need the blood to survive. Most are good with paying a donor, but some enjoy the thrill of the hunt. Fear tastes very sour in the blood, but everyone has their own preferred tastes. Unfortunately, when Vampires hunt, they have to give in to their instincts. The human rarely survives then."

He leaned down and stepped through the window. Andrew followed right after. "Having to hide meant they had to hunt more often than not. Donors have always been available, but only because a few knew about us. That is all changing though. There are many people in California that chose to become donors because it kept the Nightwalkers from hunting. Yes, they get paid, but they are also protecting their families and their friends. Now, these two gentlemen are going to make sure you get taken care of. I am pretty good at reading people, so I trust them to take care of you."

He set her back on her feet, but instead of letting go, she jumped up and hugged him, then kissed his cheek. She was blushing profusely, and it was cute. When she saw Andrew, she hesitantly stepped forward. He yipped and stuck his tongue out like he was panting. She giggled and scratched behind his ear. The growly laugh was hilarious.

"Thank you both." She told them. They nodded once, then took off running.

The kids kept the camera on them for a few seconds longer, then shut it off as they, hopefully, called for help.

"What do you think now, Rick?" Neil asked haughtily, as the video screen disappeared.

Rick seemed a little pale. "I want to say it's still a bunch of BS, but that is getting harder to do. We have reports coming in from all over. Police are being called to similar scenes, just to clean up. In most cases, the supernaturals are long gone. In a few, they aren't. One man in Wichita was walking his dog when he was attacked. He said the perp came up from behind him. Before he knew what was going on, someone was biting his neck. Next thing he knew, the perp was dead on the ground. He said the weirdest part was the man who saved him. He licked his neck, and the wounds disappeared. Guess we know now how the vampires were able to stay hidden for so long."

"Hey!" I shouted when the screen turned off suddenly.

Deacon set the remote back down. "Now you know he is fine. He is cleaning up the streets. And now you are going to focus on me."

I squealed in delight as my greedy, and impatient mate's teeth sank into my neck.

Chapter 23

Carrie

Colton woke us up when he came back a few hours later, the adrenaline still pumping through him. The next morning, we met Clarise, Andrew, and our guards downstairs for breakfast. A few people were gawking at us, but no one dared come up. At least not until we were leaving.

“Are you really a witch?” A little girl with blonde pigtails asked, stepping right in front of me, her little hands on her hips.

I knelt down on her level to answer, I may have had a little help getting down there. “I sure am. And I used to teach kids your age too. Now, I have to babysit the big ones that never grew up.” I threw a thumb over my shoulder to my two mates.

She giggled and then stopped herself. “Can you prove you're a witch?”

I tapped my chin, realizing just how much I missed teaching the little tikes. They were so innocent and loveable.

"Hmm, maybe. Do you know what a lie is?" She nodded emphatically. "Alright, then tell me two truths and lie. I will tell you which one is a lie. But make it good. Make it sound like the truth."

She tipped her head side to side, tapping her chin like I did. I felt a wave of nervous intent, wavering on whether they should come grab her or not. I looked up and saw a lady with the same nose and eyes, but with brown hair. I smiled at her and nodded my head. Her intent shifted to letting her daughter learn something new, and herself with her.

"Got it. My name is Tabatha. I am seven years old. And I hate Math."

"Hmm. I see what you did there. First, what's your real name?"

She giggled again. "Sammy. My best friend's name is Tabatha."

"Well, I think both are very pretty names. And how old are you for real?"

"Wow. You're really good. Today is my eighth birthday."

"You are such a big girl. And don't worry, I never liked math much either. I prefer to read."

"Me too! What's your name?"

"Carrie."

"That's a pretty name, too. Can he really run that fast?" She looked up at Deacon.

He chuckled, the wind blew my hair, and then he was handing me a handful of strawberries. The hotel cafe was on the other side of the hotel. Our growing audience started mumbling to each other.

Sammy pointed at Andrew next. "Does he really turn into a wolf?"

I nodded and sighed. "He does, but it tears his clothes. So first he would have to take them off." I made a stink face. "Nobody needs to see that."

She nodded like that was a logical conclusion, thankfully. Then she pointed at Clarise. "What does she do?"

I straightened my back and pointed at my belly. "See this big sucker, here?" Sammy nodded. "I got two babies in there that like to fight already. They drive me nuts!" I leaned down and pretended to whisper in her ear, looking up at Deacon and winked. "They must take after their daddy."

Sammy giggled.

"Clarise is *my* best friend, and my own personal doctor. Her power is so cool, she can make people feel calm. She is a healer to my people. She can sense my babies when she touches my belly. She can even calm them down if they are beating me up from the inside. Wanna see?"

Sammy looked at her confused, not quite sure how she would. Suddenly, the room filled with a soothing feeling, like everyone had just been wrapped up in a warm blanket.

"Do you feel that?" I asked.

"Yeah, it feels like when I am sick, and my mommy holds me until I fall asleep." She said in awe. A few people around the room had to wipe a tear.

"That's why she is my healer. She helps us be calm so she can help fix us." My knees were starting to hurt, so I lifted both arms up and my mates stepped forward again to lift me up the rest of the way. "We need to catch our plane. But it was really nice to meet you, Sammy. Thank you for being brave enough to talk to me. Sometimes, when people are afraid, they get mean. Remember, it's always better to be nice, and get information about someone, before you decide they are bad people." I winked at her. "Good luck with math. And happy birthday."

She waved, "Bye, Carrie!"

Her mom stepped up and pulled her daughter to the side so we could all pass. The others did too, watching us carefully. A few phones were still out, recording us.

No one spoke again until we loaded into our rented SUVs.

"Well done, sweetheart." Colton kissed my cheek. "Very subtle."

"I miss teaching. Kids are so much easier than adults." I sighed and laid my head on his shoulder.

"You can. Once we get settled into California, you can teach anyone you want, angel." Deacon kissed my hand softly.

"Hate to change the subject, but what's next?" Andrew asked from the front seat, next to Clint.

"I don't know. For now, just keep cleaning up the streets, I guess." Colton told him. "The Tijuana gate has not been fixed, but it's not exactly accessible for large groups to go through."

"I'm done with all this. Pick a place. Tell Gracey to fake a vision. He will come for us. It'll be a trap of course, but we can end this once and for all." I griped.

"Not a bad plan. Will he bring her with him?" Andrew asked, hopefully.

"No. He will leave her protected in his house. Just as Carrie will be protected in ours." Deacon stated firmly.

"Like hell I will." I spun on him.

"You are not going to war. You can barely hold yourself up as it is."

"I am not saying I will fight, but I can't stand the idea of you both fighting in some place, far away from me. Besides, I need your blood every day."

"Let's do it on my compound. She can be in a cabin off to the side, with guards." Andrew broke in.

I stared into Deacon's eyes silently daring him to not agree to that. He clicked his tongue and kissed my head. "Fine."

We loaded onto our chartered plane and flew home to Colorado. We were only a few hours from Andrew's pack lands, so he planned to run from there. I insisted he stay for dinner first.

The moment we walked in, Colton and Deacon froze. Everyone else looked around trying to figure out the problem. My mates were wary, but I didn't know why.

"Kenny!" Clint shouted, dropping the bags on the floor, and walking quickly to a young man who reminded me of Emmett from *Twilight*.

"Hey, dad. Long time no see." He embraced his father happily but was shooting worried looks at my mates. Something was wrong.

Clint released him, then grabbed his head to kiss the top of it. "How are you? When did you get in?"

"I'm good. I got here yesterday, just in time to catch the news."

Clint finally caught on to the fact that not all was well. "What's wrong?"

Colton cleared his throat. "Let's take this in the other room."

"I got the bags." Carter said, sauntering into the room. "Welcome home." He kissed my cheek and bowed slightly to Deacon.

Being out of Curtis' influence had helped him to mature a bit. He was still a tad cocky at times though. I was starting to see why the Nightwalkers needed the influence of their overlords. I hoped the others would react the same as well.

"Thank you, Carter. How are the kids?"

"They're all fine. They are downstairs playing video games."

I nodded and followed my mates, Clint, and Andrew. As soon as the door was closed, Clint started in.

"Someone want to tell me what's going on?"

"On our way to Vegas, after rescuing Deacon and Carrie, you mentioned Kenny. Before that, I had a plan in mind, but couldn't think of someone who would fit the bill for it. Then you mentioned your son, who still hung out on the beach. I realized he was who I needed. A vampire who was already out of the regular social circles within the clan. Someone who has been trying to live as a human. Someone who could easily slip in and convince Curtis that he wasn't happy with things here." Colton explained carefully.

Clint sighed and sat down. "You sent my only son to spy on Curtis."

"Sort of. Curtis wasn't his only target." Colton glanced at me, then Andrew. "I also sent him in as backup for Grace. I was hoping he could get close enough to keep an eye on her. At least find out where she was being held."

"I told Curtis I wasn't happy with my life. He was wary but gave me a chance to start over. He said I could change my name, change my looks, change everything I thought was holding me back. I gave him the name I have been surfing under for the last decade. Ryder."

"Because we weren't sure how careful Curtis was, he agreed to go with no options for contacting us." Deacon added.

"It was a good thing too. Curtis is very careful. He had me search Grace's things the moment they left to go finish the wall. I found her cell phone, but I kept it hidden where she left it. I told Curtis she was clean. Over time, I met the others. He has, at least, half a dozen Vampire Borns on his side. Mark, Timothy, Kyle, Randal, Ethan, and myself. Mark is in charge of the Southern Region. Timothy has the Northern. The rest of us have been running ops for him, always on the move. Man, I don't know how you guys found out about Seattle, but I was freaking. I was never alone, I didn't know where you all were, and I did *not* want to kill a bunch of shifters and humans."

"It was Grace. She freed my shifters and sent the message." Andrew folded his fingers together into a fist and moved them like he was popping them. Seattle was still a touchy subject for him.

"Yeah, she is something else, let me tell ya."

I lurched forward. "Have you seen her?"

Kenny nodded. "Yes. I went shopping with her, Curtis, and Mark. Maybe a week or so before you blew the wall. They had plans to go to Mexico after that. Grace had never been out of the country. Curtis panders to her. She isn't really comfortable with it, like she isn't used to it. I heard him talking in the beginning, when she first showed up. That was his plan to get her on his side. Give her the attention and affection she's never known."

Andrew jumped out of his chair and started pacing. Kenny watched him carefully as he continued.

"By the time I got back from Seattle, things were different. Curtis was different. Now he does it more out of love than necessity. It's tearing her up. I doubt the pregnancy hormones are helping much either."

My breath caught. "How is she? Has she been sick?"

"She's okay, I guess. The hormones hit her really hard. Like *way* hard. When they get strong, she gets fevers. Curtis mentioned it to Mark once. She can't be alone for long either. If she doesn't feel someone near, her dreams get wicked bad, and she is majorly uncomfortable. I had to take Curtis to check out the feeding centers in San Diego one night. He had to sneak out of the bed and Mark had to sneak in."

Andrew growled and pushed one of the rolling chairs across the room.

"You might want to be careful about some of the things you say, right now." Colton told him softly. "We believe Grace is Alpha Andrew's fated mate. He is her contact. They message on and off. He is not handling some of this very well."

Kenny cursed under his breath. "Grace is holding up. Her baby develops quickly. Like wicked fast. We had to take her shopping for maternity clothes, and she was only a few weeks along. She doesn't take crap from anybody. Even Curtis walks on eggshells half the time. I heard she has tamed Lucas too. At least around her."

"This is why no one could do this but Grace. If Curtis' fated mate was who I think it is, they look a whole hell of a lot alike. I'm willing to bet Curtis is reliving the past with her." Andrew met my eyes as I spoke. "Which means he will protect her as such. She will not be harmed. She will be cared for."

"Kenny. Why are you here now?" Colton asked. "What went wrong?"

Kenny licked his lips and leaned forward. "Curtis was not happy about Seattle. I explained what happened. I told him my plan. I told him no one showed up at the safe house, where we were to meet after. That wasn't true. One vamp did. He told me how he killed a human and bit a shifter before running for it." Kenny looked at Andrew, who was staring daggers at him. "I killed him." Andrew relaxed a smidge, then started pacing again. "I spun his story as my own. Curtis wasn't completely convinced. Timothy had told them you all had a spy in the house. A few days later, every member of his harem was killed. Curtis is on a spy hunt. Then the wall blew. The only people that knew the place of that door was him, Lucas, the six of us Vampire Borns… and Grace. You blew it just days after he showed it to her. It was only a matter of time before his eyes were opened. I snuck out the hole the first chance I got. With me missing, and my failure in Seattle, they will believe it was me. I figured this would be the best way I could protect her."

"Thank you." Andrew croaked out. "If they had figured out it was her, she would have been chained down until the baby was born, and then kept as a breeder."

Kenny nodded sadly. "This will only buy her a little more time. Her visions are becoming stronger. Too strong if you ask me. I overheard Mark and Curtis talking about them one night. She feels in real life what happens in the vision. I guess when she saw the vision of getting pregnant, they debated having Lucas feed her blood, so Curtis wouldn't risk weakening his freezing power. Her vision showed her baby dying. Grace felt the pain and the sorrow. The feeling still haunts her. Her dreams and visions are blending, and she's talking in her sleep. It's only a matter of time before she says something she can't take back or explain away."

"Fine. Then when we lure him out, I will go in and get her."

Colton stood and walked over to Andrew. "I don't think you should go." Andrew shook his head, not planning to let his friend finish. "Andrew, we don't know what you will walk into. Your wolf may not be able to handle it. Then what will happen? You will be putting both of you at risk. Send Morris. He promised he would get her out."

"I know where she is. I know the layout of the property. I can get this Morris guy in and out. And maybe you could somehow place her, so Curtis loses it. If he thinks you took her, he will act in anger, not using logic."

"*She is not bait*!" Andrew's voice took on a double layer, his eyes darkening.

"Woah, woah. Alpha, no one is going to use her as bait." Colton tried to reason with him.

"We have lots of planning to do if we are going to be running two missions at once. Then, as soon as we hear from Grace, we tell her what to do and when. In the meantime, we need to prepare." I pushed to stand up. "Colton, tell our troops to start heading to Grand Lupine. Andrew, call in your pack. Get them ready. I will call my coven leaders and tell them to send whoever they can. We don't know how many people Curtis will bring, so we need to prepare. Oh, and we should probably ask for a human squad or two, at least so they can testify that it is done and over with."

Chapter 24

Grace

I waltzed into Curtis' office, without knocking, and marched right around his desk. I hardly looked at the man standing in front of the desk, not caring in the least bit beyond the fact that I was dying here. Curtis just laughed as I unzipped his pants and straddled him. I sighed as I sank down.

"You alright there, love?" He smirked, amused by my behavior.

"No." I waved at my chest. "Fix it."

"Feel free to continue. As you can see, my mate is extremely pregnant and very needy." He lifted one side of his shirt that I was wearing, again, and dove right in. He had both hands on my back, keeping me right where I needed to be.

"The Mayors in Palmdale and Lancaster have a list of all those needing jobs still, and their qualifications." The man ended with a bit of a whimper, one he was trying to reign in.

I turned my head and laughed, then moaned. “Hello, Ryley. Long time, no see.” I lifted the shirt slowly off my head and threw it on the floor, he whimpered again.

Perfect, it had been too long since I got to torture someone. I grinned and rocked harder into Curtis. He was enjoying this as much as I was.

Ryley licked his lips and rubbed himself through his jeans. “Some of them have qualifications for jobs available in Santa Clarita. They want permission to move them.”

“And why did they come to you with this?” Curtis asked, cleaning up his mess from the first one.

“Ooo, is there any left for me?” Lucas walked into the room and practically skipped around.

“Please.” Curtis said politely, pulling my head down. “It leaves me open for other things.” I smiled as I kissed him.

Ryley shifted and grimaced. “I was there collecting new donors. With the Nightwalkers all through the wall now, we need more. Those cities had not donated yet. I took some of the unemployed ones and brought them here. It inspired the mayors to work harder on finding them jobs.”

“Good. No one will be caught not pulling their weight. That’s where the humans went wrong. Too many people were living off taxpayer money.” Curtis kissed down my neck, making sure Ryley had a view of his hand on my chest the whole time.

Curtis spanked me, Lucas bit me, Ryley had to unzip, and I yelled out. It was a long one too.

Lucas pulled away with a grin, smacking his lips. I reached over and grabbed him. Ryley wasn’t bothering to hide his whimpers anymore.

"Anything else, Private?" Curtis asked him, a smug smirk on his face.

"N… no, sir."

I could feel his eyes watching me and Lucas, who was petting my head and calling me a good kitty.

"How old are you, Private?"

"43 years since I made the change, sir."

Curtis nodded, rubbing a hand down my side. "You are still young. You are still learning control. Lucas here has been by my side for centuries. It takes time to get that control, to earn trust. To earn the ability to keep a pet."

Lucas sighed and stepped away. I licked my lips and Curtis felt my forehead.

"You're still warm."

"I have been for hours."

"Ryley. Come help my Queen. She will show you why it is important to always behave and to never step out of your rank."

Ryley walked over and checked me out hungrily. Curtis lifted me up and motioned for me to get on my knees. I didn't wait. I knew what we both wanted. Ryley on the other hand just stood there, shocked.

Lucas laughed as he went behind him and pushed down his pants. "Come on, go ahead."

Painfully slow, he moved. He got into it eventually, but it wasn't helping me any. If anything, it was making it worse. I could feel the fever climbing again.

Then I heard a slap, a yelp, and a deep chuckle. He got much better after that. The sounds of Lucas spanking him helped me more than that did though.

“Keep working on it, Ryley. You’ll get there.” Lucas laughed. “My Queen?”

“Please.” I gasped out, this was getting ridiculous.

Between him and Curtis, I finally got what I needed, and Ryley got a lesson.

“Tell the mayors I approve. As long as housing is available.” Curtis collapsed into his chair and pulled me onto his lap.

Ryley nodded and practically ran out the door.

“He never would have been able to handle you.”

“Or anybody for that matter.” I laid on his sweaty chest. “It’s getting harder and harder to get that release.”

“I noticed. And that’s the second time today we had to empty you. Didn’t Lucas do it when you woke up.”

I rolled my eyes. “How do you think he woke me?”

Lucas shrugged. “I know how they look when they are too full, and you were tossing and turning in your sleep, trying not to touch them.”

“They wouldn’t keep filling up so much if you two weren’t constantly emptying them.”

“Hey, you are the one who came in here and practically shoved it in my mouth.” Curtis poked my side.

I squirmed. “You started it and now I have to live with it. Are you saying you don’t want to do it anymore?” I turned to face him, my lips hovering right over his. "Should I save that pleasure just for Lucas?"

Curtis kissed me hard and fast. "Don't you dare." He grabbed them both and massaged them roughly. "These belong to me. I only let the others borrow them once in a while." And I was flying. He chuckled. "I think I just found a new trick to the fevers. Lucas?"

"Yes, master."

"Bring your bags of toys to my room, but make sure they are clean first."

Lucas' eyes sparked up. "Can I watch, sire?"

"What do you think, love? Can Lucas watch us?" When I didn't answer they both laughed. "I think she is okay with that."

Lucas ran out of the room and Curtis moved us to the floor. I may have had a bruise or two by the end of it, but my blood was finally cooling. Maybe that was where the fevers came from. The fire in my son's blood was burning me up. He couldn't control it yet, for obvious reasons.

I waited on Curtis' couch reading one of the many books lying around the house. Whoever lived here before had an odd taste. I'd been through their movie collection, which was boringly normal. The books must have been their hidden weird side. I really shouldn't talk though. I was living some of these. Got a few ideas from them too.

Curtis' phone rang, I tried to ignore him. And got that guilty inkling that I should be trying to eavesdrop. That inkling was getting more than a little annoying.

When I heard the window smash into a thousand pieces, I jumped and screamed. Curtis had thrown the lamp out the window. I ran over before he could throw anything else.

"Curtis? Baby? What happened?" I tried to pull him down to look in my eyes, but he was seething too hard and staring over my head with his glowing yellow eyes. "Curtis, please, you're scaring me. What happened?"

Lucas came running in a minute later, searching the room for a threat, his eyes glowing as well. Guess my son wasn't the only one struggling to control that fire.

Lucas looked out the window last, seeing the remaining pieces of the lamp, and blinked his eyes.

"What happened?"

I kept patting Curtis' cheeks, tears rolling down my face. "I don't know." I hiccupped. "He got a call, and then that happened. I wasn't paying attention. I rarely do when you guys are talking about business. Baby, please. Answer me."

I wrapped my arms around his stomach and sobbed. I really hated being pregnant sometimes.

"Baby, I need you. Don't leave me, yet." Okay, so maybe I was channeling some other unresolved issues.

Slowly a pair of anaconda arms wrapped around me, holding me. I sobbed harder, my legs giving out as I crumpled to the floor. We reversed roles. He was now trying to soothe me until I was quiet enough for his words to make sense. After a few of my hiccups, and using a tissue, he spoke.

"Why would I leave you?"

I shrugged. "Everybody does, eventually. Story of my life."

He sighed, frustrated. "When are you ever going to believe that I am here for the long haul?"

I shrugged again but didn't say anything.

"What happened, boss?" Lucas asked like he was tiptoeing through a bed of nails.

"Deacon had teams all over the country last night. Hunting. It was all over the human news and social media. Witches, shifters, and Royals. They cleaned out over a dozen cities of Nightwalkers. And I am sure they will be back at it tonight."

"We have more men on this side, than we do on that side."

"Yes, but most of the ones out there were my good fighters. They were raiding the cities. Deacon is also showing his hand to the clan and to the humans. They will see him as an effective ruler. With the humans handing them *my* kingdom on a silver platter, no one else will be coming to our side."

"What now, then? Do you want me to send more men out? Fight them in the cities?"

Curtis shook his head, then held me tight as he stood up. "No. No more small battles. Now we go for the head of the snake. Take out Deacon, and they won't have a choice but to follow me. I am going to take Grace to lie down. Call my council. Tell them to come. It's time to discuss strategy." He walked to the door and stopped. Without turning, he asked "has anyone heard from Ryder yet?"

"No, my Lord. He seems to have disappeared."

Curtis sighed deeply. "I didn't want to believe it, but it looks like we have our spy. Ingenious, really. Kenny was a lot like Deacon. Both raised after the curse. Both refused to hide. I think I took him on, feeling like I was getting my family back, in a way. Tell me when they are all here, Lucas."

From over Curtis' shoulder, I saw Lucas bowing. Both of us were worried about the deep sadness in Curtis' voice. He took his time on the stairs and walked down the hall. He laid me gently on the bed and moved a familiar looking bag onto the floor.

"Isn't that the bag that had those tools you used to pull my IUD out?"

He pulled my shirt gently over my head, then moved to my skirt. I obediently laid down and let him put the blanket over me. His clothes came next. I held the blanket up for him and he slid in next to me, holding me tight.

"Yes. It's Lucas' bag of toys. It's what he uses to play with his pets." His voice was still lifeless.

I lifted onto my elbow so I could look down on him. "What's wrong? I know losing a lot of men is bad, but what else is it?"

He pulled me back down and turned me so he could hold me from behind, his hands cupping my stomach.

"I think, subconsciously, I had been hoping to find a way to *not* kill Deacon. He is the only family I have left. He reminds me of me, of who I used to be. I think, on some level, I always expected him to join me at some point. I'd like to think I would have let him keep his mate, at least the female. Expanding our clan is a good thing. You and she could have been sisters. You could have raised our babies together. We could have been a family."

"That would have been nice. Why can't we still have that?" My life would be so much easier if it was.

He sighed and buried his face in my neck. "Because he has grown into a leader. His mate will not come to our side. She will not let him. I can see how she will win over the humans. She's already started."

"What's so bad about that? Isn't peace a good thing? Aren't we safer with peace, then with war?"

"You would think so. There would be a honeymoon period. Everyone happy and getting along, but then it would fade. Humans say they are tolerant of those who are different, but in reality, they are not. Look at the Blacks and the Hispanics in America. Even the Native Americans, who were here first. They get the raw end of the deal every time. All immigrants and descendants of them do. If one vampire loses control and bites someone unwilling, the riots will start. And the war begins again. Humans are like Nightwalkers, they need to be controlled, they need to be watched. They cannot be trusted to govern themselves."

I completely disagreed. Which was the only reason I hadn't completely succumbed to him yet. Our differing opinions was my life preserver at times.

"How are you going to find Deacon? Do you know where he is?"

"No. I hate to ask this of you, love. I know how much the visions of war hurt you, how all of them hurt you lately, but I need you to find him for me." He growled softly against my back, frustrated with himself, frustrated at the situation, but I wasn't sure if it wasn't frustration with me too.

He pushed me to my back and hovered over me. I knew what he saw. He saw the tears that matched the fear he smelled. He cursed.

"Forget it. I hate the idea of hurting you. I will find another way. Maybe I can send Timothy. His father has asked him many times to come home. I would send Mark, but you said Colton saw him."

"Are you sure?" I whispered, hoping he would say yes.

"Yes. If at all possible, I want you to avoid looking into the future, at least until this is over. I want to spare you from that pain. After our son is born, we can cut back on the blood, maybe that will help them weaken again."

I opened my mouth to protest that idea, then mentally kicked myself. I needed to break that habit.

He thought it was funny. "Trying to pretend you aren't as addicted to my blood as I am to yours?"

"No." I moped. I leaned up and licked his neck, he shivered. "I guess if you are going to cut me off, I should get it while I can…"

"Is my kitty hungry?"

I didn't know what came over me. I meowed.

I mean, what the hell, Grace? Did you have any dignity left?

He laughed happily and bent over to our side table, where he kept a small pocketknife for just such occasions. I was mostly happy he didn't sound lifeless anymore.

The knife wasn't the only thing he had in his hands.

He dropped most of the items, so that he was only holding the one thing and swayed it over my head. "Wanna play?" I licked my lips, and my heart began racing. "That's what I thought. Now lay there like a good little kitty while I put your collar on."

I even stinking purred when that sucker clipped on me. He twisted his wrist multiple times, wrapping the leash around it.

"Blood first. Finger, or wrist?"

I glanced down, to what was sitting pretty on top of my stomach. He barked out that laugh very loudly.

"I haven't actually done that before. But I'm willing to try it. Under one condition."

He bent to the bag on the floor and unzipped it. When he came back, it looked like he was holding another leash. My eyes widened when I realized what it was. I watched as he slid to my feet and sat down, he very carefully made a one-inch slice on himself, with the knife. He shook and breathed heavily. I enjoyed every minute of it.

I blamed the pregnancy hormones for what happened next.

We were sleeping, upside down, when Lucas came in a few hours later. Curtis had dried blood on him, and my leash wrapped around his wrist.

"Try a new place to feed her from, boss?" Lucas' face was stuck in a weird sort of grimace and intrigue.

Curtis sat up and laughed. "Yes. It was better than I expected. Would you mind?"

"Not at all, boss. Would be my pleasure."

I cackled loudly, happily, when Lucas jumped on the bed. He didn't leave after sealing it either. Curtis ended up falling back onto the bed. I just sat there and watched. Of course, the one time I tried to move Curtis pulled my leash even closer. The second Lucas moved, I grabbed it and took over. He then went behind me.

He planned that. I knew he did. I just didn't care. Lucas loved to be behind me. I heard the snap of the whip on the ground and jumped. He must have found it on the bed. He didn't even need to hit me with it, the sound was enough to bring back the memory of early.

"So much for just watching." I teased Lucas a few minutes later.

He shrugged. "The council is downstairs, my Lord. They made great time."

Curtis pushed himself to stand up, lengthening my leash. He turned and looked down at me. "Your face is flushed again." He sighed. "I think this may be our only son." He grazed a finger down my cheek. "These near constant fevers worry me. They are becoming more frequent. As does the speed in which he grows."

My eyes teared up. I cursed and started wiping them quickly. Curtis sat next to me and carefully removed the collar.

"Are you worried about our son, or sad about not having any more after this?"

I huffed. "I don't really know. I am so tired of crying! I am tired of these stupid emotions always getting the best of me." I growled and crawled off the bed. "And I am tired of always having to freaking pee!"

They were laughing, I couldn't hear it anymore, but I knew, and I flipped them off. Then their mutual arousals hit my nose.

"Not helping!" I shouted as I slammed the toilet room door closed.

Curtis was waiting on the bed for me, my new favorite outfit next to him. I didn't bother apologizing for my outburst. He wouldn't let me say it anyway. I just stood there while he dressed me. He had gotten the hang of twisting the shirt up pretty quickly.

Chapter 25

Grace

"Did you want to come down with me? Or do you want to stay up here? I can have Charles bring you some dinner."

I folded my arms and hissed. They were filling and getting hard again already. Still, I kept my arms there.

"I'm tired of always being in this room. Can't we go outside or something?"

Curtis rubbed my bare belly. "Not with you dressed like this. It is too cold outside."

I sniffled, again. "I need air, Curtis. I'm going crazy being trapped inside all the time. And maybe the cool air will cool me down. Maybe I just need fresh air."

Curtis cupped my chin and kissed my head. "No. And that's final."

I pressed my lips together, fighting back the urge to snap at him. Which made my skin heat up.

“Bottling it up makes it worse. You know that.”

“Yeah, well, it’s not like arguing with a brick wall is going to do me any good either, so just drop it.” I looked into his eyes. “And that’s final.” I mocked him as I turned and started walking out of the bedroom door.

Almost made it too, before a wave of dizziness got me. Curtis cursed, caught me, and carried me back to the bed.

“Curtis.” My voice barely came out. My vision filled with black spots, and I could feel the sweat beginning to brim all over me. “Curtis.” I pleaded.

“Lucas! It’s happening again!” Curtis bellowed through the door I had left open. Half a dozen men came bursting through seconds later, Lucas and Mark in the front.

“What’s going on?” Mark ran around the bed and started mopping sweat off my brow the sheet. “Why is she burning up?”

“This is what happened before. We don’t know why. It’s probably the baby.”

“It is, my Lord. I saw it in the human breeders. The fevers were common. Not all could survive them. How did you bring it down last time?” Timothy asked.

“Blood trade. But she runs fevers on and off all the time. Her hormones go to extreme levels. She was trying to control her need to curse at me a few minutes ago, right before that she was crying. A lot.”

“Mark.” I whispered. I lifted a hand and caressed his face. “So good to see you.” I added a purr at the end.

“Think about the wall, my Lord. She needs to release the hormones. Do the same as you do for the smaller fevers. Let us help. We need our Queen.”

I wasn't paying attention to the rest. Curtis was telling them something about his theory from earlier, something about the bag. I was too busy caressing Mark's very nice chest.

Oh, look, I could see it better now. Hmm, much better.

"Timothy. I need you to go join your father. We need to know where Deacon is."

"I thought you were going to have Grace look, sir." I saw Lucas walk around the foot of the bed - his pants were already long gone.

"No. I will not subject her to that. I do not want her to have any visions for a while."

I heard a whimper then a small chuckle. "Fine. Since you are risking a good deal for us… Love?"

I tore my attention from where Lucas was purposely putting on a show for me and looked at my mate. His eyes were glowing.

I bit my lip and reached for him. "My mate. Hmmm."

His chuckle was only half there as he kissed me. "Timothy needs to go spy for me, so you don't have to have any visions of fighting."

I closed my eyes, feeling someone sliding their hands on my thighs. I purred again. Pretend to be a pet cat long enough and apparently you turn into one.

"He should be rewarded, yes?"

I opened my eyes and looked down at the vamp who looked like Legolas. I hummed and moved my legs for him. While he worked, two people emptied the coconuts on my chest. I flinched when I felt something cold hit both my wrists. Both arms met restrictions when I tried to move them. I looked to the side and saw that I had been cuffed to the bed.

The next thing I was aware of was the extreme need to pee. The problem was that I couldn't reach the edge of the bed. There were naked men everywhere. The grip on my waist tightened and a head popped into my vision, from over my shoulder.

"Hi." I said, somewhat shy.

Mark laughed. "Hi. How are you feeling?" He kissed the side of my head, lingering for a minute, probably checking the fever.

"Fine, except I *really* have to pee."

He winked, slid a hand under the pillow his head and been on and pulled out the whip. He smacked it across the two chests huddled together in my pathway. The sheet over them automatically tented up. I sucked my lip into my mouth and moaned. Mark laughed and did it again. This time, his arm that I had apparently been laying on, slid under the sheets and held me in a different way.

He whacked them again and my back arched against him.

Before I knew what was happening, one of them was on their stomach, the other behind them. The whip now only hitting the one on the back end.

"My mate has a thing for torture." Curtis said, walking back into the room.

"I was actually just trying to get them to move out of her way." Mark laughed, snapping the whip again. The last time was enough to send me over.

"She's full again, my Lord." Lucas fell to his butt, which was bruised now. I hadn't looked at faces, but I still should have known it was him.

"So is my bladder, now move it!" I shouted.

I ended up climbing over the one that passed back out on his stomach. I yelped and jumped when the whip hit my back.

Curtis followed me, insisting on me washing more than just my hands after.

"Did I burn up again, last night?"

"You don't remember?"

"Yes and no. It's a bit hazy. Why didn't you just do the blood trade again?"

He backed me to the wall carefully and lifted me up. My legs habitually wrapped around his waist. "We did. We tried many things. You went through all of us, and it was still high. No more bottling up. If you have to curse and yell at me for no reason, do it. If you have to spend an hour crying and rambling nonsense, do it." He started kissing down my neck. "If you have to break me and a few of my men, do it. I will not risk your life. I can't lose you again." The last part was barely a whisper, but it was enough.

Curtis loved me for who I looked like. Not me for me. And maybe that was what was missing, why my hormones and emotions could not find the outlet or the comfort they needed. I needed more than just physical love and devotion. I needed the real thing. I needed a heart behind it.

For me, not for some dead woman.

By the time we reemerged, the extra bodies were all gone.

"Do you mind if I just rest for a while? I am still very tired." I asked him quietly, despondently.

He could tell something was wrong. "As long as you need. I will send Charles up with food." He lifted my hand and kissed the back of it. "If you need anything, holler. Yes? No bottling?"

"You are the first person I will find. Unless I need to bottle feed Lucas."

He laughed and kissed me softly.

I sat on the bed and waited until he was gone. Then I pulled out the phone.

Me: You look better on tv than you do in my visions. They say the camera adds ten pounds. Was it all muscle on you?

I waited. And then I waited some more. I looked at the time and cursed myself for my stupidity. Not everyone followed vampire hours.

I slid the phone quickly under the pillow when someone opened the door. Lucas was back.

"Uh. hi. What's up? Curtis is already downstairs." I stood up and walked to the closet, holding my towel tight. Please don't let him go near the bed. The phone was on silent, but he might hear a vibration.

"The master told me to come check on you. He fears he said something earlier that he shouldn't have."

I closed my eyes and swallowed. "No. It's fine."

"You look like her. But you are not her. And he knows that. The Master has only loved two women in his life, and oddly, they both look the same. I never met her, but I knew of her. She was rumored to be stubborn, a bit on the impetuous side, but a very loving person. But never in a million years would she have allowed so many men in her bed."

I snarled and spun. "Is that supposed to be a compliment or are you wanting to be locked out next time?"

Lucas didn't seem phased in the slightest. He came closer, not even flinching at the death look he was getting. Not like he used to. Those were the good ole days.

"I am only stating the differences. The pain from losing her scarred him deeply. It changed him. Then he met you. I have seen more of the Master I devoted my life to all those years ago, in the last few months, than I ever have before. They never got to have a life together. He sees his chance in you. He hadn't mentioned her in centuries. Now you are here, and he is telling you who he is. He is entrusting you with it. He *cares* about you. Don't lose faith in him because of one slip of the tongue. He needs you."

I sniffled and turned my face away from him. "He needs her. Not me. I am just a replacement."

Lucas looked at the ceiling, cursing his master out quietly. "He is not who he was back then. Conrad died the night of the curse. Curtis was born the next day. He is not the same man. Not even close. *Conrad* needed her. *Curtis* needs you. You have reawakened his heart. He is like a toddler learning how to walk. Give him time?"

I lifted my hands to wipe my eyes and ended up losing my towel. "See, even towels don't like me anymore."

Lucas laughed and lifted a finger to poke me. "I would be more than happy to walk around all day, acting as your clothes. I think you would find that my hands are quite large enough." He demonstrated. I hissed but still laughed. "Would my Queen like me to help her this morning? You would rest more comfortably."

I laughed and rolled my eyes, shaking my head. "Is this for me or for you?"

He bowed, his eyes sparking as he came back up. "Is it a bad thing to enjoy my job?"

My breath grew labored as he leaned down, one hand on my back to bend me, the other doing what it did best elsewhere.

"They say if you love your work, then you never work a day in your life." He gave me a thumbs up, then put that thumb to some very good use.

He eventually had me off the ground and against the dresser, not the wall. Lucas had no qualms about pushing me into the drawer handles. Me either.

I never thought I would kiss Lucas, but I was really glad I did.

"Always a pleasure to serve you, my Lady."

"Ya huh."

He laughed, spanked me once, then left. Thankfully locking the door behind him this time. It took me a few minutes to wobble back to the bed. I laid down, sliding my arms under the pillow to snuggle it, then froze. The phone was vibrating against my arm.

I cursed, something I had been doing more of lately. I wasn't exactly pure when I got here, but it was safe to say that the vampires corrupted me.

Hill: I am so sorry. I was out hunting with Colton late last night. I overslept. How are you?
Hill: Dang it. I waited too long, didn't I?
Hill: Okay, I'm hoping this phone is hidden really well. I need to say something, and maybe this way is easier. Look, we know you are pregnant. We know about the Queen thing. There were cameras inside the vault. And I must say, you are a vision. The only thing missing is the light in your eyes. Those men around you must really be stupid not to see that your smile is not reaching your soul. I swear, Gracey, I will make sure you always laugh from your soul.

Ryder is Deacon's man. He knew everything would come back to you, so he left to make it look like it was him. He told us a lot, more than I ever wanted to hear. But I am glad that they are taking care of you. But, sweetheart, no one will ever take care of you the way I can. The way I WILL. I will love your son and raise him as though he were my own. As he should have been all along. We danced around this last time. But you are mine. You are meant to be mine. And I will love you and take care of you the way you deserve to be. Just tell me when and I will come get you. We have a plan to trap Curtis and end this mess. We just need you to tell us when. He won't see a trap coming from you. I hate putting you in this position. I fight my wolf every minute of the day to not run in there and get you now. As is, they won't let me when the time comes. Morris will come. We don't trust my wolf to not lose it. He needs you. I need you. We all need you. And not for your ability to birth an heir, or for your ability to see the future. Just for your heart, your spirit. You are part of my soul, Gracey. Come home.

I didn't bottle-up the emotions that time. I let them roll. I closed my eyes, willing the vision to come. I saw him there, pacing in a large living room. It looked homey and comfortable. It looked like him. I saw Morris talking to him. Hill kept looking at the phone, then up at Carrie on the couch, Deacon rubbing her feet. He looked down at his phone again.

Me: I'm sorry I messaged so early. It was my fault not yours. I forget sometimes the rest of the world sleeps when the sun does, not the other way around. Thank you for your words. I can't tell you what they mean to me. Tell Morris hello, and my sister. Kind of makes me want a foot rub too. Oh, and stop pacing in my living room. You'll put a hole in the rug I plan on burying my feet in one day.

Me: I've been told I wasn't supposed to be having any more visions, but I will see what I can do. FYI, Timothy is headed to Bryant. He's been sent to spy. Gotta go.

I turned off the phone and slid it back under the mattress, my head going down at the same time, willing the visions to come. I got something else instead.

I spun in circles, running my hands over the familiar trees. I knew as soon as I stepped through them what I would see. Steadying myself, I pushed through.

“You’ve done well, my child. I’m sorry it has been so rough.” A familiar woman with long black hair sat on the edge of a large pool of water, the green ribbon still tied around her wrist.

“When you said I would have to sacrifice, I thought it meant sacrificing having my family with me. I wasn’t even close.”

“You still aren’t to that part yet. I know it feels like it now, but what will happen next is unavoidable. I’m sorry for that.”

“You’re her, aren’t you? You’re Angela.”

She sighed sadly. “It’s been so long since I heard that name. But yes. I am.”

“Are you dead then?”

Her laugh had a self-deprecating tint to it. “I have wished for death many times, but not once has it come to me. But it will soon. Soon I will be released from my misery.” She stood up and dusted off her light white dress. “Time is of the essence. You have fulfilled your mission. It is time for you to go home. And it is time for me to step in. I have done my best to withhold the vision from you, trying to alleviate some of your pain. I will give you what you need now. I fear giving you everything would change the future. But that is not written. Are you ready?”

I gulped. “Will I feel the sorrow and the pain? They have been so real lately.”

“No, you are getting this second hand, I will act as mediator. Are you ready?” I nodded and she put her hands on my cheeks. “Good luck, my child. I will see you in the flesh soon.”

I opened my mouth to ask what she meant, but she vanished, in her place was a large field with cabins. The biggest one had a porch, one I watched Hill put a hole in. I turned and saw Curtis and his men hunched over and sneaking around. The sun was up, but a storm was getting ready to roll in. At least, that is what it looked like at first. I knew it wouldn't last though.

The fighting would go on for a while, both having many men fighting. Then things would change. So many things were blurry, I couldn't see them. Then it all went away.

My eyes blinked and I looked around mine and Curtis' room. Only 5 minutes had passed. I grabbed my clothes, quickly tying up the shirt and ran out of the room.

They were all in the conference room when I got there, all eyes jumping to me when I ran in. Curtis sprang up, a panicked look on his face. His hands started pressing all over my face, neck, and down my arms.

"What's wrong? Are you alright?"

"I'm fine. I know I wasn't supposed to, but sometimes they just come on their own. I don't know how to stop them." Dang it. My lip started quivering.

Curtis moved in and stopped it with his teeth. That worked.

"Now, slow down, start from the beginning. What did you see?"

"It looked like a large base. That cargo plane you showed me, the one that disappeared, was there. Or one like it anyway. I saw a storm brewing, allowing you to move during the day. Deacon is there. All of them are there."

"Yes!" Lucas shouted, a fist in the air. "That's perfect. They won't expect us during the day. They will be resting."

"Did you see where this base is?" Mark asked from his chair.

I shook my head. “No. There were lots of mountains. There was a sign that said Grand Lupine, but I don’t know where that is.”

All the men looked at each other, grins sliding up on each face.

“They’re staying with the Alpha. Everyone, call your men. Get whoever you can. Tell them there will be an open bar on the shifters. Lucas?” Curtis wrapped me up from the side. “I need you to stay here. I need you to watch Grace.”

“But…” That stupid lip again. “You’re leaving me?”

Curtis quickly picked me up and carried me to the table, setting me down. “No. I am not leaving you. I am protecting you. I will be gone 24 hours, tops.” He lifted a hand and slowly started lifting my shirt. Why did I even bother getting dressed? “And when I get back, with my crown, we will have a proper celebration.”

Hmmm, I loved when his hand did that. His other hand was on my back, which he used to slowly lay me down. He was over me a second later, that hand now on my stomach, while the other moved him in. Each of the others sat around the conference table, their eyes on us, not losing a beat with their phone calls. Every now and then, I would see one stand up and work himself where I could see him, his eyes watching me the entire time.

They were all naked, and the room stank of sweat and arousal, by the time Curtis got off that table. He just left me there like I was a feast. And then, one by one, they each took a turn. I fell asleep on that table, and woke up back in my bed, with a tray of food on the dresser.

Before eating I pulled out the phone. I ignored the message I had missed and quickly sent my own to Hill.

Me: One week from today, a storm will come at midday. It won’t last long. But that’s not what I told them. I am being left behind with Lucas. Good luck.

I turned the phone off and put it away. Mark came in a few minutes later, as I was returning from the bathroom. He met me in the middle of the room with a deep and passionate kiss.

“I noticed you don’t kiss the others. Is it just me and Curtis?”

“It was. At least until this morning. Lucas thought he would take a shot.”

“Hmm.” He kissed me again, pulling me against him, then sighed and let me go. “If I had found you first, I never would have shared you. Ever. I’d let you break my manhood off first.”

I laughed and took his hand, pulling him to the bed with me. “Did you have a reason for coming up?” I sat down and let him crawl over me as I laid down.

“Yes, I wanted to make sure you were comfortable and resting well.”

I lifted my arms around his neck and pulled him down to kiss me again. “Does Curtis know you are up here?”

“No, my Lady. The master of the house had to step out for a few minutes. I promised to look out for you.”

I grinned. I loved it when he pretended we were sneaking around. It made it more fun. “We best hurry then, I don’t want you to get caught and in trouble.”

His lips left mine for a split second before he was back, minus the clothes. “At least I would die a happy man.”

Chapter 26

Grace

Curtis' council left two days later, needing time to prepare for war. Mark slipped into my room a few more times, under the pretense of checking on me. Lucas was a little mopey about it. Oddly, I believed Mark meant it when he said he would have kept me.

Things had been intense around the house. No one had heard from Timothy. I was too chicken to check my phone again with the council wandering around, and Mark frequently sneaking in.

Curtis was different when it came to me and Mark. With the others, Curtis was usually around. But Mark, he wasn't. Lucas had his moments, but still, there was something different about it. I didn't have the guts to ask either.

The closer we came to the big day, the worse Curtis got. He was terrified about leaving me, he was worried about the fevers.

"Curtis, baby, calm down, please." He was leaving in a matter of hours, and he was pacing a hole into the floor. Much in the same way I had seen Hill do.

"I should have had Mark stay and taken Lucas with me."

"Huh." Yeah, why didn't you? I'd have been down with that. "Why? Do you not trust Lucas? Is he a better fighter than Mark?"

Curtis rolled his eyes, which moved his whole head. He needed to work on that. He sank to the floor in front of me. I was sitting with my legs crossed and under me, on the foot of the bed. He put his hands on my waist, and I put mine on his face.

"I noticed that when Mark is here, you rarely burn. You were calmer, happier. Does he do something different than me? What is it about him that keeps your blood calm?"

Uh. Hadn't thought about it before. I took my time answering, wanting to give him something. He wouldn't like the truth. Mark was loving when it was just him and I. I felt cherished, not just desired.

Not like a pet.

Not like a replacement.

"Nothing is standing out to me. Baby, I was with you a lot during that time too. Maybe your fears are playing with your imagination?"

He dropped his head to my lap. "Probably." He bit my leg playfully and I laughed.

"I'm going to miss you." I kissed the back of his head.

He lifted up to look at me, then kissed me as he pushed me onto my back. An hour later, Lucas knocked on our open door.

"The men are ready to leave, sir."

I bit down on the bloody thing in my mouth, not quite done yet. Besides, I knew this would be the last time I tasted vampire blood, his blood. Lucas just laughed. He was a little jealous that I couldn't drink his blood now. Curtis at least let him seal him every time. Curtis had found he liked a little pain, so this was our go to method lately.

I kissed him slowly at the front door, Lucas' arm around my back.

"Keep her safe." Curtis commanded, before kissing me one last time. "I love you, Gracey."

"Love you. Be safe. Be quick."

And then he was gone. He was meeting the others at the hidden door in Mojave. That was the only one large enough for a truck to go through. Curtis wanted his soldiers to save their energy for the fight.

Kyle had gone ahead of them, finding an empty warehouse for them to hide out in until the clouds rolled in.

The reality of what was about to happen settled deep into my gut, and I began to slowly crumble. Lucas didn't let me fall, he took me to my room, and just held me. A little before sunrise, I woke up to him being helpful once again. I gripped his hair and rolled to my back, he came with me, invading my private space.

"He will be back soon. Everything will go smoothly. You saw it for yourself." He said, making my back arch.

"When did you learn how to multitask?" He froze and looked down at me. I laughed. "Usually, your mind can't function beyond one thing."

He laughed, catching on. At least he stopped talking until we both finished.

"Shall I get breakfast for my Queen?"

"Yes, thank you. Did you sleep at all last night?"

"Some, but I will be fine."

I sighed. "Lucas. When was the last time you fed from your pet? You've been with Curtis and I almost every day."

He blushed and looked down, scratching the back of his head. "Your fevers scare all of us."

I couldn't help the smile. "Lucas. Go feed and rest. You are no good to me if you are low. Please. I know you hold back with me. Get what you need. I will be fine. Just have Charles send something up."

Lucas bowed, an excited grin on his face as he picked up his bag of toys. "Thank you, my Lady. If you need anything, just holler."

I shook my head as he left and grabbed my phone. I read the missed one first.

Hill: You weirded everyone out. Thank you. I needed a good laugh. Be safe.

I giggled, imagining that in my head. Then moved to his latest one.

Hill: Find a way out of the house around sunrise. If you take too long, he will come in after you. Morris means to get you out safely.
Me: Sorry, I wasn't left alone all week. I will do the best I can. See you soon.

I walked to the closet and put on a full set of clothes for the first time in weeks. I was not meeting Hill for the first time dressed like a pregnant hooker. I grimaced as I pulled a pair of leggings on, and a maternity t-shirt. I had to shake my arms a few times. It just didn't feel right.

I recognized the knock on the door and ran over to let Charles in. I was starving. He looked me up and down and sighed before walking in further. I closed the door without needing his reminder.

“At least eat before you go. I assume you have a plan?”

I grabbed the breakfast sandwich and ran to the window. He was barely noticeable, but he was there. A large brown wolf, hiding in the bushes.

“Yes, and it looks like my ride's here.” I ran back to Charles, shoving the last bite in my mouth, I was going to pay for speed eating later. I kissed him swiftly on the cheek. “Is Lucas in with his pet now?”

He grimaced. “Yes. She was stronger than the others in the beginning, but I do not see her lasting much longer. You must hurry if you are going to go.”

I slipped into my shoes, grateful I was lazy that day we shopped for my fat clothes and was already struggling to see my feet. These were lace less tennis shoes. I tiptoed down the hall and down the stairs, my phone in my pocket. Charles stayed with me just in case I needed help. He said farewell one more time before I ran out the door and down the beach.

Morris’ wolf ran out and ran around me in circles.

“Alright, pup. Let’s go, we are in a time crunch here.”

“Grace! Look out!”

My face paled and I turned in time to see Morris jump between me and Mark. I patted the wolf’s shoulder and stepped around him.

“Mark? I thought you went with Curtis?”

His eyes refused to leave the large wolf, but his hand was stretching out to me. I refused to take it.

“I was. Curtis sent me back. For some reason he thinks I am better equipped to keep your fevers down than Lucas. I do too, frankly. They just don’t know what you really need.” I sighed and pulled my arm away again when he tried to grab it. "Grace? Please, this isn't a normal wolf."

I twisted my fingers in front of me and looked down at the ground in shame.

"Grace, what are you doing? Come back inside with me. You will be safe there."

The tears came and he cursed. I wasn't given another choice, he pulled me in and held me to his side, him partially between me and the wolf. The wolf growled.

"I'm not meant for this life, Mark. I'm not meant for Curtis."

"I know. You were meant for me. If sharing you with Curtis is the only way to do that, then I will. He knows it too. Why else would he have sent me back?"

I choked on the hiccup. Everything happened so fast from there. Morris lunged, and Mark went to catch him with his knife. I screamed and jumped between them.

Mark pulled back in time, barely cutting my arm. I stumbled back. Morris yelped and tried to come to me, but Mark dropped his knife and shoved him away. He ripped the bottom of his shirt and wrapped it around my arm.

"Good thing I'm only part witch, huh?" I was trying to use levity as Mark was shaking so bad he had a hard time tying the knot.

"Witches are immune to silver."

"Oh, That's good then."

"Your son is not a witch."

"When you said I would have to sacrifice, I thought it meant sacrificing having my family with me. I wasn't even close."

"You still aren't to that part yet. I know it feels like it now, but what will happen next is unavoidable. I'm sorry for that."

"This is what she meant." I half-whispered; half-moaned.

"Who? Gracey?"

"Angela."

Mark's hand froze on my arm. "You've spoken to Angela? Conrad's Angela?"

"Only in… NO!!!" I pushed out of Mark's arms right as the silver dagger dug into his heart from the back. "No!! Why, Morris? Why? He would have let me leave!"

Morris stood behind a frozen Mark on his knees, his eyes looking at me with betrayal.

"He was not going to let you. He wanted you. You belong with the Alpha."

I sighed and then quickly closed my eyes. "Not what I need to be seeing right now, trust me." It was a good thing it was so cold outside. Only thing keeping me cool.

"Sorry, ma'am." Morris ran to his bush and grabbed a pair of pants. "We need to behead him before he unfreezes."

I stood in front of Mark, not letting Morris get near him. "You will not. Mark has been good to me. I won't let you hurt him. He's most likely the reason this kid hasn't killed me yet."

Morris grumbled under his breath. "Fine, we at least need to go before it wears off."

I turned and knelt in front of Mark. "Why?" He pushed out, barely able to move his lips.

"Angela wanted me to heal Curtis. She's not dead, Mark. I'm sorry. I really am."

"Spy."

My tears fell faster as I confessed, finally. "Yes."

"Gracey!" Morris warned.

I kissed Mark's head one last time. "I'm sorry, Mark. For what it's worth. If my fated mate weren't on the other side of that wall ready to dig his way to me, I would have stayed with you. Not Curtis. You."

With that. Morris swooped me up into his arms and ran. I just cried.

"I know this is hurting you right now, but I promise it will be better soon. He was right though. Your baby is not a witch, and that silver is in your blood. We need to get you to Clarise, the witch healer, as soon as possible."

I would have responded, if not for the black spots running across my vision.

Somewhere in the distance I heard a helicopter engine.

Blacking out was probably for the best. There was no pain and sorrow when you blacked out. Maybe I could finally get that mini vacay.

Chapter 27

Andrew

“They’re here. I can feel them. They are walking onto my land now. Do they not know that an Alpha knows when people trespass?”

Deacon huffed in annoyance. “Doubtful. Are they close enough yet? I’m bored, and Carrie won’t stay asleep much longer.”

“I still don’t know why you drugged your mate with your blood, forcing her into a coma.”

Deacon answered me by pointing at Clarise, who was in the corner with a couple other healer witches.

“It was better than the stress she would be under if she were to be awake during this.” Clarise said, walking over to us.

“I don’t mind.” Colton grinned. “I’ll be the only person she likes for a while.”

Judging by Deacon's frown, he was right. I felt a tingle run up my spine.

"They're moving in. Over a hundred of them."

"No worries. We got the numbers. Shift so you can communicate with your men." Deacon stood up and walked to the front door. Colton behind him, patting his back in support.

I shifted, my breakaway pants falling to the floor in the process.

Clarise whistled.

Deacon stalked out to the top of the porch steps. Colton and I were on his sides.

"Deacon. Long time." Curtis grinned at him.

"*Uncle* Conrad. I'd like to say it is a pleasure, but we both know it isn't."

Curtis gave a dramatic sigh. "We would have made a great team together, Deacon."

Deacon scoffed and stepped further down. On that signal, Vampire Borns stepped out of the cabins surrounding the common area and all the Nightwalkers in it.

"I'm not a murderer like you." Deacon spat on the ground.

Curtis scowled. "I did not murder *anybody*. I would have helped rebuild the kingdom. I would have helped break the curse before it got to this point. The pride of your father and mine got in the way. Don't make the same mistake."

"My only mistake was ever looking up to you as a child. For ever thinking you were anything but a mad man." Deacon pulled the sword from his back. Curtis met him in the air with one of his own.

Now. I called out to my pack. They came out of the same cabins the others had. And soon, all hell broke loose.

Fighting covered my once peaceful compound. Blood began to run, while heads and fur fell to the ground. Far in the distance, I heard the sound of a chopper coming closer.

“What is he doing? They weren’t supposed to come here!” Colton shouted at me, punching a Nightwalker in the nose.

I don’t know, but something doesn’t feel right.

Chapter 28

Angela

I was a giant chicken. That's what I was. If my ancestors weren't already disappointed in me, they would be now.

I hid at the very far end of the woods, entering the pack lands at the exact same time as Conrad. I stayed far enough away that no one would smell me. Which, strategically speaking, was the best choice.

I mean, Carrie's cabin was on this side. Why would I need to walk through a war?

It had nothing to do with being nervous to see the mate who betrayed me.

Technically speaking, I betrayed him too.

Still, the time for restitution was at hand. Finally.

I opened the front door to the lovely little cabin and stepped in. I smiled when I saw who was waiting.

“Clint.” I said calmly, greeting the man lounging in my great niece’s living room.

“Angela?” Clint smiled, rising up warily. Poor man probably thought he was seeing a ghost. “It’s been so long. We heard you had died. Libby was devastated.”

I lifted my right wrist for him to see it. “Carolyn was kind enough to cast a spell on my ribbon. I couldn’t keep feeling him. I needed him to think I was gone like all the other mates. I hated seeing everyone else’s sorrow.”

Clint opened his arms, and I quickly ran and fell into him. He had been such a good man. I was happy to see that hadn’t changed.

“I’m sorry she did not survive the birth of your son.”

He sniffled and cleared his throat as he stepped away from me. “Thank you. Why are you here? Curtis is out there, fighting. He might see you.”

I gave him a small, sad smile. “I know. I designed it this way. It is time he and I finished this. Don’t you think?” I tilted my head to the door behind him. “But I need Carolyn’s great granddaughter to do that.”

“Carolyn’s… you mean Carrie?”

“Yes. She and Grace are the keys to all this. Our family placed the curse and started this fight. It must be our family that puts an end to it.”

Clint shook his head regrettably. “I can’t let her out. And I can’t let you in. I have my orders. Our Queen and her unborn heirs must remain protected.”

I placed a hand on his shoulder. “I know. They will not come to any harm. I promise. I have seen it all.”

"What do you mean, you have seen it? You do not have that power."

I chuckled softly, patting his arm. "I have held many powers over the centuries. Now, time is running out. I need Carrie. And I need her now. Either you open that door, Or I will."

Clint laughed, looking down at me, folding his arms. "And how exactly are you going to do that?"

I sighed and lifted my hand up to his cheek. "As I said, I have held many powers. I kept a few. Like dreamwalking. Say hello to my cousin for me, will you?" I closed my eyes and focused.

I opened them again after I felt him fall from my hand and heard the loud thunk as he hit the ground. Shaking my head, I reached down and grabbed the key from his pocket. Carrie was sitting on the foot of the bed, her eyes watching the door. She was visibly fuming.

"You know they were only doing what is best for you and the babies, right?"

She stood up and dusted her maternity jeans off. "Yes. Doesn't mean I can't be irritated about it though." She stepped over to me and kissed my cheek. "I had a feeling I would be seeing you today. I assume the time has come?"

I grinned proudly. "You have grown into your mantle well. May I?" I pointed to her rounded stomach. She nodded.

I placed a hand on each side of her stomach and hummed a small tune. When I stepped back, Carrie was crying.

"What did you do?"

"I helped them rest, much like your healer does. They will be safe and will allow you to focus on what must be done. I also blessed them."

She wiped her eyes. “What do you need from me?”

“I need you to come to the battle with me. When I say so, you are going to say a spell, and remove this ribbon from my arm. It is the only thing hiding me from Conrad. And then….” I pulled a dagger out of the bag I carried over my shoulder, “I will need you to place this in my chest. I will tell you when.”

Carrie stepped back, pulling her hands into her chest, like she would get burned if she touched it. “I can’t do it. I can’t kill you.”

“You must, child. By killing me, you will be killing Curtis. He is too strong, and too fast. He was once the greatest warrior in the land for a reason. He has had a millennium to get better. If you don’t, he will kill all you hold dear.”

I lifted the dagger higher, she slowly reached out and gingerly took it from me. Holding it to her chest she bowed. “I will do what you have asked, my Queen.”

“No, you hold that title now. Once upon a time it was mine, but I passed it over in the name of love. Respect it better than I did. Now, we must go. Grace is nearly here.”

Carrie grabbed a small shoulder bag of her own and slid the knife in. Together we walked out to the living room. She gasped but did not otherwise move.

“Please tell me you didn’t hurt him.”

I chuckled softly. “No, He is just having the best dream of his long life. He is with his mate, Libby. At least, that’s what it will feel like.” I frowned and looked down at the man I once knew so well. “It may feel like a curse later, I hope not though. He was a dear friend, once upon a time.”

“It will be both, I’m sure. He has missed her greatly. Welp. Let’s get this over with.” I watched as she marched out the door, her blonde hair and the light created the silhouette of a crown on her head.

She reminded me so much of my dear sweet sister. She was deserving of having a name so close to hers. I knew Carrie would change over the course of these few months, growing into her tiara. Tiara*s*, actually. Seeing it was nice though.

Let's just hope seeing her in person would be enough to pause Curtis at the right time.

I pulled Carrie toward the back, insisting we stay behind the cabins a bit longer. When we reached the main one, we waited.

Andrew

Grace. I could smell her, and her blood, as the helicopter lowered.

Everyone in the center scattered to different sides, making room for it to land. The fighting ceased, everyone's eyes on the surprise inside.

Kenny turned off the engine and jumped out before opening the back door, holding it for Morris to climb out. He had Grace in his arms, her head and arms hanging down. My wolf ran to get closer, but Colton stopped me.

"Wait. Not yet."

She's hurt!

"I know."

I growled. I watched as Curtis took off running, just to be blocked by Kenny.

"Boy, you best be moving right now. I will deal with you later." His eyes landed on her arm and reached to grab it, as he pushed his way around Kenny. "What happened?" He hissed.

"She tried to stop your man from stabbing me with a silver dagger. It hit her arm instead. Now move so I can get her to the healer before it kills her son." Morris explained in a flat voice.

"No! I will heal her. She is my mate, give her to me. Please." His voice cracked on the last word, stunning us all.

Morris looked at me.

Do it. If he can heal her, we need to try. As soon as she is better, we will take him out from behind. I made sure to include Colton in that.

He nodded once, understanding, and stalked closer.

Morris carefully, and unhappily, handed her to Curtis, who put his sword back in the scabbard on his back, before falling to the ground with her. He bit into his wrist and placed it on her lips.

"Come on, love. Drink it. Wake up. Please. Please." He kept begging her over and over again.

I held my breath, waiting. She wasn't dead. She couldn't be dead. She was a witch not a vampire. But she would wish for death if her child died.

We waited minutes, hours, it didn't matter, nothing changed. Grace remained unconscious.

Chapter 29

Angela

"Now." I lifted my arm to Carrie. "Take it off, now."

"But shouldn't we wait? Let him heal her first."

"Your sister will live. It is too late for her son. He was not developed enough to fight off the effects of the silver. Now, Carrie."

She nodded and pricked her finger, one small drop landed on the ribbon with a quiet sizzle.

"What's yours is his, what's his is yours. What once was parted is now reunited." She pulled the ribbon off my arm, and I felt a great pain stab my chest. Curtis was in pain, and not from a wound of his own.

Grace did it. She humbled the hidden prince.

I stepped forward, passing one soldier after the other. Carrie stayed by my side.

"Why isn't this working? It should be working! My blood is supposed to heal my mate! It has been for months." He cried, dropping his wrist, and holding her up so his face was in her neck.

"It didn't work, because she is not your mate." A male voice called from the side. He was completely naked and not caring in the slightest. "She's *mine.*" His wolf laced the last word with enough power that all the wolves standing cowered before him.

Conrad snarled at him. "I marked her months ago as mine. How can she be yours?"

"Because fate is the master at screwing with people. You cannot mark more than one, Conrad."

I watched as he sniffed the air in confusion, his head beginning to spin until he turned all the way around. He looked down at the sleeping girl in his arms, then looked at me and Carrie again. A slight snarl came up when he saw Carrie.

"You were dead. She said you were dead." He spat out, looking at Carrie and not me.

"Oh, I didn't say anything. I've never met you before. But would you mind handing my sister over to the Alpha. We have healers waiting nearby, they will fix her up. You know… since you aren't her mate and all."

Conrad stood up part way, ready to pounce, then froze at the mumble coming from his arms.

"Hill."

"Gracey? Wake up." Conrad begged again.

"Hill." She whimpered again.

The Alpha walked all the way up and started taking her out of the shocked and confused vampire's hands.

"Alpha Hill, at your service. I will take my mate from here. Thanks."

"Let them go, Conrad."

His attention came back to me. The Alpha swiped Grace away while Curtis was distracted.

Curtis look back at them as they stepped away from him, then back to me. He was torn on which way to go. On whom he was supposed to be fighting for. The alpha had no such qualms. He took his mate and ran, the way behind him was immediately blocked by both Vampire Borns and wolves.

Curtis turned back to me and slowly came closer. When he was two feet in front of me, he closed his eyes and sniffed deeply. Then dropped to his knees.

"She said you were dead." He turned his face up to me, his eyes shining from tears, but not fire.

"No, she said she lost her sister. I was only dead inside. I had her bind my soul with the very ribbon we used to bind our souls to each other. It kept you from feeling me. And me from feeling you. I knew that as time went on, I would feel the evil that had entered your heart. I was lost to my own anguish and guilt. I should have punished you instead of all the others. I wanted you to suffer. I wanted them all to suffer the way I did. Most of you were not worthy of your witch mates."

I looked up to Deacon and Colton, walking over to be near theirs.

"At least that lesson was learned." I looked down to the man kneeling before me.

"I did betray you though. I thought I could solve the problem on my own, but instead I made it worse. And I betrayed your memory further when I fell in love with Grace."

Feeling his sorrow, his guilt, they both erased so much of my past hurts. I dropped to my knees in front of him and held his face in my hands.

“No, you didn’t. I sent Grace to you. I told her about the waterfall and what to do. She loved the softer part of you, but her mate has been here, waiting for her to come home. It was cruel of me to keep her from that. But it was needed. You, my prince, needed to humble yourself to a witch mate. Fate brought us full circle. Our time is done, my love. We have poisoned this world long enough.”

I closed my eyes and leaned my forehead against his.

Carrie pulled the dagger out of her bag and raised her arm behind me. But she wasn’t fast enough. Conrad saw her out of the corner of his eyes, yanked the sword off his back, and stood up swinging.

“No!”

At the same moment the sword hit flesh, a dagger went through my stomach. I looked up, blinking, into the glowing eyes of Deacon.

“I’m sorry. There was no other way.” I whispered my plea to him, begging for him to understand why this had to happen. To understand why Grace wasn’t the only one who was going to be mourning this day.

Chapter 30

Carrie

That was the sign, putting their heads together was the sign. As fast as I could, I pulled the dagger out of my purse and raised my arm. I was shaking so bad, I worried that I would drop it.

I saw Conrad jump up and yell. Next thing I knew, I was on the ground.

I looked at the body at my feet and screamed. I should have known he would be right there. Right by my side.

I vaguely saw Deacon stab Angela, doing what I failed to do. If I had done it better, faster, this never would have happened.

The bodiless head at my feet attested to that.

I heard another body begin to fall and turned to look for Deacon. He was already at my side, holding me. Together we watched Curtis go from his knees to his side, holding his stomach. His eyes stayed on Angela.

It took effort but she lifted her hand to him, and he took it. A moment later, she slumped next to him on the ground and their eyes closed.

I tore my eyes from them and stared at the open ones of a man who managed to find a way into my heart, despite it already being occupied. My body began racking with sobs, my heart tearing into two, Deacon's right along with mine.

The sun broke through the clouds right then, making us all jump and cover our eyes. Screaming broke out all over the large field. I watched through blurry eyes as Nightwalkers tried to run into cabins and trees, only to be blocked by a large wolf or a Vampire Born.

I looked up and to my right, feeling a soft palm on my cheek. I stared in confusion at the face in front of me.

"Sleep, my sister. Let your mind recover."

A warm blanket wrapped around my heart, getting tighter, until I fell asleep.

Andrew

The moment I grabbed Grace, I ran for the pack house. "Coming through!" I yelled, barging through the open door. "Clarise! She needs your help!" I laid Grace on the couch, wanting her to be comfortable.

The spunky blonde came running over, a male witch called Tyler was on her heels - where he'd been ever since he showed up a week ago. Much to Steve's chagrin.

A true mate trumped all.

"What happened? I thought Morris was taking her to the Rockies." She dropped down and started unwrapping Grace's arm.

"One of the vamps in California put up a fight. She jumped in the way and got cut with a silver dagger. Can you help the baby?"

Clarise dropped the arm, Tyler picked it up and started rubbing a foul-smelling ointment on it.

"The baby is too quiet. I don't even feel a heartbeat. Tyler? Can you jump start it?"

"I don't know, but I can try." They traded places, and Clarise picked up where he left off with rewrapping her arm.

Tyler's power was the opposite of Clarise's. Where she was like Novocain, he was like adrenaline. She could calm a room, and he could cite it up.

Tyler placed both his hands on my mate's stomach and closed his eyes. His face contorted in different ways as he put as much as he could into it. After a few minutes, he dropped to the floor, out of breath.

"I'm sorry. My guess would be that that baby died within minutes of her getting cut."

I dropped my head to hers, crying for the pain that she would undoubtedly feel. "Why isn't she waking up?"

"She has enough vampire blood in her from Curtis that the silver is playing havoc with her system. She will survive it, but the longer it is in there, the higher the chance that it will cause damage." Clarise explained methodically.

"What do we do?"

"Well, we do have to remove the baby anyway, she will bleed and that will help flush her system. Plus, we will have to give her a blood transfusion. Normally, mothers with stillborn babies push them out. It is a very heartbreaking thing to go through. Going through the process of giving birth, only to bury your child. If we do it while she is already out, it might help her cope later."

I nodded. "Where?"

"I can do it all here, or at the hospital. Your choice."

"Here. Please." I sat on the floor and put my arm under her head, cradling her. "I'm so sorry, Gracey."

I vaguely noticed someone running in to grab Clarise, and then both of them running out quickly.

A few minutes later, Morris ran in, searching the room with his eyes.

"I'm here."

His face fell as flat as my voice. He walked around and dropped to his heels beside me. He reached up and grabbed her hand. My wolf didn't have it in him to growl about another man touching her.

"How is she?"

"The baby died within minutes of her getting stabbed. The silver is mixing with Curtis' blood, which could be bad in the long run. They are preparing to remove the baby. We are hoping she will bleed out most of his blood, and they will pump in fresh blood."

Morris' eyes looked haunted. Probably reliving the past.

He had been one of the lucky ones. He met his fated mate when they were teenagers. She got pregnant right out of high school. Neither of them survived.

When they met their mates so young, shifters waited to officially bond until they were legal adults and moved out of their parents' home. Living separately after mating would have been painful. In this case, it had saved his life. Physically anyway.

"She will be okay." I told him. "Thank you for getting her out of there. Did you have to go inside? How did Lucas get to you?"

He shook his head. "She came out to me on the beach. We were getting ready to leave but Curtis had sent one of the Royals on his side back. He and Grace had had some type of connection. He mentioned something about being one of the few that could keep her fevers down. He said it was because they were a better match than her and Curtis. She had agreed. Told him if she didn't know you were over here, she would have picked him. She told me he had been kind to her. He freaked after hitting her and dropped the knife. I waited long enough for him to wrap her arm with a piece of his shirt. Then stabbed him. She wouldn't let me cut off his head though."

That sounded like my girl. All heart, even for the enemy.

"What happened outside? Is it over?" I probably should have stayed with my pack, but my mate came first.

"Yeah. That new chick was Curtis' original mate. She had a spell muffling their bond all these years. Said it was time for it all to end. I think it was planned. Carrie tried to stab her, but Curtis saw it and grabbed his sword. Deacon took out the girl while Colton protected Carrie."

"So, Curtis is gone then?"

Morris opened his mouth, then closed it, his voice shaky. "Yes. But his sword caught Colton. We lost him. Clarise had to knock Carrie out, she was hysterical."

I cleared my throat as the tears fell. I would miss my friend. "Deacon?"

"Barely holding it together. And only for Carrie's sake. He took her back to their cabin. They will need time to process."

"And the Nightwalkers?"

"Grace was right. The clouds didn't last. They broke, and all the Nightwalkers were trapped. Our people blocked all the exits."

I leaned down and kissed my mate on the head. "She's the bravest little witch I've ever known."

"That she is, sir."

I couldn't help the chuckle when I saw the look in his eyes when he looked at my mate.

Ask her, before you ask him. My wolf grumbled. I laughed at him.

Would you be willing to share her, after all of this?

It is not uncommon. And he would protect her, he already has. She will need it, especially after this.

"My wolf says I should ask her first, but I'd rather get your opinion before I do that."

Morris raised an eyebrow at me.

"If my mate is willing, would you be interested in joining us? Obviously, not the same setup the vampires have. Had. I love you, but not like that."

We both shivered and laughed softly. My best friend used his other hand and pushed hair off her face.

"If she is willing, then yes. I'd give it a shot. After Jill died, I never thought I would be able to look at another female the same way again. But there is something about this one. I can't explain the relief I felt when she came running out of that house. Or the fear when she passed out in my arms."

I nodded. I understood the feeling. Although I had yet to look her in the eyes, to hear her voice. At least I could hold her and comfort her with more than my words on a screen now.

Morris and I both stood to the side a little later, when Tyler came to pick her up and carry her to the room they set up to use. I finally looked around at the makeshift hospital that my living room became. Nearly two dozen witches, shifters, and humans were lying around on various surfaces and on the floor, with patches and gauze on them in different places. Some were sleeping, some were laughing. The tension of an upcoming battle, of a war being fought was gone for them. For them, it was over.

I stepped outside and saw a mix of the various species collecting burned and chopped off parts. There was a giant fire in the middle, a large pit at the bottom. The Nightwalkers were being unceremoniously dumped there, along with any traitor Royals.

Timothy got lucky that he had been sent home to spy. Otherwise, he would have ended up there too. All of Curtis' little friends, that didn't die in the battle, were being locked up. With silver chains. For now, they would be held somewhere in California.

I walked along the side, toward different piles with blankets over them. Those we lost would be given a proper send-off, depending on their traditions.

I stopped at the one form on a table, off the ground from the others. I stood next to it, knowing I needed to look so it would feel real, but not ready yet.

"How many?"

"Three witches, five humans, two wolves, and… one Royal.

If the helicopter hadn't landed when it did, we may have had more. The healers were able to get to the seriously wounded fast enough to help them."

We had been lucky on many fronts. Over the last week, nearly a dozen healers had shown up with other witches that had fighting powers or talents.

I held my breath, hoping, praying, we were wrong somehow. I pulled the blanket and my head fell, followed by my body. They had laid him respectfully, his head where it belonged.

"He went out the way he would have wanted. Dying to protect us."

I spun and saw Deacon standing nearby, tears still falling down his face unabashedly. I walked over to him and hugged him. I let him cry into me for a minute, letting him be the weaker one for now. When he was ready, he pushed back.

"I'm so sorry, Deac."

Deacon's eyes stayed on his mate, and best friend's, face. "Me too. It doesn't seem right. He's been by my side the majority of the last 400 years. My constant companion. He left once in a while, doing his Royal duties with my father. It wasn't until Carrie awakened our hearts that we saw what was there all along. When we first found out Carrie was pregnant, Grace looked into the future. She cried but wouldn't tell us what the difference between the two were. I think I know now. Part of me wants to know what we could have done differently. The other part knows that regret just makes things worse."

I nodded. "How is Carrie? The babies?"

"She's sleeping, and not by my hand this time. It's the oddest thing though. Clarise said the babies are wrapped in a magical cocoon, protecting them from any outside influences, including Carrie's emotions. She said it will wear off eventually, but for now it is for the best. Otherwise, Carrie would risk early labor. Clint was asleep too. In a heap on my living room floor. Clarise said he was only in a deep sleep, and happy. She told me about Grace. I was coming to find you. Check on you."

I put the blanket back over Colton. Deacon was struggling to move his eyes away from him. His breath caught but he pushed on.

"I'm alright. Clarise and Tyler believe she will be fine. The real work will be when she wakes up and finds out about her son. What happened out there?"

Deacon explained it all to me as we walked back to his cabin. We left him there but took Clint with us. They needed to mourn in peace. Morris carried Clint to the couch Grace had been on. A witch brought a blanket over and laid it on him.

I moved to the hall, across from the room Grace was in, leaned against the wall, and sank to the floor. Morris sat next to me.

"Where is she?" A vampire ran in, a crazed look in his eyes, nearly an hour later.

Morris jumped up, in defense mode, snarling. The man saw him but came over anyway.

"I don't want trouble. I just need to know that she and the baby are okay. I'll never live with myself if I hurt her."

"She is in surgery. The baby is dead. The silver was mixing with Curtis' blood in her body. They are trying to give her a blood transfusion before any permanent damage is done. Your boss is dead, along with half your army. Because you were kind to my mate, I am giving you one shot. Run. If I ever see you again, I will kill you." I didn't even look at him. My eyes were glued to that door, willing it to open already.

"Thank you. If I had known she had a fated mate…"

"Just go. Please."

"Right. Thank you. Take care of her. She honestly has no idea how special she is."

I huffed out an ironic laugh. "I know that better than anyone."

I listened to his footsteps turn and leave. He didn't wait long, he booked it out fast. Just because I gave him a chance didn't mean the others would too.

Chapter 31

Grace

I sat on our back porch, rocking my baby to sleep, a soft smile on my face.

My smile grew when two figures loped out of the woods, shifting from animal to man. They stopped only to pick up the pants they had left on the bottom step. Both walked up the stairs and bent down to kiss me, and then the baby.

"How has our angel been?" Hill asked.

"A demon. That's how. She has cried nearly nonstop since you left this morning."

Morris laughed from beside me, rubbing a hand down my pure black hair. "We had to go, sweetheart. It's part of our agreement with the humans in the town."

"I know that. You know that. But your daughter does not. She wants her fathers when she wants them." I pushed the sleeping tyrant into Hill's arms, they were the closest, and stood up. "Now. Your *angel* kept me up all night again. So, you two are on diaper duty, she has already eaten enough to last a week. I am going to go take a nap. Good luck."

As soon as I closed the door, the crying started again.

I smiled as I opened my eyes. I wondered if they survived. I looked around the room and saw the men in question asleep in chairs by my side. They looked like hell.

I moved to sit up and gave a mix of a hiss and gasp.

Why did my stomach hurt so bad?

"Woah, sweetheart. Take it easy. You don't want to rip out your stitches." Hill grabbed my hand and took it off my lap and helped me lay back down. "Hey, it's nice to finally meet you. I was right to, you are a vision."

I tilted my head, confused. Then it hit me, none of that had been real. But maybe it was a vision.

"Hill?" My voice croaked, making me grimace. That hurt.

He picked up a cup with a straw from the side and handed it to me. Morris sat up and felt my forehead.

"Morris? What happened? How long have I been out?"

"First off, I think it's time you start calling me Andrew. And him Roger. Second, nearly a week. Your body needed to replenish a lot of blood." Hill chuckled, it sounded too forced.

I looked down at my semi flat stomach while taking a long drink before giving him back the water. The water had felt like heaven going down. I laid my head down and gently placed my hands on my stomach. My empty stomach.

"Angela said I would have to make a sacrifice. So many times, I thought I knew what it was. Most of the time I was sure it was my sanity."

They both reached over and grabbed one of my hands. Definitely a vision then.

"Alright, so tell me. How is all this working? Cause I'm not sure I'm up for multiples any time soon." I laughed as they both growled. "Vampire pregnancies are the absolute *worst*."

Andrew blushed. It was adorable. "I know I should have talked to you about this first, hell, talk to you in person about anything first, but it is common for shifters to have more than one mate. Not like the vampires do. Hell, no. He's my friend and only my friend. But we don't have many females in our community."

"What he is trying, and failing, to say" Roger cut in "is that he already asked if I wanted to join you guys, but it's your choice. I lost my fated mate ten years ago. The Army was my out. It kept me alive. For the first time, I feel again, and it's because of you. But no multiples. Just… no."

I laughed. And squeezed their hands. "I'm okay with that. Honestly. I need time to process everything. My power helps. Just before I woke up, I had a vision of the future. It was beautiful. It was perfect. And it was the four of us." I rubbed my empty stomach and choked up. "I may not have fully wanted the father. The pregnancy may have nearly killed me. But I wanted my son."

Andrew quickly climbed on the bed and held me while I cried. Roger kissed my hand and held it in both of his. Both were supporting me in my hour of need.

Carrie

"Come on, Carrie. You can do this. One more push."

“Clarise, if you say one more, one more time, I will kick you in the throat right now!” I screeched.

Deacon sat behind me, trying to hold me up. We had practiced this many times. We just hadn’t practiced for Colton not to be there to keep Deacon from freaking out. He was stepping up though. He was channeling Colton from the other side.

A calm feeling came over the room and I started cursing Clarise out. She laughed it off.

Another contraction hit and I curled up to my legs, screaming loud enough that the wolves a town over howled at the moon. I collapsed back, my breathing heavy, my face covered in sweat, my hair a complete and utter mess from 30 freaking hours in labor.

I was ticked. Grace finally woke up yesterday, but no one would let me go see her. I had refused to leave the compound until I got to see her for myself.

It was a good thing Clarise went everywhere with me. These boys baked in four months, but they were taking their sweet time coming out.

My heart fluttered when I heard the most beautiful sound.

“Gimme, gimme, gimme.” I shouted, raising my arms for my son.

Clarise and Deacon laughed. “Hold on, mama. He needs to get cleaned up. Oh, he is a big boy… and… uh.”

“What? What’s wrong? Is he missing a toe or something?”

Deacon put a hand on my arm to calm me.

“Or something. You two really are an odd couple. First twins, now this.”

“Just tell me already!” I demanded, hitting the bed under me.

"Well, it looks like at least one of your boys is a witch."

"Wait. What?" Deacon asked, completely floored by this. Their line had only ever birthed vampires, no matter the race of the mother.

I used that moment to scream as the next one was ready to come. Apparently it was just the oldest that took his time. My younger son seemed to be in more of a hurry.

I wasn't planning to play favorites, but if I did....

Clarise handed my apparently witch son over to her mate, Tyler, and came back to me. I was passed caring about my best friend seeing my girlie area already.

Ten minutes of screaming later - yeah, no favorites - and we heard that beautiful sound again.

"Alright, mama, you are all done. You have two beautiful... uh..."

"Oh, for Pete's sake. What now?!" I shouted.

Tyler carried over my son and set him in my lap. My anger and fear went away as I looked at the most handsome little man.

Deacon stroked his cheek with one finger. "He's a pure-blooded witch alright. I can smell it."

"How is that possible?"

"Well, you had two powers, which is unheard of. It must have made your eggs split into two. Your babies are fraternal twins. One took all the witch genes, the other took all the vampire ones." Tyler walked back to Clarise to help her clean up my other son.

Considering that he was pure energy inside, Tyler was a laid-back kind of guy. Which kind of fit. Clarise was calming inside, but she was *not* a calm person.

There was a light knock on the door, and it opened a bit. Andrew's head popped through. "You up for visitors yet? I got a very impatient mate who wants to see you."

"Yes, please!" I gleefully shouted at him. He disappeared, only to push through a wheelchair. "Oh, Grace. I would hug you right now, but I'm not sure I'll walk ever again."

Grace laughed. "No worries. So, how are the little guys?"

I watched her carefully, and even felt Deacon getting concerned. I figured we'd get to it later. I held up my baby boy for her to see.

"Apparently this one is all witch. Pure blooded. So, the royal line can continue on with tradition." I stated proudly, kissing his little head.

"What do you think about naming him Colton?" Deacon asked me carefully, like he was afraid I'd say no.

I sniffed, feeling that now familiar ache in my chest. "I think it's perfect."

Clarise walked around the other side of my bed, holding my other baby.

"Is he okay? What made you freeze like that?" I looked at her desperately. I couldn't handle any more bad news right now.

Clarise sniffled and wiped her eyes with her other hand. "Nothing is wrong. Your daughter is absolutely perfect. And one hundred percent vampire."

No one made a sound. Not even baby Colton.

"That's not a funny joke, Clare."

"I'm not laughing, Car. Here."

Deacon picked up Colton and I took the second baby. Carefully, I lifted the small diaper and gasped.

"We have a daughter. A vampire female." Deacon whispered reverently.

"How is that possible?" Grace asked.

I looked over to her and smiled. "Because of you. Angela told Curtis, a prince who had been hiding who he really was, that she sent you there to humble him. *Because of your betrayal, your kingdom will wither and die. Your females are gone, and you will have no more. The curse will be broken when the hidden vampire prince accepts his witch mate and humbles himself to her.* That was the curse. You humbled him, Grace. He chose you over the power. He stopped fighting when he saw you unconscious, he even handed you over to Andrew, so you could get to the healers, when his blood would not work. You sacrificed so much to end the curse on the Royals. Angela was right, they had come full circle."

Deacon gulped down a ball in his throat. "My people owe you a debt of gratitude larger than we realized. The shifters as well, as they had received ripples from the curse."

Grace shook her head. "Don't thank me. You of all people should not be thanking me."

"Why? Gracey, I told you. We love you. None of what you did over there matters to us." What I wouldn't give to get up and hug her. And then slap some sense into her.

She shook her head. "In the vision of the last battle, Colton wouldn't have died. Curtis was set to bring both a dagger and a sword. I insisted on the sword only."

Deacon tensed up behind me, our son giving a small cry, not liking that.

"What would have happened if Colton lived, Grace?" I asked softly.

She sniffed. Andrew dropped to his knees and just held her for a minute.

"Curtis would have reached for the dagger, instead of the sword. He would have gone low, not high. You would have fallen onto the dagger, and one of your babies would not have made it."

I held my miracle daughter to my chest and held back the sobs trying to come out.

"You picked the right future, Grace." Deacon told her gravely. "Colton died to protect his family. Just as he would have wanted it. Given the choice, he would do it again. As would I. You are free to let the guilt go. You made the right choice."

Grace closed her eyes, a weight lifting off her chest.

"Just one more thing. Did you see the twins when you first looked at the future for me? We already know Colton being gone was the difference." I was dying to know.

"Yes, but I didn't know it. The part I saw was right before she handed you your daughter. I assumed that baby was hers."

"That makes sense, a lot of this we weren't expecting. Go, rest. You and I both need a nap, and a long vacation." I smiled, hers was small but it was there. A promise of better times coming.

"Do you mind if I go shout the news to everyone waiting outside?"

I laughed at Deacon. "Go ahead. Bring me back some food, I'm starving.

Deacon

I carried my daughter out of our bedroom a few minutes later and stood in the hall staring at her. She looked just like her mother. I smiled and looked to the sky.

"We have a daughter, Colton." I whispered.

Wiping the small tear, I walked outside. I knew they would all be there. A good portion of my clan. Waiting for news.

"Conrad had once been a prince to our people. He betrayed his mate, who then cursed our people. We all know the story. We can all recite it perfectly. He hid who he was until a witch, who was a descendant of his mate, brought him to his knees."

I licked my lips and gave a small laugh and cry. Off to the corner, I saw Andrew stop the wheelchair. He was close enough for her to hear.

"She sacrificed a lot. She made hard choices. But she made the hidden prince humble himself to a witch mate. I know you are all expecting two baby boys. Baby Colton was too greedy to wait, he's eating." A few of them chuckled. "He is a pure-blooded witch, so I left him with his mother to learn his lesson."

Steve barked out a laugh.

I took a big breath. "It is my honor to introduce you all, to Angela Grace Michaels. The first *female* vampire to be born in a thousand years." My voice cracked.

The clan went silent for two of my daughter's heartbeats, then the cheers went up. Hugs and backs were slapped. Bryant made it to me first. Kissing my daughter's head.

They were all beyond thrilled, taking pictures and beginning to spread the word. If only Colton were here to share this moment with us. It would be perfect.

I kissed her head again, holding her tight. “You ready to go back to mama? Let’s just hope she doesn’t turn me into a toad for naming you without her.”

Epilogue

Deacon

I kissed my mate, and our one-week-old twins, then left the small cabin. Andrew, Clint, and Kenny were already waiting by the chopper for me.

"I'm surprised. I expected you to take at least another ten minutes for your farewell." Clint laughed.

I smirked. "And I might've, but I started to smell something foul and ran. I do *not* do diaper duty." I shivered.

Andrew scoffed. "Liar, just yesterday I saw you volunteer to do it."

I shoved his head to the side as I passed by him. "Let's get this show on the road. We only have an hour until sunset."

Kenny and his father stepped into the pilot seats, while Andrew and I got into the back. As per-usual, he was only wearing a pair of breakaway pants. When the mechanical bird began lifting into the air, he waved goodbye to his mates.

"You two seal that deal yet?"

He shook his head, keeping his eyes on Grace. "No, she isn't ready. She needs time to heal, and my wolf and I are giving it to her. Roger as well."

"I wasn't talking about you and Grace." My hand caught his fist as it flew at half power to my stomach.

"We are not like you. We will each mate with Grace, not each other."

"Ya huh, we'll see about that. Just wait until the witch's binding ceremony. There are some things you just can't fight, nor should you."

"Shifters are different. We aren't focused on self-gratification."

"How does a mating work with shifters? We exchange blood, witches literally bind with a ribbon and a spell, what do you do?"

His wolf growled a laugh and his eyes darkened. "The mates bite at the right moment. We mark the other as ours. Similar to how I marked Morris as my Beta. Only on the neck, instead of the wrist. We do end up with a small bit of blood, but just a touch. Enough to blend our scents and souls. When one mate cannot shift, the biting is only one way. But it still works the same. Grace will one day carry two marks. Mine on the right, as her fated, and Roger's on the left."

"The witch's ceremony will have all three of you bound to each other. And you will share her power, to an extent. Carrie is more sensitive to intent than I am. Colton was too. But I could spot the lies better."

He shrugged. "What will be will be. If it gives her comfort and stability, then so be it. Like now, I would not be able to leave if he wasn't there. She still has nightmares, from the visions of what would have been, from losing her son, from lots of things she won't talk to us about. It is better when she is not alone."

I chuckled. "Not much room when there are three in the bed, is there?"

He gave me a wary look.

"Just because you didn't lie, doesn't mean something wasn't left out. Besides, with a mate in distress, you both would want to comfort her." I laughed some more as he shifted in his seat. I decided to play nice and give him a break. "Have you three decided where you are going to live? Carrie mentioned reserving a cul-de-sac of houses for all of us and the teenagers."

"Grace had a vision of us, she didn't give a timeline, but we will have a daughter of our own. We will still be on my land, working with the town nearby in some way. Maybe one day we will need to go behind the wall, but for now…"

I nodded. "Carrie is thinking of taking the three regions that Curtis divided and giving them to each magical species. The witches in the North, the vampires in the center, and the shifters in the south. The humans will be spread throughout. Everyone will have the freedom to live where they want, but that species will run that region. This way it is equal for all of us."

"Makes sense."

"I agree." Clint said from the front, finally admitting to eavesdropping.

He had been quieter than normal the last two weeks. Which was saying something for the naturally stoic man. He slept for 24 hours and woke up with a grin on his face. It took less than that for him to realize it had all been a dream. He won't talk about what happened, but there were times I saw him smiling into the distance.

Sometime later, Kenny landed us in the backyard of a large house. By the time we all climbed out, we had a greeting party.

“Yeah, kind of figured you’d be coming eventually. I wasn’t sure how much was the ramblings of a man left half dead on a beach, and how much was true. As soon as one of his little witches healed him he took off like a bat out of hell. So, tell me. Was she the spy all along?” Lucas asked. He was leaning against a small brick wall that ran around a pool.

“Yes.” I told him flatly, putting a restraining hand on Andrew’s shoulder.

Lucas sucked on his front teeth with this tongue and nodded. “And Angela really sent her?”

“Yes. She worked through both our mates. Because Grace was able to humble Curtis, the curse is now lifted. Carrie gave birth to a son and a daughter. Our people can move on. We can finally begin to heal.”

Lucas nodded again. He waved a hand to an older gentleman, a human, standing nearby. He stepped forward.

“This is Charles. He runs the house. I had him clean up all the rooms. They are ready if you want to use the house for a base or what not. When Curtis didn’t come back, the few Nightwalkers that came around regularly scattered. Charles can help you with anything you need.”

I lifted an eyebrow and stepped closer. “Are you planning on going somewhere?”

“No.” He looked resigned to his fate. “Just kill me and get it over with.”

I stepped up close enough to put a hand on the back of his neck, hitting him roughly and squeezing. He didn’t even flinch. I laughed.

"While the thought is tempting, especially to the wolf behind me, we still have need of you." I let go and moved to walk past him. "Oh, and just so you know, that wolf was Grace's contact, and her fated mate." Lucas finally flinched. I laughed. "Play nice. Charles, is it?"

The human bowed. "Yes, sir."

I offered him my hand and he shook it, albeit a bit warily. "My name is King Deacon. I am in charge now. Grace is my mate's sister. She told us of your kindness and the part you played in caring for her. My mate wanted me to give you her deepest gratitude."

The old man's eyes watered. "She is well then?" I nodded. "And her unborn child?"

"Did not survive. She is healing." I gestured to the house, and they followed. "Come, we have work to do. I promised to be home as soon as possible."

A few tense hours later, we escorted Lucas as he returned a much quieter and reserved version of Alicia to the feeding center. I planned on closing her room for business for a long time.

Standing in the lobby, with a giant grin, was a familiar face.

"Deacon! It's good to see you!"

I laughed and hugged my old friend. I laughed harder when I heard the grumbling from my side.

"What's wrong Lucas? You didn't know Lou was a friend of mine?" He shook his head, eyes on the ground. "Who do you think told me it was time to run?"

"I take it this means you are in charge now? I saw the news report."

"Yes. Curtis is gone, along with all the Nightwalkers he took with him. How did you manage to escape the draft? I worried you were among the burnt."

"Nah, I talked Lucas into putting me in charge of the feeding center. I rounded up as many of your donors from the bar as I could and brought them here. Ryley has been helping me. He brought a few over from other cities, unwillingly. I put them in rooms on the bottom floor, but never told the Nightwalkers about them. They have been left unharmed. How is Carrie?" He laughed at the proud grin on my face.

"Perfect. And so are our twins."

"Twins?" His eyes bugged out.

"Yes. A male witch and a female vampire."

Lou pulled me in for a congratulatory hug. Over the next few minutes, I filled him in on everything that happened. He gave his condolences over losing Colton. Then we turned to business.

Lucas somberly took us around most of the city that night. My bar was still there. Left untouched. I planned to ask Carter to run the place for me. I was sure Todd would help him. We passed many Nightwalkers on the street, most of them I already knew and were happy to see me.

Lucas didn't like that much.

He had been in charge of this region from the take down on. He never knew I was there, right under his nose. And he never knew how many allies I still had there.

Neither did I frankly. I guess by always giving them a place to be true to who they were, bought me a bit of loyalty.

When we returned to the main house, he showed me around the office and how to record a message for the drones. I did a video conference with each area and Nightwalker commander, telling them about the change in command. As was expected, most didn't care. They were still going to be free.

The only ones not being granted freedom was Curtis' council of Royals. The traitors. We had all but Mark now. We weren't actively searching for him, at Grace's request.

The only person she confided in was Carrie, so, in a way, it was my angel's request.

If he ever came sniffing around again though, it was game on.

"Citizens of California. My name is King Deacon of the Royal Borns. If you were able to watch the Live news report with President Price a few weeks ago, then you know who I am. For now, I only have a few things to say. Most importantly, Curtis is dead, and the war is over. We have all lost loved ones. We have all had to make sacrifices. Together, we will heal, we will move on, we will prove to the world that coexistence is possible. Over the next few weeks, and months, there will be many changes. You will be free to live where you wish but know that you will be living next door to a magical creature. Everyone, including us, will work to live in harmony. Donating blood will still be needed, but only from those willing to do so. Any vampire found hunting, will be killed by our own law enforcement. Anyone purposely killing anyone, no matter the species, will have to face judgement from that same law enforcement. Which will be made up of humans, witches, shifters, and Vampire Borns. You have no need to fear me or my people. If you do not want to remain here, then you may apply to leave. Technically, this is no longer considered part of the United States. However, we will be allies with them. Look to your local leaders for guidance. Just be patient with them, they will be struggling to, once again, learn a new system."

I ended my message and ordered it to be sent out near midday. While Clint helped me with office stuff and contacting different people, Kenny and Andrew left to find any other shifters still being held captive. There were still missing members from packs.

Lucas told us of another base that held some captive. When I asked why Curtis hadn't sent them to Seattle in place of the ones they lost…

"By the time we knew about the lost shipment, time was short, and he was distracted. Grace had the vision of getting pregnant. His priorities shifted. She had a vision of losing her child if they used my blood, which nearly incapacitated her. His focus blurred. If it wasn't for that, we would have sent them."

Andrew said he would make sure to tell her that she saved more than she realized with her sacrifice.

The next morning, just after sunrise, every human mayor logged on to a zoom call. I had messaged them in the night, from Curtis' account. The moment they saw me, many started crying. They had seen the news. They knew what this meant. We spent hours going over logistics. I wanted a report from each city on how they were doing. We scheduled to meet again in a week, after they had time to meet with their people and get an idea of what they all wanted, in regard to where they wanted to live. I was perfectly happy to let them go back to the careers they had before.

I didn't believe humans were any less than us.

I returned home with Clint and Kenny at the end of the day. Andrew stayed to fly back on a cargo plane with the four dozen shifters they found. Most weren't even soldiers. Andrew contacted their packs, and representatives would meet them in the morning to take each of them home.

Roughly 24 hours after I left, I walked quietly back into our little cabin, afraid to disturb the babies, just in case they were asleep. I smiled when I saw my angel sitting against our headboard, holding our children.

As quietly as I could, I stripped down and slid in, just in time to catch their bedtime story.

"Once upon a time, many years ago, all sorts of creatures lived free in the land. The shifters ruled over their own land. The Witches ruled theirs. But the Vampires had the most land for they ruled over the humans."

Thank you for joining Carrie and Grace on their not so fun adventures. Please remember to leave a review and let others know what you think.

Feel free to browse through the destination list in my weird world, check out some of my other stories. If you like romance with a dark tint and some humor, check out my mafia series'. Want some shifter fun? Check out the Silver Moon Collection.

***

Don't forget to leave a rating and/or a review, and let others know what you think of the book.

Follow me on Facebook (@tjleebooks), Instagram (@tjlee2.0), Goodreads (tjlee), TikTok (@tjleebooks) and bookbub (@tjleebooks) for updates on new releases.

www.weirdworldoftjlee.com

THE WEIRD WORLD OF TJ LEE

The Cooper Family Chronicles

- Love, Devotion, and Trust...with a side of Brownies (Levi & Callie)
- For Ellie (Emma & Freddie)
- For Emma (Emma & Freddie Cont./Rick & Rachel)
- Forgive & Forget (Tim & Alicia/Zack & Zoey)
- Avenging Angel (Mitch & Charity)

Dark Protectors (frequent crossovers with the Coopers)

- Daughter For Sale (Eli & Vanessa)
- Heartbeats (Alyssa & Ryan)
- Sins of the Mother (Trixie & Ty)

Million Dollar Duet (Crossovers with the Coopers)

- Million Dollar Angel (Elizabeth & Antonio)
- Million Dollar Screw Up (Stacey & Ricky)

Standalone novels (still have crossovers with the others)

- Finding My Sunrise (Samantha/Sarah & Jackson)
- 2 Doors Down (Rose & Ryan)
- Last Christmas (Trish & Noah)

The Yin & Yang Collection (you guessed it, slight crossover here too)

- Oil & Water (Mia & Theo)

The Silver Moon Collection

- Ivory Snow (Snow White - Shifter Style)
- Now Until Forever (Jessica & Jake)

The Cursed Ones

- Revolution
- The Birth of a Queen
- The Witch's Curse

ABOUT THE AUTHOR

TJ is an avid reader. Reading was always an escape for her in her crazy messed up world. She's always had a vivid imagination. It wasn't until she was locked in her house for a year and a half, with only her two young kids, and two dogs to talk to, that she finally started writing. She found an even better escape.

TJ is a High School English teacher and a single mom. She holds a Bachelor's degree in Cultural Anthropology and Master's in Cultural Responsive Education. Her life motto, one she says with her students regularly, is to "fly your weird flag high!" She wants everyone to learn to be true to who they are. Accept yourself the way you are. Love yourself the way you are.